The Commissioner

The Commissioner

Stanley Johnson

C

CENTURY

LONDON   MELBOURNE   AUCKLAND   JOHANNESBURG

An imprint of Century Hutchinson & Co Ltd
Brookmount House, 62–65 Chandos Place, London WC2N 4NW

Century Hutchinson Group (Australia) Pty Ltd
16–22 Church St, Hawthorn, Melbourne, Victoria 3122

Century Hutchinson Group (NZ) Ltd
PO Box 40–086, 32–34 View Road, Glenfield, Auckland 10

Century Hutchinson Group (SA) Pty Ltd
PO Box 337, Bergvlei 2012, South Africa

Typeset by Inforum Ltd, Portsmouth
Printed in Great Britain by
Anchor Brendon Ltd, Tiptree, Essex

ISBN: 0 7126 15873

To Jennifer
and
Alexander, Rachel, Leo, Joseph,
Julia and Maximilian

Chapter One

Isobel Morton's hairdresser was the kind of person who prided herself on knowing a good deal about her clients. She had built up her business through contacts and word-of-mouth recommendation. She knew perfectly well that the women who came to her comfortable establishment in Knightsbridge did so not just in order to have their hair done, their legs waxed or their hands manicured; they came because they knew, without ever saying so in so many words, that they could talk to Patricia about more than the time of day, particularly about their husbands and children and lovers, and that Patricia would guard their confidences.

The system, of course, was never watertight. Not absolutely watertight. But then it wasn't meant to be. The good ladies who sat beneath the drying-machines were not all dunderheads. Some of them told things to Patricia hoping, or at least half-hoping, that she might pass them on, that the ripples might spread and one day rock the boat. It was part of Patricia's professional skill and her personal charm to be able to distinguish between genuine confidences and deliberate indiscretions.

But Isobel Morton, partly because she was an American, tended to flummox her. She didn't use the same code as the others. The signals she sent out were confusing. That particular morning, as Patricia attended to the business at hand, Isobel spoke in particularly vehement terms about her husband and his way of life.

'It's cuckoo, absolutely cuckoo, completely and utterly

1

crazy. They're there all hours of the night. As far as I can make out they just have to stay there until the whips decide it's safe for them to go home. I thought it might be better now that James has a job but it hasn't made the slightest bit of difference. He gets home just as late at night; what's worse, he has to go off to the office in the morning whereas before he would sometimes be around until lunchtime before going over to the House. I'm not sure I can take much more of it.'

Patricia looked at the handsome, faintly petulant face in the mirror in front of her. This was one of the rare occasions when she couldn't quite decide whether the message, if indeed there was a message, was intended for her and for her alone; or whether Isobel was voicing for eventual publication the terms and conditions to be applied in the not-too-distant future if the Morton marriage, deemed by most to be a great success, was to continue on an even keel.

She picked up a comb and gave the hair above Isobel's left temple a few tentative twiddles.

'Quite a few Members' wives come here, you know. They all say they won't stand for it. But they do. Apart from the ones who don't.'

Isobel grimaced. 'Most of them are old bags. They put up with it because they don't have any alternative. Nobody else would have them.'

She stood up to go. Tall. Imperious. There was one thing you could say about Isobel, thought Patricia; she would never lack for alternatives if she ever did finally decide that being an MP's wife was a mug's game and gave poor old James the boot.

'Are you going back down to the country tonight?' Patricia asked.

'Not till tomorrow morning. I'll drag him away then if I have to. Either we have a life of our own or we don't. Do you understand me?' She was suddenly serious.

Patricia looked at her with affection. Over the last two or three years since Isobel had taken to coming in on Thursdays to have her hair done, she had found herself responding to the frank and outspoken nature of the woman's character. There was nothing bland about her. Nothing wishy-washy. Once

2

again, Patricia reflected, it was probably the American background. American women either did very well in London, ran the place the way they liked it, or else they packed up and went back home. As far as Isobel was concerned, Patricia still wasn't sure which way it would go.

She held the door open for her friend and client. 'Do you want a cab?'

'No, I'm parked on a double yellow. If they've clamped me, James can send someone to get it out. That's what "having a job" means, doesn't it?'

In the event, the car had not been clamped. Isobel drove fast and dangerously through the traffic, her sense of dissatisfaction a hazard that other drivers had to reckon with. She was rich; she was meant – she knew it – to come out on top of the tree, yet somehow she had ended up picking the wrong guy. There were many qualities she admired in James Morton. He was tall, that was a start. She had always preferred tall men. And he was a kind man, who had done his best to humour her over the six years of their marriage. At the time of their wedding she had thought she was in love with him, and she probably was, but now she was looking for more. When she had decided first to come to England and then to stay; when she had cast her determined eye on James Morton, one of the eligible bachelors of his day; when she had devoted herself to Morton's emerging political career, she had done so, not so much because she was ambitious for him, though she was, but because she was ambitious for herself. One day she wanted to be able to call up her crummy folk back home, and tell them, guess what, that she'd made it all the way from the smokestacks of Trenton, New Jersey to Downing Street, London. In her farthest dreams, she saw herself installed at Number 10 itself, a twentieth-century Lady M, dispensing patronage and influence in her own inimitable way. More prosaically, she would have settled for Number 11. After all, the role was not without precedents. Hadn't Jenny Jerome, once considered the most beautiful girl in Philadelphia, married Lord Randolph Churchill? And hadn't Randolph Churchill been – at the age of thirty-five – the youngest-ever Chancellor of the Exchequer?

Well, she thought, as she turned into Beauchamp Place, it

3

didn't look as though she was going to make it to Downing Street in any capacity whatsoever, unless she decided to become a tea-lady. James Morton simply didn't have what it took – that was the sad conclusion she was forced to. He had been in politics now for almost fourteen years. His constituency, down in Berkshire, was one of the safest in the country. His Party credentials were impeccable, both his father and his uncle having been Conservative MPs before him. The galling thing for her was to see others whom she considered less intelligent and less qualified overtaking James in the race to the top of the greasy pole. What he lacked, she supposed, was the killer instinct, the urge to succeed at almost any price. If you didn't have that in politics, you had nothing.

Isobel Morton was no slouch where self-analysis was concerned. She didn't need long sessions on the psychiatrist's couch to learn that if there was one commodity which she herself possessed in abundance, it was precisely the one that her husband seemed to lack: the killer instinct, the urge to succeed. Down at the far end of Beauchamp Place, she pulled abruptly on to the pavement in front of a pretty Georgian-fronted shop, where a range of chintzy fabrics was displayed in the window and an elegant hand-painted sign proclaimed *Isobel*. This little venture had netted her, she estimated as she trotted up the steps, profits well into five figures – and it had only been going for three years. That was what drive and determination could do for you. *Isobel*'s, under her vigorous direction, had virtually cornered the market as a purveyor of high-priced materials to high-priced salons. Isobel Morton had, moreover, discovered in herself a talent for interior design. Nowadays, among the rich and super-rich, having a drawing room arranged by *Isobel* was like having a Chagall or a Matisse on the wall. In fact the two very often went together.

'Hi girls!' She breezed into the room, not an absentee landlord, more a visiting potentate. 'What's new?'

The girls were three sweet-looking but hard-as-nails Japanese, all in their early twenties and all hand-stolen by Isobel from competing establishments.

'I'd never employ English girls,' Isobel had once confided to

4

Patricia. 'They're lazy, they're dirty, and they're usually dishonest.'

The senior of the three Japanese, Chiko Muramatsu, jumped to her feet, pressed the tips of her fingers together and bowed. The two others followed suit. Isobel waved them back to work like waving a puppy back to its basket. The place was busy, though not yet frantically busy since Christmas was still thirty-eight shopping days ahead. Isobel didn't mind so much about having a full store. The place was classier when it was emptier. She wasn't running a penny bazaar. In any case, the people who looked in off the street were not normally the big spenders. The rich and super-rich didn't come to see you; you went to see them. On such occasions she would take one of the girls along. She would get the business; the girls would do the donkey work. It was a good combination.

She walked straight through the shop and up the stairs to her office on the first floor. Interior decoration, like charity, began at home. Isobel Morton's business quarters combined comfort, elegance and efficiency. Functionalism was not a word to be found in her vocabulary. There wasn't an angle-poise lamp in sight.

The telephone was on a small inlaid table next to the sofa. Isobel sat down, hooked one deeply tanned leg over the other, picked up the receiver and dialled a number.

'I'm on my way.'

She replaced the receiver, took a Museum of Modern Art address book from the table, jotted down a series of numbers and then pressed the bell on the wall. When Chiko appeared in the doorway, Isobel handed her the list.

'I want to visit all of them in the next ten days. There's work for a season here.'

Chiko nodded. 'Will you be back later?'

'I may look in. If I don't, you can manage, can't you, Chiko?' Isobel smiled a wide, dazzling smile, showing a row of large and flawless white teeth. (That was something else she couldn't stand about the English. The dentistry was so bad or else the people were such cheapskates that they didn't go till it was too late.)

Chiko smiled back. 'We all prefer it when you're here. We

work harder too.' She gave a short laugh, as near mirth as she ever came. Her head bobbed and her short dark hair fell forward.

'I can't imagine anyone working harder than you three do.' Isobel meant it. She gave the girl a kiss on the cheek and swept out.

This time she was not so lucky. There was a traffic warden standing by the car, writing a ticket. He was about to tuck it under the windscreen wiper when Isobel said: 'Don't worry, give it to me. It's my car. I'm sorry, it's been one of those mornings.'

Surprisingly, that brief encounter with authority put her in good humour. Isobel Morton never minded people doing their jobs. What she minded was people who *didn't*. If she got a ticket for illegal parking, that was her tough luck. If you didn't play by the rules, you had to be prepared to pay the consequences.

If parking on the kerb in Beauchamp Place was one example of Isobel Morton's propensity for ignoring the rules, Tim Kegan was another. Isobel had 'discovered' Tim six weeks earlier at some evening festivity organized by the Conservative Group for Europe. Tim, like James Morton, was a Tory MP. He was widely regarded as one of the brightest young men in the Party. At thirty-four, he was two years younger than Isobel, but she didn't hold it against him. The fact that he was slightly shorter did, marginally, concern her. She had to make a conscious effort to adjust when she was with him. Not that she had been with him very much. Not so far, anyway.

As she turned into Dolphin Square she found herself wondering what her real intentions were. Two lunches and one quick drink before dinner didn't add up to adultery. Not yet. What was she looking for? What was *he* looking for?

Tim Kegan's seat was up in the Midlands, an area which Isobel vaguely knew to be somewhere 'north of Watford'. That was where he kept Mrs Kegan and three little Kegan children hidden. Isobel had no special desire to meet any of them, home or away, but the fact of their existence could not be denied.

6

She took the lift up to the fifth floor. God, what a dump this place is, she thought, as she walked along the corridor. It reminded her of the worst of the apartment blocks in New York – dark, stuffy and overheated. Take a human being, tip him on end, draw a box around him and you have a room. Do it a hundred times and you have a building; do it a thousand times and you have Dolphin Square – without the dolphins.

'You've got to get out of this place,' she said as he opened the door. 'It just won't do.'

He was taken aback. Tim Kegan was a man who had made his own way up in the world, a new-mould Conservative. He was quite proud of where he had managed to get so far and the flat in Dolphin Square was part of it. People normally waited for years for their turn in the queue, but someone fortunately had pulled strings and Tim had slipped in ahead of the field.

A frown crossed his face. 'I thought it was all right. Come in anyway.'

Isobel threw her coat on a chair in the hall. 'I need a drink. I've been going since nine this morning.'

He brought her a large whisky. 'Who did the hair? It looks great.'

'Patricia. She has a little place behind Harrods. I've gone there for years.'

He looked at her with something approaching wonder. Of course, he held his own in the everyday cut and thrust of political life and that included the social side but deep down he knew he didn't have the confidence, the savoir-faire of those bloody old Etonians. They expected to end up with the best-looking woman at the end of a party; he didn't. That was the difference. He still didn't know whether Isobel Morton liked him for what he was, or for what she thought he was going to be. He suspected it was more the latter than the former. Either way, he felt himself flattered and enthralled. He found her beautiful, dazzling, golden – and he was ready to make a fool of himself.

He gave a sideways glance at himself in the mirror, trying to see himself as other people saw him. As Isobel saw him. He thought his face was rather white, pasty in fact. He knew he had been working too hard and it showed. His trousers were tighter round the waist than they used to be. Even junior ministers had a lot of official lunches and dinners to go to. He turned to her, glass in hand, holding in his stomach and feigning a confidence which he did not feel. He wanted to sound suave, nonchalant, as though he knew about these things, without of course seeming to know *too* much about them.

'How long can you stay?'

She leaned back on the sofa, tilting her head so that the light which slanted in through the high window caught the underside of her chin.

'How long do you have?'

A raw day in the middle of November was hardly the time for smoked salmon, but that was what he had fixed and he'd probably picked the wine – a predictable Muscadet – from the Hugh Johnson pocket book. But she didn't care; the trappings would come in due course.

'Are you going to the House later?'

He wasn't sure what she meant by later, but he nodded anyway. 'Your husband's down to make a statement after Questions, about power-sharing in Northern Ireland.'

'Oh is he?' Isobel sounded wholly unconcerned. 'Why don't you just get shot of Northern Ireland? James spends half his time over there on some piddling job. He's not interested; Britain's not interested; even the Irish don't seem to be interested any longer.'

'Someone has to do it.' Tim Kegan knew as well as anyone that Morton had been less than a howling success in his junior ministerial post in the Irish office, but he refrained from saying so.

Isobel, feeling hungry after her busy morning, helped herself to another plateful of salmon.

'I hear you're being tipped as a possible Chairman of the Party. Congratulations.' She lifted her glass.

'How did you know?'

'Little birds . . . . ' She laughed, looking at him across the table. He was so different from anything she could have imagined; so much the antithesis of her husband. What a mess she was going to make of his life, of both their lives!

8

She turned to him, lips half open, the unspoken question hovering between them.

He got up from the table and stood by the window. A barge was making its way up the river towards Teddington.

'This kind of thing isn't really my scene, you know. Other men's wives.'

'Other women's husbands. What's the difference?'

He thought about that. 'There is a difference. You've never met my wife. You don't even know her name.'

It was true, Isobel realized. Mrs Kegan could be Helen or Nicola or Tracey for all she knew.

'What is her name?'

'Phyllis.'

God, thought Isobel, some men really knew how to pick them.

She came and joined him by the window. 'Let's be clear about this. We're both grown-ups, we both know what we're doing, know what we're looking for.'

For a man whose scene it wasn't, Tim Kegan turned in a creditable performance. He followed her into the bedroom.

'I want to watch you undress.'

'Feel free.'

She still thought the surroundings were scruffy, cramped, but that couldn't be helped, she supposed. She stepped out of her skirt, unbuttoned her blouse, turned her back to him. 'You do this one.'

As he unhooked her brassiere he noted the pale golden skin, the unblemished sheen of a well-cared-for body. He ran his fingertips lightly between her shoulder blades. Out of the window, downstream, he could see the Houses of Parliament. About now, he imagined, James Morton would be on his feet talking about Northern Ireland.

Suddenly, Tim Kegan didn't want to think about the House of Commons, didn't want to think of Northern Ireland, didn't want to think about James Morton. For a moment, Isobel was more important than any of that. He pulled her down on top of him, a poor boy making good, the gold-digger hitting paydirt. He would never have admitted it, not even to himself, but the truth was that for Tim Kegan, as for so many other successful

9

politicians, sex and ambition were closely linked. The same kind of urge was involved, the same rewards.

She was surprised by the intensity of his passion and, being surprised, she found herself responding in a way that brought back memories of those hot, sticky, glorious nights in the days when coeds at Harvard still had a touch of novelty about them. He reminded her of Seth Wiederman who had banged her one whole summer, up there in his place off the square, as though his very life depended on it.

'You're not Jewish, are you?' she asked.

James Morton, less than a mile away, was having a much less agreeable time. The responsibility for making mistakes on Northern Ireland should not, rightfully, have been his at all. But the Secretary of State had clearly realized that this was not to be a propitious occasion and had discovered some urgent business elsewhere, leaving the field to his junior minister.

In a half-empty, but none the less hostile House, Morton had done his best. On a good day, he had considerable presence at the despatch box. His voice could sound properly sonorous, with more than a hint of authority. At the age of forty-eight, his hair had begun to recede from his forehead, but only moderately so. No one could say that James Morton looked boyish (not a negligible asset even in the rather trad eighties), but he was not, on the other hand, in any way avuncular. As the French would say, he looked good in his skin.

'I do not believe, Mr Speaker,' he addressed the Chair as he embarked upon his concluding paragraph, 'that the Government's decision should be seen as a retreat in the face of terrorism, or as a concession to violence, far from it. Our policy remains unchanged. . . . '

There were a few half-hearted cries of 'That's the problem' and 'It hasn't changed for four hundred years' from the opposing benches, but James Morton ignored them. He ploughed on, head held high, both arms placed firmly on the table in front of him.

' . . . remains unchanged. Honourable and Right Honourable friends on both sides of the House know this as well as I do. The Government stands firm in its determination to preserve the integrity of Northern Ireland and its links with this country. If we have been able today to announce a further measure of devolution, this should in no sense be seen as any indication that the bonds which have knitted the destiny of our peoples together over the centuries are in any way to be weakened or severed.'

He wondered, as he resumed his seat on the front bench to a smattering of applause, whether 'knitted' was really the right word. Shouldn't it be 'knit'? He would look it up and make the correction later, before Hansard appeared, if he had to.

Outside, in the lobby, he ran into the Chief Whip. Harry Braithwaite, bluff, jovial and corpulent to go with it, took him by the arm and steered him towards the Smoking Room.

'Are you free on Sunday? The PM wants to see you for lunch at Chequers. Can't say what it's about. Don't know.' He saw Morton's look of alarm and added reassuringly: 'Don't worry, she didn't hear the statement; anyway, I thought you did your best in the circumstances. Dirty trick, Maurice shoving off like that and leaving you holding the baby.'

Morton did his best to sound only mildly interested, but in reality the opposite was the case. For him, a summons to Chequers was either good news or bad news. He had never been in, or anywhere near, the Inner Circle consisting of a handful of ministers who might drive over to the PM's Buckinghamshire retreat on a Sunday morning with nothing more in mind than roast lamb, mint sauce and a glass or two of the house claret. Admittedly, the net was thrown rather wider at Christmas, but Christmas was still too far ahead for him to have been caught by some casual trawl.

'Thanks, Harry. I wonder what she wants.' In spite of Braithwaite's reassuring words, Morton still felt a twinge of uneasiness. As an afterthought, he asked: 'Is Isobel invited too?'

'I believe so.'

Later that afternoon Morton met up with a small party of his constituents, half a dozen loyal workers – the people who got

11

the vote out on polling day and they were the people who mattered – and took them to tea in one of the rooms overlooking the river. He found himself repeating, as if by rote, the familiar patter:

'Yes, they found the old William Morris design and printed it up again. It *is* pretty, isn't it? Scones? They have a very good line of scones here.' He wondered whether, after fourteen years in the House, he was getting stale. Had some of the zest gone?

'We saw your name on the screen as we came in.'

Morton recognized the speaker as one of his branch chairmen, Mrs Blenkinsop, who usually asked him a question about hanging at the Annual General Meeting. 'It *was* Northern Ireland, wasn't it?'

Morton spent a few moments going through the main points of the statement he had made earlier that afternoon. His constituents did not seem specially convinced.

'The scones are very nice anyway.' Mrs Blenkinsop seemed to speak for them all.

He took them up to the Strangers' Gallery, more in the hope than the expectation that they would find something amusing or interesting going on down below, and then went back to the small room which, by virtue of the modest office of profit which he held under the crown, he was permitted to occupy on the first floor of the Palace of Westminster. He decided to ring his wife with the news about Sunday.

Chiko answered the telephone at the shop. 'Madame was here before lunch, but she has gone. She didn't say if she was coming back.'

Morton had a brief mental image of pale skin and dark hair. Like his wife, he approved of the Japanese. They were honest, conscientious, knew how to work. Much as he admired his wife's drive and energy, the way she could sweep through life like an express train heading for its destination, he sometimes wondered whether her commercial success didn't owe as much to the unstinting efforts of Chiko and her colleagues as it did to Isobel herself.

'If she comes back, could you ask her to call me at the House?' He wondered idly where Isobel could have gone.

When he was first elected to Westminster, James Morton had bought a house just off Smith Square. Those were still his bachelor days but, suspecting he would at some stage tie the knot, he made sure he had space for a family. In the event, Isobel had never had children. Though at first she had seemed to regret it, Morton suspected that she was happier without. It gave her more scope. And though he himself had once had visions of walking back to tuck up young Thomas or Amanda before returning to manly, breadwinning activities in the mother of parliaments, he had to resign himself to the fact that he was now unlikely to have a chance to practise his skills as a father. None the less, on the nights when he and Isobel were in London, rather than in the country, he would always try to get home for a drink or for dinner. Having the bell installed had made a world of difference. At a fast walk Morton could make it to the Division Lobby in three and a quarter minutes.

Isobel seemed glad to see him when he came home around seven-thirty. She was, he thought, looking specially radiant. He'd have to tell her to tone it down a bit before Sunday; the PM was sensitive about that kind of thing; she seemed to expect Conservative women to look the part, sensible if not downright frumpish. Of course, Isobel could always put it down to being an American, a foreigner.

'You're looking marvellous.' He gave her a kiss on the cheek and poured himself a Scotch from the decanter on the side-board.

Oh shit, thought Isobel, I spend the afternoon screwing one of his colleagues and he doesn't notice a thing. Enter Morton centre, kisses wife, moves right to sideboard, pours drink. Can't he smell it, she wondered?

'How was your day?' There was a bright interested note in her voice. 'How did the statement go? Maurice rather dropped you in it, didn't he?'

Morton would never be drawn about his colleagues, not even where his wife was concerned. It was another one of the things she found insufferable. The life had so many draw-backs, late hours, a ludicrously small salary, uncertain prospects at the best of times – and he couldn't even gossip about his mates.

13

'Oh, I wouldn't say that,' Morton replied. 'We have to share things out a bit. The Minister had urgent commitments elsewhere.' He sounded as though he believed it.

She could have kicked him. Why couldn't he see when he was being used? Tim Kegan, she reflected, would never have let himself be set up in that way. She couldn't help thinking about the contrast between the two of them No doubt at all, Morton was the nicer man. But there was no doubt either, in this particular race, which one of them was going to bring home the gold.

'We've been invited to Chequers on Sunday,' Morton said, 'I don't know why. Harry Braithwate stopped me in the lobby and told me.'

Isobel looked at him curiously. 'Aren't you going to try to find out beforehand?'

'I don't think so. We'll know soon enough. Perhaps she's planning a visit to Berkshire or buying a cottage there for her retirement, putting down roots. She can't stay at Chequers for ever.' He smiled. 'Of course, that's for the *distant* future. The PM expects to be around and running the show when the next millenium dawns. Tell me about your day.'

She knew he wasn't deeply interested. That made it easier. Isobel had long ago discovered that James Morton believed rather vaguely that women should have something else to do apart from what they did, but that he had no clear ideas on the subject. It was enough to tell him that you were busy and you could see him heave a mental sigh of relief, and switch his mind to something more congenial. He didn't actively believe in female emancipation or equality of opportunity or other similar notions, but he accepted that some steps along this road were a necessary part of domestic harmony.

'I called you at the shop this afternoon, but I'm afraid I missed you.'

She was grateful for that. She hadn't been back and she hadn't had a chance to check with the girls. In any case, they might not have told her that James had called.

'It was a busy afternoon. I thought I might make it back, but I didn't manage it. There's a lot of work to do in Cadogan Place.'

14

She almost believed, as she said it, that she had spent the afternoon in Cadogan Place.

She looked at him across the room, their room. How typical it was, she thought sadly, that he wasn't interested enough even to find out where she had really been that afternoon. If he had persisted, perhaps after all she would have told him. Perhaps she wanted him to know, wanted some air-clearing explosion, some cataclysmic thunderstorm after which the sky might once again seem blue and serene while the ship sailed majestically onwards towards the sunlit horizon. She felt a little sad. Some women, it seemed to her, had unfaithfulness thrust upon them when they discovered, too late, that they had married good and worthy men who were quite simply too dull to be getting along with.

She wanted to blurt it out, to say that she had seen Tim Kegan, gone to bed with him, enjoyed it, and that what's more, she planned to do it again.

They were still having dinner when the Division bell rang.

'I shan't be late,' he said.

'I'll probably turn in. Let's leave early tomorrow.'

'I'll have to look in at the office to see if there's anything to sign, but I should be through by eleven.'

'I'll be ready.' There was no point in hanging around in London over the weekend, she thought. Nobody stayed in London at the weekend. By lunchtime, anyway, Tim Kegan would be on a train to his constituency. It was absurd, but she was missing him already.

When Morton had gone she lay in the bath thinking about her life. On the face of it she had everything she could want or need. A loving husband, homes both in London and the country, a defined status in the land where she had chosen to live. She flexed her long slim toes, raised one knee in the bath to admire the curve of the calf, followed the line of the thigh up to the mound with its blonde curly crown. Tummy still firm, she thought; tits more than passable.

She looked at her face in the glass at the end of the bath. It was a good face. She liked it. She had got used to it. Once, when she was a teenager in high school back home, she had been voted the prettiest girl in her class. What the hell, she thought, your looks were like your life. You had to work at it.

Chapter Two

As the crow flew, the Mortons' country home in Berkshire, not far from Newbury, was barely sixty miles from Chequers. Invited for noon, they took a cross-country route enjoying the bare fields and the winter sunshine. In spite of the ravages supposedly inflicted on the landscape by modern agricultural techniques, Isobel couldn't help thinking that a good deal of rustic beauty still managed somehow to survive even here, within a hundred miles of the capital. She enjoyed the quiet villages; the pubs with their hand-painted signs doing a thriving trade this bright morning; the sense of permanence. Precisely because she *was* a foreigner, an American, she appreciated qualities in England which others, native to the place, came to take for granted. If you were brought up in Trenton, New Jersey, any quiet traditional English village, any uncluttered landscape, tended to seem like Paradise.

She glanced at Morton as he drove. He looked good in the country; it was where he belonged. Mortons had farmed in Berkshire for over a century. She liked the hint of brown in his suit; much better, she thought, than those ghastly pinstripes most Tories wore when the House was sitting. She liked his straight nose and firm chin, the way he gauged the road and took the bends as though saying, this is my country, my land, this is where I do what I do best. She sighed, half admitting that the problem lay not so much with him as with her.

'What's the matter, darling?' He half-turned towards her.

'I was thinking of the fête I have to open next week.'

'A fête worse than death.' It was an old joke, but they both laughed.

They knew they were getting near when they saw the police cars. You didn't see police cars around on Sunday morning in the country, not normally. But when the Prime Minister was at Chequers for the weekend, the Buckinghamshire constabulary worked overtime.

'It's not just the ones you see and recognize,' Morton told her. 'They'll have unmarked cars out as well with plain-clothes police in them. The chap who gave Chequers to the nation didn't have security in the forefront of his mind. I can think of better places for prime ministers to relax from that point of view.'

The Prime Minister herself was just returning from church as they arrived. How graceful she looked, thought Isobel, watching her as she stood in front of the elegant Elizabethan facade, welcoming her guests; how supremely proprietorial. Age had in no sense withered her. On the contrary, she seemed to thrive with the passage of time.

'Ah, James, Isobel! How good of you to come!' She ushered them inside the panelled hall with its unique collection of Cromwellian portraits. 'We're going to have a rather informal lunch. Do you know Gordon Cartwright who runs United Chemicals? Of course you do. Gordon and Rose are staying with us for the weekend.'

Beyond the fact that he was a major donor to Party funds, Morton knew very little about Sir Gordon Cartwright. Unlike some of his predecessors as Chairman of United Chemicals, Sir Gordon preferred to stay out of the limelight. He was a tall man, of sallow complexion with dark hair slicked back from his forehead in the Robert McNamara manner. His wife was a dumpy Scottish lady, who seemed ill at ease with the splendours of Chequers. Nor had Isobel's arrival done much to increase her confidence. Isobel exuded glamour and vitality. As far as Rose Cartwright was concerned, she might as well have come from another planet as from the other side of the Atlantic.

The Prime Minister decided to leave what she half-ironically referred to as the 'men' to have drinks in the library before lunch while she took the 'ladies' on a guided tour of the establishment. Morton found himself being gently quizzed

18

by Cartwright on matters about which he had very little knowledge. Sir Gordon seemed especially interested in Morton's view on industrial policy.

'Wouldn't you say we're over-regulated? Tied down in too many ways? Don't you agree that industry needs a much freer rein if it's to develop its full potential?'

Cartwright lobbed the questions at him in quick succession, leaving Morton with an uneasy floundering feeling. Apart from a handful of directorships of the kind any Tory MP tended to accumulate, Morton had very little experience of industry. He had lived most of his life in the country; he represented a constituency where the main interest was farming though latterly some high-technology industries whose nature Morton did not profess to understand had sprung up along the axis of the motorway; there was precious little unemployment where he came from and, as far as he knew, no effective trade union movement, except for the farmers, which was another story.

'Yes, absolutely.' The best course, he felt, would be to agree with Sir Gordon. Presumably the man knew what he was talking about; otherwise he wouldn't be Chairman of United Chemicals.

'Above all,' Gordon Cartwright continued, striding up and down the room with his gin-and-tonic in his hand, 'we have to clip the wings of those bureaucrats in Brussels. Clip their wings, keep them under control, don't you agree? Fair trade and competition is one thing, but bloody-minded interference is something else altogether.' Cartwright ranted on.

This was safer territory. Over the years Morton had addressed meetings of his constituents and potential electors in village halls and schoolrooms up and down his constituency. There were certain phrases one grew to recognize like 'Brussels bureaucrats' and 'interference in our day-to-day affairs'. There were knee-jerk questions and knee-jerk responses. He gave one now, faithfully echoing the other man's viewpoint.

'Couldn't agree with you more . . . cut them down to size . . . never believed in harmonization for harmonization's sake. . . '

To his surprise, Morton realized that he seemed to have passed the test, if it was a test, when Sir Gordon took him by

19

the elbow and steered him towards the dining room. 'Mustn't keep the Prime Minister waiting; she likes to have lunch on time.'

It was an enjoyable, though hardly festive, meal. The Prime Minister clearly regarded Isobel Morton with some suspicion. It crossed Isobel's mind, just for an instant, that the PM might know about her relationship with Tim Kegan, if indeed it could be called a relationship. Did MI5 keep tabs on ministers, even junior ministers or perhaps especially junior ministers? And had perhaps material of this sort formed part of some 'briefing' given to the Prime Minister before the arrival of her guests? But then she dismissed the notion as absurd. This was Britain, not the Soviet Union. Things just didn't work that way.

'Why *did* you decide to settle in Britain?' The Prime Minister smiled sweetly across the table.

What you mean, thought Isobel, is why don't I get back home where I belong. She smiled just as sweetly back. 'Because I met James and decided to marry him.' If she does know about Kegan, she'll certainly enjoy that one!

'How romantic!' The Prime Minister turned to her other female guest. 'And you, Rose, decided to stay in England after you met Gordon?'

'Oh, no. It was the other way round. Gordon met me in Scotland and decided to stay there. He spent his first fifteen years with United Chemicals in Scotland. He worked his way up, you know.'

The Prime Minister laughed. 'I worked my way up too. There's nothing like it.'

James Morton listened to this banter and wondered what it was all leading up to. But not until the end of the meal did the Prime Minister give any kind of clue. 'What was your majority, James, at the last election? Wasn't it over twenty thousand?'

James Morton felt absolutely sure that the Prime Minister knew the answer to the question. But he gave it anyway. 'Twenty-three thousand two hundred and twenty-two, actually.' He looked across the table at Isobel, involving her in what he chose to think of as a joint achievement. 'We're in the

Guinness Book of Records for having the largest majority in Britain.'

'Excellent.' The Prime Minister, seeming satisfied, turned to Gordon Cartwright. 'Did you two have a good talk this morning?'

Gordon Cartwright spoke for both of them. 'Very good, Prime Minister. We certainly see eye to eye on the main problems.'

After lunch Morton had a few moments alone with the Prime Minister in her study. They sat in leather armchairs either side of the fireplace.

'I know it will be a wrench, James, but it's for the good of the country and the good of the Party. And I think it will be good for you too. And for Isobel, perhaps.'

James Morton didn't know what to make of this, particularly the last remark.

'What are you referring to, Prime Minister?'

The Prime Minister seemed surprised. 'The by-election at Newbury, of course. You're going to Brussels.' She leaned forward and tapped him on the knee. 'I want a man there I can trust, a man with a certain weight and clout back home. It could be four years, James; it could be eight years. That will depend on you. Central Office will be circulating the constituency vacancy this weekend; we're going to move very fast; we don't want to give the other side time to get organized, particularly the Alliance. They often seem to do rather well in these Home County seats if you let them get their act together.'

James Morton was mildly surprised to hear the Prime Minister using an expression like 'get their act together', but then he recollected that she had once had teenage children running around at home and there was no knowing what could rub off in that process.

'I'd like to discuss this with Isobel.' It sounded lame but he meant it.

'What's Isobel got to do with it?' the Prime Minister snapped.

Morton emerged from his interview with the Prime Minister

21

feeling shaken. This was not a new experience. On the two or three previous occasions when he had had a tête-à-tête with the leader of the Government (and the Party) he had not found it easy going. The Prime Minister had a habit of making her own mind up and then telling you in no uncertain terms precisely what she had decided. He caught a glimpse of the Cartwrights driving away in a chauffeured limousine. What link, he wondered, had there been between Gordon Cartwright's presence at lunch that day and the Prime Minister's surprising announcement? That there had been some connection, he felt certain. It was almost as though the PM had asked Cartwright in to vet him.

Isobel, it appeared, had been taken on a guided tour of the portraits by one of the staff. Morton found himself standing somewhat aimlessly in the hall until she reappeared.

They drove home together in silence. Isobel waited for him to begin but Morton was reluctant. He had been married long enough – married to Isobel long enough – to know some subjects should be approached gingerly. This was going to be one of them.

One village after another slid past. They were half-way home before Isobel, looking straight ahead, said: 'I'm not going, you know.'

Morton played for time, feigned innocence. 'What do you mean?'

'Wild horses wouldn't drag me to Brussels. You should have told her that.'

Morton sighed. 'I didn't have a chance. You don't actually have conversations with her, you know. That's not the way it is. Anyway, how did you know?'

'That drab old doormat Rose Cartwright told me as soon as you went in. Apparently they've known for weeks. It's so like you to still be in the dark when obviously half of London has heard and is having a fine old laugh. Talk about being booted upstairs. This is like being booted out of sight.'

Morton felt his anger rising and resisted an urge to stamp on the accelerator. He spoke very slowly and precisely, using the softest of tones. She knew he was angry when he called her 'darling' twice in the same sentence.

'Look, darling,' he said, 'I think you've got it wrong, darling. This was just a preliminary discussion. Nothing has been decided.' He paused, playing for time. It was not imposs-ible that he could win her round. 'Actually, going off to Brussels isn't like going off to Siberia. Brussels isn't a political backwater, you know, not nowadays.' He adopted a concili-atory tone. 'We don't have to take any decisions now. We can let it ride, think about it. Why don't we go over and have a look at the place? It's been years since I've been to Belgium.'

For the first time Isobel turned to face him. Suddenly she felt sorry for him. She knew she wasn't making it easy. The Prime Minister's news must have come as a terrible shock. Here was a man who, deep down, still nurtured hopes of high or at least higher office, who might have aspired to the Cabinet itself and then, suddenly, ruthlessly and without any warning at all, those hopes, those aspirations had been destroyed in half an afternoon.

She patted his knee. 'I'm sorry, James. You must feel rotten. You're not going to make it, are you? It's a tough world. Yes, I'm sorry, but don't try to pretend to me that things aren't decided when they are.'

'If you don't want to come to Brussels, I won't go. It's as simple as that.'

Morton didn't mean what he said and she knew it.

'Don't be absurd. You know you'll never get anything else and this might be better than nothing. She'd drop you at the next reshuffle anyway if you turned her down. But don't count on me. All that "whither thou goest I go" stuff doesn't apply, not now, not any more. Not with me anyway. I've got certain clear ideas about how I want to lead my life and I can tell you now that Brussels, Belgium, doesn't feature.'

Morton permitted himself one small vicious kick on the accelerator. 'I still think we should talk about it.'

She relented then. 'Of course, we can talk if you like. No promises, though.'

They had the constituency chairman and his wife to dinner that evening. It was the kind of chore that Isobel had come to hate. Morton sympathized with her, but insisted none the less.

'Once a year; that's all it takes,' he told her. 'It keeps them happy; surely that's a small enough price to pay.'

Isobel wasn't so sure. She found many of her husband's constituents excruciatingly dull and Walter and Elizabeth Clegg were no exception. They were neither farmers nor landed gentry. He had made money in the City some years earlier and had decided to retire to Berkshire where part-time activity as an officer of the local Conservative Association suited him very well. Mrs Clegg seemed quite happy in the role of loyal wife.

'Why didn't you tell them?' Isobel turned on Morton when they had gone.

'We haven't even decided ourselves yet. What should I have said?'

He followed her into the kitchen where he made feeble gestures with a drying-up cloth. He was still trying to be conciliatory. As he looked around the room, he thought that maybe he should promise her a new kitchen on their return from Brussels. If you can't persuade them, bribe them. But in his heart he knew that Isobel would take more convincing than that.

'Make up your mind then.' Isobel shrugged her shoulders, suddenly bored by it all.

After she had gone to bed he sat downstairs a long time. Make up your own mind, she had said. Could one, finally, make up one's mind in isolation? Weren't other factors always involved? When he tried, he could see Isobel's point of view. He had married her precisely because she had a will of her own, knew where she was going and what she wanted. That had been one of the things that most attracted him to her. He certainly didn't want to lose her and he knew he ran the risk of that if he took the job. And yet what choice did he have? Either you kept your hat in the ring, or you didn't. Even Brussels was better than nothing. Isobel was right about that.

He drank his way steadily through half a bottle of whisky. Isobel, he supposed, would stay in the house, so perhaps he could get over at weekends. Of course, she'd be spending quite a bit of time in London. It was lucky they had a place in town as well. Thank God there weren't any children; at least that made things easier. He realized as he sat there looking out at the moon as it rose over the downs, that he was thinking and talking as a man might think and talk who is contemplating divorce rather than some temporary separation thrown up by the necessities of his job. He took a grip of himself, drained his glass resolutely and put the top on the bottle. He had always regarded his marriage to Isobel, difficult though she sometimes was, as one sure landmark in his life. They would have to find some way of working things out.

He went upstairs, hoping to find her still awake. He was disappointed. She lay face down with her golden hair spread out over the pillow, breathing gently and evenly. It was clear that the dilemmas that so troubled Morton were for Isobel much less threatening.

He went into the dressing room, closing the door behind him so that the light wouldn't disturb her. He stood there looking at the lines of ties all neatly arranged in rows. A collection of ties, he thought, was as much a curriculum vitae as an entry in *Who's Who*, besides being a good deal more colourful. His school ties were there: house prefect, house colours, school prefect, First Eleven, First Fifteen, Old Boys. The regimental ties were there – he belonged to the last generation of National Servicemen and his father, himself a Brigade of Guards man, had seen to it that his son spent his two years profitably – and enjoyably. The university ties were there; the select dining clubs; Vincents; the Bullingdon. And then there were the ties he had accumulated during his time as a member of Parliament, some of them with the famous portcullis emblem emblazoned in different forms; others more discreet, indicating only that the wearer belonged to some coterie whose members were numbered in handfuls.

Looking at those serried ranks, he wondered where he had gone wrong. On the face of it his credentials were impeccable. He had been 'tipped for promotion' almost as soon as he entered the House. His marriage to Isobel had helped as well. Or so it seemed at first. She had brought a degree of flair and a bravado to the role of being an MP's wife. In those early days she had thrown herself into the work wholeheartedly, held

25

coffee mornings, visited sickbeds, even deputized for him at the AGM on one occasion when he had been held up in town on a three-line whip. Yes, in those first years, Isobel had certainly been a plus. She was a world apart from many of the good ladies of the constituency, yet she had seemed to take to them and they to her. And there was even one season, he remembered, when Isobel had ridden to hounds on Saturday and accompanied him to church on Sunday. They had loved her for it.

He straightened a couple of ties on their hangers, took off his jacket and put it away. It had begun to go wrong, he reflected, a couple of years ago. He had just passed his forty-sixth birthday. Looking down the list one day, he had been surprised to see that several colleagues whom he thought of as his contemporaries were actually half a decade younger and by any reckoning now held more senior positions. One of them had made it to the Cabinet; others, like him, held junior ministerial office but in ministries which were not, like his, political backwaters. And, of course, men like Douglas and Nigel – though not absolutely contemporary in the sense of having been born in the same year – could hardly be thought of as belonging to a different generation. He had had to recognize that his rate of ascent had slowed fairly dramatically. Unless some new impetus emerged from somewhere it was clear that the early promise was not going to be realized. He seemed to have reached the kind of position where, after a decent further interval as a member of the Government, he would be retired once more to the back benches – possibly with a knighthood (though one of the lower orders).

James Morton was not a man much given to self-analysis. Though he had read Greats at Oxford, his was not a pro-foundly questioning spirit. He did not, for example, spend much time contemplating the meaning of existence or, for that matter, the meaning of meaning. He was a practical man concerned, more than anything else, to get things done and to pass a fairly agreeable time in the process. Being a farmer, even a part-time farmer, meant that you saw things from a more down-to-earth point of view than your average ivory-tower academic. But tonight, at the end of this long and tiring day, he was forced to take stock. 'Hmm, Morton?' he could hear the Chief Whip's report. 'Loyal. Not quite a high-flyer. Well liked in the Party, though, and among his colleagues. How about Brussels, Prime Minister? Wouldn't Morton do very well? After all, we've got to send someone. We had better find a chap from here or else those Euro-MPs will start saying it's their turn and that wouldn't do. I know that means a by-election, Prime Minister, but Morton's got the safest seat in the country.'

Was the end-of-term report true? Was it fair? Did it say all that needed to be said? No, of course it wasn't and didn't, but that was life in politics. So much depended on luck and on temperament. Perhaps he wasn't the man for the time. The modern Conservative Party was a very different affair from what it used to be. Men with broad acres and broad bottoms were beginning to find themselves in a minority. There was a new breed around, exemplified by chaps like Tim Kegan, people who were upwardly mobile, hard-working, articulate and – for his money at least – deeply nasty. What he could never understand was why Isobel, who ought to know better, seemed to be attracted to a person like Kegan. The problem was, Isobel being an American didn't quite see things the way they should be seen. She didn't always grasp the subtleties. Someone had told him the other day, the way people do, that they had run into Isobel having lunch with Kegan at Wheeler's. Well, as far as he was concerned, Isobel could have lunch with anyone she liked. That was her concern and he certainly didn't propose to start asking his wife how she filled in the hours between noon and 3 p.m. But quite why anyone, let alone Isobel, should want to have lunch with Tim Kegan he couldn't understand. The man might be the cleverest fellow to emerge in the Conservative Party since Disraeli, he might in the long run (and Morton hoped it would be in the very long run indeed) eclipse not only Douglas and Nigel, but William and Chris and John as well, but that didn't mean to say you had to like him!

He put out the light in the dressing room and slipped back into the bedroom. He got into bed beside the sleeping form of his wife. He was never much into poetry, though he had from time to time turned out some workmanlike verses as any good classicist should; but a line of poetry came to him then as he gently moved her hair from the pillow on his side of the bed: 'Lay your sleeping head, my love, human on my faithless arm.' He couldn't remember who wrote it and he couldn't quite work out who was talking to whom, but he liked the sound of the lines.

He closed his eyes. Good God in heaven, he thought, Brussels! What an epitaph to a political career that never really took off! But then, as he drifted off to sleep with the owls hooting down from the gibbet, an idea occurred to him. Not a brilliant idea, not an alpha-plus idea, but a solid, serious idea for all that. Why couldn't he totally confound all those who wanted to write FINIS to James Morton's political career at the premature age of forty-eight? Why couldn't he show them that Brussels was a place where a man could make a name for himself just as much as at the despatch box of the House of Commons?

Cold reality intervened the next morning. *The Times* had the story on the front page. Morton read the concluding paragraph with gloomy comprehension. The piece had been filed from Brussels, by the paper's resident correspondent – Murray Lomax.

'Officially,' Lomax wrote, 'the Government is maintaining that it is sending a senior political figure to Brussels, thus indicating a continued commitment to the European ideal. Privately, Ministers were saying last night that Morton, though a capable middle-rank performer, was a suitable appointment for what is regarded as a cul-de-sac post. It is certainly true that, up till now, no British politician has emerged from a stint in Brussels with his reputation enhanced. Much will depend, of course, on the allocation of dossiers in the new Commission. If the Prime Minister pushes strongly for a major portfolio, such as external relations or agriculture, to be given to her appointee, and if she is successful in achieving this, those who now regard Morton's translation to Brussels with some scepticism may have to eat their words.'

He was just finishing the piece when Isobel came down to

breakfast. Without a word he passed the paper over to her, tapping the story with his forefinger.

'Don't worry. I heard it on the *Today* programme while I was having my bath.'

Before Isobel could say anything more the telephone rang. Morton walked into the hall from the breakfast room and picked it up.

'Oh, hello, Walter. No I couldn't tell you last night; it wasn't official then. Actually, I didn't know it was official *now*. I asked the PM for time to talk it over with Isobel.' He gave a short laugh. 'I guess I should have known better. Yes, of course there has to be a by-election. You can't be Commissioner in Brussels and a Member of the House of Commons at the same time.'

He came back to the table. 'That was Walter Clegg'. He reached out and took her hand. 'I'm sorry, darling. It seems a brutal way of going about things. You had a right to be consulted and you weren't. I did my best, honestly. But won't you give it a try? I know most people will say Brussels doesn't add up to a hill of beans, but we might make something of it.' He used the plural deliberately.

She hadn't come all the way from back of nowhere to throw it up without a second thought. She was too canny for that. Hell, Senators and Congressmen commuted to Washington and came home at weekends. Weren't they heading for a United States of Europe? Was Brussels so much different from Washington? She liked their house in the country, their flat in London, the shop in Beauchamp Place, lunches at Wheeler's, love in the afternoon even in a stuffy little flat in Dolphin Square. And she liked Morton, liked him a lot, had loved him once, might love him still. The man had been good to her. Besides, he paid the bills. Whatever else you said about men, they were good at paying the bills! That morning, after a good night's sleep, she was in a mood for compromise. She poured him coffee and helped herself.

'You go ahead, James. Set things up, see what it's like. I don't just mean the place, I mean the life. I don't know anything about Brussels except that they've got that statue of a little boy peeing and that it's where the sprouts come from. It

29

may not be a great place to visit, but maybe it's a great place to live.' She laughed, suddenly cheerful. Perhaps, after all, it could be a good formula, the best of all possible worlds. She could fly over to Belgium for the occasional weekend; Morton could come back from time to time; Tim Kegan would be around, wifeless, the nights she spent in town. Yes, on reflection, Isobel thought it might all work out fine.

She walked round and stood behind his chair, resting one long-fingered hand on his shoulder, leaned forward and nibbled his ear. 'Just give me time, James.'

Morton heaved a deep inward sigh of relief. More than anything else, he hated to be alone.

'All the time you need. I'll get things organized. You keep an eye on things here and come over when you're ready. By the way,' he added, 'we shan't be paupers on a Commissioner's salary.'

Isobel gave a merry little peal of laughter. 'Don't be too sure! I ran into Nancy Tate at the US Embassy the other night. She and Jack have just come over to London after a posting in Belgium. She told me they all spend money like water over there just to stop themselves dying of boredom. There's nothing else to do.'

'I'm sure you'll be just as successful in that respect, darling, as you are in everything else.'

Isobel looked at him in surprise. There had been more than a hint of irony in Morton's voice.

Phineas Fogg, he recalled as he walked up the steps a few minutes before one o'clock, had started off from the Reform Club on his eighty-day journey around the world. Lunch with Sir Rupert Evans, head of the diplomatic service, in the same crusty environment was another valedictory occasion. Brussels, as far as Sir Rupert was concerned, may not have been darkest Africa, but he certainly managed to give the impression that it was a place to be visited, if at all, only under protest. In spite of Britain's more-than-fifteen-year membership of the European Community, Sir Rupert was one of those who believed in old-fashioned diplomacy, the relationship between sovereign states, the exchange of plenipotentiary representatives. The European Community didn't fit neatly into that mould. He didn't think it was what Britain really needed but naturally he had kept these doubts to himself, otherwise he would not have been where he was.

They sat at one of the tables above the atrium with their pre-lunch drinks. Sir Rupert, a tall man with thinning sandy-coloured hair and the somewhat faded complexion that comes from years in the tropics, chewed on an olive.

'The black ones are so much better than the green ones, don't you think?'

Morton was not an expert on olives but he supposed he would soon have to become one since olives, whether in the form of trees or oil, seemed to loom large in the European Commission's preoccupations.

'Hmm,' he replied non-committally. Then he added: 'Talking of olives, do you think we ought to go for the agricultural portfolio? Britain has never had agriculture.'

'We've never had a qualified candidate,' Sir Rupert sounded rather tart in his reply. 'Henry Plumb might have done it at one stage but he preferred to stick to the European Parliament. Can't think why.' He looked at Morton over his drink. 'You've got a farm, haven't you? Up on the Berkshire Downs, isn't it? Used to walk there in my youth. Wonderful country. Yes, perhaps we should try to get the farm job. Mind you, Britain also has a real interest in the external relations dossier. We haven't had that one since Soames left Brussels.'

They went on into lunch. The dining room of the Reform was full of senior civil servants stoking up before Christmas. Morton felt warmed not only by the food and wine but also by his encounter with the head of the diplomatic service. It was clear that the Government would be pushing him for one of the key posts in the new Commission which would take office at the beginning of January.

He spread some salmon mousse on a thin and curly slice of toast. 'It goes without saying that I'll do whatever job I'm given, but of course I would welcome, as I am sure anyone in my position must welcome, the chance to carry out one of the major assignments.'

They left it at that. Later that afternoon, when he was at the

House clearing his desk (the by-election having already been announced), Morton rang Isobel. This time he found her at her shop.

'It looks like they're going to come through with the goods,' he told her.

Isobel, revamping her schedules for the coming year now that she was committed, however reluctantly, to spending at least some time in Brussels, wasn't quite sure what he was referring to.

'The portfolio, I mean,' Morton explained. 'The Government's going to push for either agriculture or external relations.'

'Not agriculture.' Isobel sounded adamant. 'We have enough of that at home. External relations could be interesting, I suppose. Didn't they have a commissioner once who was always flying off at public expense to exotic places? He was the external relations man, wasn't he?'

Morton was momentarily surprised that Isobel should have recalled the minor scandals of a previous era. 'That's not the point. Travel would be a necessary part of the job.' If he sounded stuffy, he meant to. He'd already noticed how quickly people got the wrong end of the stick. There'd been quips both in the House and in his constituency about high tax-free salaries and expense-account living.

'Sorry if I sounded less than enthusiastic, darling. We're under pressure at the moment. I think it sounds splendid and I hope you get it whatever it is.'

More olives, thought Morton. Branches this time. Isobel, he reckoned, would come round in the end.

At the beginning of the following week, with his Parliamentary career now a matter of historical record and a successor already designated in his constituency, Morton flew to Brussels. He was met at Zaventem by a young man from the British mission to the European Community.

'I'm Peter Simpson from UKREP.'

'That sounds fairly nasty,' Morton commented as they walked over to the diplomatic parking lot.

'Actually, it stands for the United Kingdom permanent

32

representation to the European Communities.' Simpson stressed the last syllable. 'Strictly speaking, we deal not just with the European Community as such, but also with the Coal and Steel Community and Euratom. Since the merger treaty, the Commission services all three bodies.'

Morton suppressed a sigh. He hoped that Brussels wasn't going to be full of intelligent young men like Peter Simpson. Foreign Office high-flyers could be rather tiresome. He smiled amiably. 'I expect I'll learn the jargon in due course.'

UKREP had produced an expensive-looking Rover for him. It was a low, sleek, powerful-looking car. Simpson explained that it spent most of its time in the garage being repaired.

'We've got it on one of the good days,' he indicated sarcastically. 'Mind you, it goes splendidly when it's on the road.'

They flipped from one motorway to another. A few minutes later they were entering Brussels. Some senior Conservative politicians like Peter Carrington, Morton reflected, could put on their CVs that they had liberated Brussels at the appropriate moment and had been decorated by the King of the Belgians. He had missed out on that. Looking at the rash of ugly buildings on the outskirts, he rather wondered whether the place had been worth liberating. An uncharitable thought. He decided he would have to pull himself together. He had a job to do and was going to make the most of it.

'There's Monty,' Simpson informed him. 'And this is Square Montgomery. Actually, it's not a square, it's a circle.'

Morton looked with interest at the larger-than-life statue of the great general. He stood there, hands clasped firmly behind his back, gazing down at the traffic as it ran through the underpass beneath him. Monty's back was firmly turned on the city; the Rhine, of course, still lay ahead.

'Have they got a Churchill Square, as well?'

'They have an Avenue Winston Churchill.'

'How about Heath? He signed the Rome Treaty here, didn't he? What about an Edward Heath Boulevard? Is the Foreign Office pushing for that?'

Simpson laughed. 'I don't think it's high on the list of our diplomatic priorities. Not in present circumstances.' Morton wondered whether the Belgians had ever named a street or

33

even a cul-de-sac after a British Commissioner. He rather doubted it.

A couple of minutes later he was ushered into the office of the British Ambassador to the European Community. The UKREP building lay on Rond-Point Schuman itself, facing – at a distance of a few hundred feet – that vast expanse of glass known as the Berlaymont which housed the civil servants of the European Commission. Morton had seen pictures of the place but, as he walked into the Ambassador's room, to confront the massive star-shaped construction rising across the way like a great shining cliff, the reality surprised him.

The Ambassador, Sir Oliver Passmore, caught the direction of his glance. 'No, it's not pretty is it? Still, I expect you'll get used to it. I'm told they all do.' He gave a dry, brittle, ambassadorial laugh. Sir Oliver had been ten years in Brussels already. He had seen Commissioners come and he had seen them go but, like the proverbial stream, he himself seemed to go on for ever. There were plenty of people who argued that the head of Britain's mission to the European Community was a far more powerful person in Brussels than the British Commissioner himself.

Passmore was a cadaverous man. He had first made his reputation in the Far East and his skin had somehow managed to acquire, and retain – as though by osmosis – a faintly yellowish tinge. He possessed one of the world's finest collections of Chinese ceremonial swords, some of which were hung menacingly along the walls of his office.

As Morton sat down on the sofa opposite one particularly magnificent specimen, he asked: 'Who did that belong to? Damocles?'

The Ambassador raised a quizzical eyebrow. 'Probably to the Emperor Kwang Su. He was the son of Prince Chun, brother to the Emperor Hsien Fung and thus first cousin to the Emperor Tung Chi. That sword will certainly have chopped off one or two heads in its time.' He laughed, another small, dry explosion.

Looking at the other man, Morton decided that Sir Oliver himself was probably not averse to chopping off the occasional head if this was what the circumstances required.

34

Peter Simpson was still hovering. 'Sit down, Peter.' The Ambassador gestured impatiently to a chair. 'Anything a Commissioner knows, his Chef de Cabinet ought to know too.' Seeing Morton's puzzled look, the Ambassador continued: 'Of course, the choice of Chef de Cabinet is entirely yours. There will be several candidates and Peter will be one of them. But I emphasize,' he repeated, 'that the choice is yours.'

'What was it Henry Ford used to say?' Morton murmured. 'You can have any colour as long as it's black!'

Sir Oliver Passmore looked at him sharply. Everything he had heard about James Morton led him to suppose that the man was an unimaginative middle-of-the-roader, certainly not destined for high office as indeed the appointment to Brussels proved. He was obviously not familiar with the way things worked in Brussels.

'Most of the decisions of the Commission are prepared by the Chefs,' he said sharply.

Morton had a brief mental vision of a group of people standing around in white hats with long wooden spoons, preparing decisions.

'What's more,' the Ambassador went on, 'now that we only have one British Commissioner as opposed to two, it's even more important to have the right man as his Chef de Cabinet. Of course, as a Commissioner you will be wholly independent' – he repeated the words – 'wholly independent. You'll take an oath of office to that effect before the European Court of Justice in Luxembourg. But you will certainly find it useful to have someone who *is* in touch with us, whoever you choose.'

During the course of this exchange Peter Simpson had remained silent. This was unusual since he was a man who had a high opinion of himself and of the value of his own views on most subjects. He spoke now with studied modesty: 'I should certainly regard it as an honour to be selected.'

Morton noticed that the young man was slightly pudgier than he should have been, a lot of heavy eating in Brussels restaurants. But he looked competent; the Ambassador would not be pushing him otherwise. He sensed that he was being put under pressure but there didn't seem to be much he could do about it. The Ambassador obviously knew the score and he didn't.

'Of course, I hear what you say,' he replied. It was a politician's form of speech, but Morton still considered himself a politician.

Sir Oliver Passmore gave no outward sign of the relief he felt. In his long experience as Britain's Permanent Representative to the European Communities he had learned that the appointment of a Chef de Cabinet was often a tricky moment. An incoming Commissioner could have his own ideas about who his right-hand man was to be and those ideas would not necessarily coincide with the views of the Ambassador or of the Government. Some Commissioners had had some most unsuitable thoughts about how to fill the top post in their private office and it had taken a good deal of effort to dissuade them.

For most of the next hour Sir Oliver Passmore briefed James Morton about the Commission and about the Community. He knew the subject and he presented it well. He had learned from experience that there was a limit to the amount of technical detail which an incoming Commissioner could be expected to absorb on his first scouting visit to Brussels, so he contented himself with the broad-brush approach.

'The theory, as you know, is that the Commission proposes and the Council disposes. Somewhere in between you have the European Parliament. When they aren't spending their time shunting between Brussels and Strasbourg and occasionally Luxembourg, the Parliament gives its advice – or opinions as they are called – on the proposals of the Commission or, in the case of the Budget, on the draft Budget as prepared by the Council. Except in the case of the Budget – and even there we are trying to limit the damage – the Council doesn't take much notice of the opinions of the Parliament.'

The Ambassador was engagingly frank and Morton listened with interest.

Towards the end of the morning he asked Sir Oliver if there had been any developments as far as the allocation of portfolios was concerned. 'I had lunch with Sir Rupert Evans. He said we'd be making a fairly strong pitch for agriculture or external relations when it came to the share-out of jobs among the Commission.'

As he spoke he noticed a shadow pass across the Ambassador's bleached features. Morton pressed the point. 'Surely it's important we go for one of the big jobs?'

Sir Oliver was off-hand in his reply. 'People *think* the foreign affairs or the farm jobs are the only jobs worth having but that's not necessarily true. There are plenty of other important things to do. But of course we shall do our best to make sure things come out right. Ultimately, it's up to the President-designate of the Commission – Dr Horst Kramer – to decide.'

Morton was disappointed to be able to get nothing more out of him. Even though the President-designate of the Commission was technically responsible for the allocation of the portfolios, the views of individual governments could have an important, often decisive effect on the outcome. He found it hard to conceal his disappointment as the Ambassador turned the conversation to other topics.

At the end of the session Sir Oliver Passmore took Morton back to his official residence for lunch. Number 21, Avenue Henri Pirenne in Uccle, one of Brussels' most salubrious *quartiers*, had been acquired by the British Government for the residence of its chief representative to the European Community as a result of some nifty footwork in the early seventies. It didn't, of course, have quite the *cachet* of the residence in Paris, a stone's throw from the Elysée, or Washington, where the Embassy dominated the upper reaches of Massachusetts Avenue. But it was a splendid establishment, more than adequate – so Morton concluded as he was ushered inside – for the task at hand.

'A quiet, informal lunch,' Sir Oliver had explained as they drove from the Rond-Point Schuman to Uccle. 'Mary will be there, of course. That's my wife. I've also asked Murray Lomax. He's the *Times* man in Brussels. You will find the press pretty persistent, sometimes downright hostile. It's as well to have a few friends among the corps.'

Morton remembered the piece Lomax had written upon the

announcement of his appointment as Commissioner. It hadn't been altogether friendly. But then he hadn't expected it to be. In his experience, journalists usually spelt trouble. He didn't, for example, want them snooping around and asking questions about Isobel, when was she coming to Brussels, and so forth. That was his business, no one else's.

Mary Passmore obviously took the same view. As they sat at lunch she approached the subject with the greatest delicacy. 'Do let us know if there's anything we can do to help when you're house-hunting. I know a lot of the good ladies of Brussels by now and I'm sure we can put together a shortlist of possible places. What area of Brussels would you like to be in? Has Mrs Morton any preferences? There's no shortage of property but I suppose if you're only going to be here four years, it would be better to rent than buy.'

Down at the other end of the table she sensed – rather than saw – the warning glance of her husband. She recovered quickly, 'Of course, I'm not suggesting that you won't stay longer than that. All I meant to say is that four years is the normal term for a Commissioner. Christopher Tugendhat did eight, of course, though I'm not sure that Julia wanted to stay *quite* so long.'

Morton enjoyed her discomfiture, if that was what it could be called. On the whole Mary Passmore – *Lady* Passmore as far as the general public was concerned – was a polished performer. Her husband's rise to one of the diplomatic service's most senior jobs had been due in no small measure to the splendid support that Lady P had offered over the years. To look at, she was rather small – *petite* would, Morton supposed, be the correct description – but she had immense poise and an ability to come to terms with the realities of diplomatic life. Twenty years earlier she had decided that her job was to do everything possible to further Oliver Passmore's career, even if that included, as inevitably it did, sacrificing something of her own ambition and interests. She had succeeded brilliantly.

'What I meant,' she explained, smiling, 'is that buying a house can be quite a business, especially in Brussels where you pay a heavy tax when you purchase, so you need to be sure that's what you really want to do.'

Morton was not the kind of man to take offence easily. He had spent too many afternoons leaning on five-bar gates, looking at cows chewing the cud, to get worked up about real or imaginary slights to his dignity. 'I shall be grateful for any help you can give. Isobel is an interior decorator, you know. Brussels could be a challenge.'

'Ah,' Lady Passmore murmured, having successfully elicited the information she had been looking for. 'I'm so glad Mrs Morton will be with you. We heard some suggestion that she might be staying behind.' She turned to Murray Lomax. 'Some article of yours, no doubt?'

Lomax was a short, red-faced man of about thirty-five. He had been transferred by *The Times* from Bonn, where he had made a name for himself through concise, accurate reporting, to Brussels, a city in which, from the journalistic point of view, the threads were much more entangled and where what seemed to be hard news had a habit of being soft at the centre when you dug into it. In spite of that, Lomax was enjoying himself. He had learned to take Brussels at several different levels. There was the European dimension, centred on the Commission and the Council – that was why he was at the lunch in Uccle that day. There was the NATO dimension, though that tended to be handled by specialized correspondents. And finally, there were the Belgians, '*les Belges*'. Lomax had already learnt that it didn't pay to underestimate '*les Belges*'. If you floated through Brussels without trying to get on terms with the natives, as it were, you risked missing out on a lot. And Lomax, whom many saw as a future editor of the paper, wasn't the kind of man to miss out on anything.

He paused, with a forkful of roast pheasant three inches from his lips, and smiled: 'Not my story. I'm afraid *The Times* is still pretty stuffy. We tend not to speculate if we can help it.' He shook his head at Mary Passmore in mock reproach.

Morton took an instant liking to the man. 'Thanks for that,' he said. Then he turned to his hosts: 'I'm sure Isobel will love it here.'

It was wishful thinking but at the time it seemed the only thing to say.

He was back in London by dinnertime that evening. In normal circumstances he would have made a dash for the House, but now there was a strange hiatus in his life. Having time on his hands, he gave Isobel a detailed account of his day, beginning with his arrival at Brussels airport, including the lunch with the Passmores and ending with a rushed half-hour in the office of a real-estate agent who had promised that finding accommodation would be the least of his problems, providing he was willing to pay the going rate. Isobel had been moderately interested. 'Did you see the Breughels? Apparently they have some splendid Breughels?'

Morton sighed. 'I'm afraid it was a question of nuts and bolts today.'

'I'd say that nuts is *le mot juste*. I still can't understand why you want to do it.' She spoke vehemently, almost bitterly. Things were not, after all, going so well in her life. That afternoon Tim Kegan had seemed to be alarmed when she suggested that with Morton in Brussels, the two of them would be able to spend much more time together.

Morton sighed for a second time. 'The British Commissioner is not a place-man. He's not a glorified civil servant. He has a job to do, a job which can involve independence both of judgement and action.'

He had spoken more seriously than he had meant to, surprising himself. But Isobel wasn't buying it. 'Tell that to the marines. I bet that old pussy-footing Ambassador had you exactly where he wanted. You've just told me he even picked your Chief of Staff, Chef de Cabinet or whatever you call him. What kind of independence of judgement or action did you show when you let that happen? Either you're your own man or you're not.'

They left it at that. Morton doubted whether she would ever understand the nuances.

Chapter Three

He flew to Cologne the week before Christmas. Dr Horst Kramer, the German President-designate of the Commission, had called his team together for preliminary discussions at a castle, a *Schloss* which had been lent for the occasion. It belonged to some high-powered industrialist friend of Kramer's, so Morton was given to understand when he made inquiries about the venue. The idea was that, closeted together in the wooded hills above the Rhine and amply supplied with food and drink, the new Commissioners – all twelve of them – would quickly get to know each other, personally as well as professionally, so that from January they would be ready to function in every sense as a collegiate body.

Before he set out for Cologne, Morton spoke to Sir Oliver Passmore on the telephone to ask for any further news or indication of what to expect. Passmore chose his words with care. He had been choosing his words with care for most of his life. 'We're not absolutely sure what Kramer intends,' Passmore told him. 'He may try to do what his predecessor, Jacques Delors did, when he was President-designate back in 1985.'

'What was that?'

'Delors wanted to avoid the "Night of the Long Knives", as they called it. Previous Commissions used to start their work with unseemly wrangles about who was going to do what job and sometimes these arguments would go on all night, leaving the press and public with the impression that the new Commissioners were behaving like a lot of squabbling schoolboys rather than concentrating on building Europe. Delors eliminated that by getting them all together in advance – he chose some watering spot in France as you'd expect – and more or less telling them the jobs he had worked out for them.'

'And you think Kramer may try the same approach?' As he spoke, Morton could imagine the parchment-faced Ambassador sitting at his desk in Brussels surrounded by his Chinese ceremonial swords.

'I do. Kramer may even try to go one better than Delors.'

'What do you mean?'

The Ambassador sounded engagingly frank at the other end of the line. 'I'm not absolutely sure. We don't seem to know a great deal about Kramer or his methods. He may spring some surprises.' Sir Oliver Passmore seemed to find the idea of some Kramer-induced surprises rather funny.

As he replaced the receiver, Morton wondered how much Passmore knew. There seemed, as he had told Isobel, always to be nuances, layers of meaning. Who pulled what strings? Who were the puppets and who were the puppeteers? There were personalities and there were institutions, there were motives and there were masquerades. Would the weekend in Germany shed any light?

A car was waiting for him at the airport when he arrived. He caught a distant glimpse of Cologne cathedral, its twin spires soaring over the city, then they swung north around the town on the ring road and headed for the hills. As they crossed the bridge over the Rhine, Morton saw a giant chemicals complex spread out along the river and extending inland well over half a mile. It was a futuristic sight, a maze of tanks and pipes and vats and chimneys from which gases flowed. He rolled down the window of the car and sniffed the air, recognizing the unmistakable odour of wealth. Back in England they talked glibly about growth in service industries – that was probably because there wasn't much growth anywhere else. But people like the Germans, above all the Germans, knew that you could never ignore the manufacturing sector. Chemicals were still at the heart of the modern economy.

The driver saw or sensed the direction of Morton's interest. 'That's Deutsch-Chemie, the biggest chemical company in

Germany. Probably one of the biggest in the world.'

Morton wound the window back up. 'Are you English?'

'Irish, actually, but I'll forgive you.'

Morton looked at the man's face in the rear-vision mirror. The complexion was reddish, flushed would be the word, he supposed, except for the unfortunate connotations. He doubted if Commission drivers drank on duty.

'What's your name?' he asked.

'Gerry McLoughlin,' the man replied. 'If I'm to be driving you over the next four years, I hope you'll call me Gerry.'

'When did you join the Commission, Gerry?'

'Back in 73, when Britain and Ireland first entered the Community. They needed a pool of drivers so I applied and got the job. I've been with the Commission ever since. It's a good job and you get to drive some lovely cars. I'm glad you've chosen the Jaguar, sir. It's been quite a time since we've had a Jaguar; the other British Commissioners have tended to stick to the Rovers. It's good to have some British cars in the pool, but I don't think much of the Rover.'

'I wonder who does.' Morton remembered Peter Simpson's earlier comment.

They left the main road and began to wind their way through a succession of villages which, Morton realized, were surprisingly pretty. Northern Germany had a bad press, he decided. People tended to think of it as the home of heavy industry, an area of dense population, the target of pollution of every kind. But once you got away from the Rhine and the coalfields of the Ruhr and into the clearer air of the hills – you could hardly call them mountains – the whole place seemed different. It wasn't Bavaria with men in *lederhosen* and women in *dirndls* and cows with tinkling bells around their necks, but it was real; it was authentic; there were people here who did a day's work for a day's pay without any assistance from telephones and typewriters, word processors and photo-copying machines. It came to him in a flash that four years in Europe might just conceivably be fun. There was nothing wrong with Newbury, nothing wrong with London for that matter, but there was always a case for change. He wished Isobel could have seen it that way.

43

Morton leaned back in the seat and watched the countryside slide past as the evening gathered. His father had fought the Germans; his grandfather had fought the Germans. Different wars, different weapons, but the same enemy. Now he was heading off to a hilltop retreat above the Rhine, where, yes, a German who had been nominated as the next President of the European Commission was about to hold a briefing session on how he proposed to run Europe. There were some ironies here, surely.

His briefcase was on the seat beside him. He opened it and took out the material which had been sent out in advance of this first getting-to-know-you meeting. He turned to the biography of Dr Horst Kramer. Who the hell was Kramer, anyway? The curriculum vitae, as prepared by the Commission (presumably on the basis of material supplied by the man himself), was relatively brief. Kramer had been born in Mannheim in 1923; he had been a tank captain during the war, being taken prisoner at the end of it. As a POW, Kramer had been sent to Canada and the United States. When hostilities ended he had returned to Germany to work with the Confederation of German Industry, at a time when Professor Erhard was beginning to sow the seeds of the German 'economic miracle'. The biography indicated that Kramer had risen in time to become the President of the CGI, had in fact served over twenty-five years with that organization before being nominated by Germany for the top job at the Commission. No wonder, Morton thought, that Kramer had a few pals who would lend him a *Schloss* for the weekend when he needed it. And his friendships certainly wouldn't be limited to West Germany. Did Kramer know Gordon Cartwright, for instance? The odds were heavily in favour.

He looked at the photograph which the Commission had supplied. How much could you tell from a face? A bland smile. Heavy spectacles. Hair thinning on a high forehead. A touch overweight too, he thought, though it was hard to tell for sure. Wouldn't fit easily into a tank today.

It was getting dark. Morton flipped on the switch of his reading light and skimmed through the other biographies. The average age of the Commission, he noticed, was around fifty-five, the *doyen d'age* being the Greek Dimitrios Kafiri, while the youngest member of the team was the Spaniard with the impossibly high-sounding and aristocratic name of Ariosto Rivera Azul de Balaquentes.

The French Commissioner, Pierre Duchesne, was only just older than Rivera. Morton knew him by reputation as a brilliant technocrat, a man who had wrought a transformation in the fortunes of Renault, France's ailing automobile manufacturer, before being named for Brussels. Those who followed French politics closely had suggested, Morton recalled reading, that Duchesne's four years in the Commission should be seen merely as a springboard back into some high-level job in the Government, perhaps at the Matignon itself. The French obviously were more bullish about a Commissioner's long-term prospects than some of his friends back home.

Morton studied the papers for a time, reading both the lines and – as far as he could – between the lines. Quite often biographies were interesting not for what they revealed, but for what they concealed. He knew for a fact, for example, that the Irish Commissioner, Paddy McGrath, had had an interesting past but there was not a hint of this in the documents. And Ippolito Camino, the Italian Commissioner, had been involved, he remembered, in the Vatican bank collapse. Not a whisper of that either.

He smiled. Perhaps the other Commissioners were at this very moment looking at his own biography with similar scepticism. He turned to the brief *curriculum vitae* which he had sent in a few weeks back. James Morton; this is your life. How many lies were there? None, as far as he could see; but wasn't there just a touch of exaggeration in that bold-typed statement 'Minister for Northern Ireland'? It made him sound like a pro-consul, wielding imperium over distant lands, while the reality was something rather different. He had been a junior minister and he might not have risen much further.

Morton didn't have time to read in detail about the other Commissioners: the Belgian, the Dutchman, the Luxemburger, the Dane, the Portuguese (the latter, as far as he could tell from the photograph, a young and attractive woman), because the driver turned round and said: 'I guess we must be getting close.'

Morton put away his papers, switched off the light and looked up as the car swung through some large stone gates and turned on to a gravel drive to confront – at a distance of around two hundred yards – a small gem of a castle surrounded by parkland and prettily illuminated by floodlights.

A policeman flagged them down. The driver showed him his papers. After taking a close look at Morton as he sat in the rear seat feeling extremely vulnerable – why didn't the fellow just shoot? – the man waved them on. Ten minutes later Morton was unpacking in his room. 'Dinner at eight,' the butler had told him as he entered. 'Drinks at half-eight.'

'Do you mean half-seven?' Morton had asked, looking at his watch.

Butlers were not meant to smile, but this one smiled.

'I'm sorry sir; in Germany we say half-eight – *halb acht* – when we mean half-seven.'

'Perhaps that's the reason Germans always get to work on time.' Morton had been to far too many country-house weekends in his life to be intimidated by one modest German castle. In his experience the best way to deal with butlers was to jolly them along.

There were no embroidered slippers to lay out, no neatly starched shirts to tuck into drawers. Morton travelled light. He hung up his suit, took a bath, poured himself a drink from a well-stocked cabinet then sat down in front of the television to watch the seven o'clock news.

His German was rudimentary, if that, but he recognized the picture of the castle when it was flashed on the screen and the words '*Der Kommission von dem EG*'. EG, he knew, stood for Europaische Gemeinschaft which was what the Germans called the European Community. It came as something of a surprise to him to realize that over here in Europe, especially perhaps in Germany, the Commission was news. In Britain the media treated the European Community as something peripheral. If the twelve Commissioners had gone to Windsor

46

Castle for the weekend, he doubted whether the BBC would have run the story. He felt suddenly cheerful. Watching the news was one thing, making the news was another. He hoped he would be able to make the news, if only the German news, at least once or twice during his tour of duty.

He went downstairs at seven-thirty exactly. The butler, hovering in the hall, pointed the way to the salon overlooking the park and the ornamental lake whose variegated statuary was clearly visible in the floodlights.

Horst Kramer, looking very much like his photograph, was standing in the middle of the room talking to an elderly man whom Morton deduced must be the Greek Dimitrios Kafiri (in Kafiri's case the Commission had tactfully produced a photograph which understated his age by about twenty years). Both men broke off their conversation as he approached.

'Ah, Mr Morton, is it not?' Kramer had a deep booming voice. 'Did you have a good journey? The car was at the airport, yes?'

'Very good,' Morton shook hands with both men. '*Guten Abend, Kalispera*.' He knew little German and less Greek, but he was willing to give it a try. Both men laughed.

Kramer waved at the butler. 'Whisky? Champagne? Or perhaps a glass of wine? After all, we have to do something about the wine lake!' Kramer laughed heavily, teutonically, at his own joke. Morton suspected he had made it before and would make it again.

He settled for whisky. He liked wine with his meals, but not before, and champagne was altogether too variable. Sometimes it could be delicious; at other times, it could leave you dry and headachey. The room filled up as they talked. Morton looked with interest at his fellow Commissioners. They were all new boys but, unlike new boys on their first day at school, this set were going to start in straightaway as prefects. Only two of them, out of the twelve, had been Commissioners before – the Irishman, Paddy McGrath and the Greek, Kafiri. The rest were as green as he was.

As Kramer moved away to greet the new arrivals Morton found himself talking to the Dane, a florid man, now in his late sixties, who had once been Economics Minister in

47

Copenhagen. 'My name is Jurgen Larsen.'

'I'm James Morton.'

Morton had always liked the Danes. In Britain, Vikings and Norsemen made an early entry into the average schoolboy's historical consciousness. Something of the legend tended to rub off on their successors in title. 'The Angles, Saxons and Jutes are going to be in a minority in this new Commission,' Morton said.

Larsen laughed. 'Bringing in Spain and Portugal has certainly changed the character of the EEC; the axis has shifted towards the Mediterranean but I don't expect Kramer will let things get out of hand.'

'Do you know Kramer?'

'Oh, yes,' Larsen replied. 'When I was Minister in Denmark, I had to deal a lot with the Germans, as you can imagine. When he was running the Confederation of German Industry, Kramer was a force to be reckoned with.'

Morton caught sight of the German at the other end of the room moving purposefully from group to group, greeting each individual member of his team, making sure they weren't standing in a corner by themselves. He exuded confidence and bonhomie. A powerful man, Morton thought; surprisingly light on his feet; probably a quick thinker too. The sort of man the Commission needed, he supposed.

'I see what you mean,' he said.

The gong sounded for dinner; the panelled doors were opened at one end of the salon; the twelve Commissioners filed in. As they entered the dining room Fritz, the butler, held out a silver tray on which twelve name cards had been arranged, following the seating plan of the table itself.

Morton found himself at the far end of the table with the Dane on his right and the Greek on his left. Kramer, he noted, sat in the middle with his back to the window. The other Commissioners were ranged about without, as far as he could see, any discernible order. It was as well, he thought, that there had been no adherents to the European Community after Spain and Portugal. The two Iberian candidates had brought the number of Member States to twelve. A thirteenth state would,

48

under the new dispensation, have meant thirteen Commissioners. They could have found themselves – all thirteen – sitting down to dinner on this first night. Hardly an auspicious beginning for a new Commission.

He turned to Larsen. 'Does Mrs Larsen know what she's missing?'

The Dane gave a sad little smile. 'I'm afraid my wife died last year. But I don't think anyway she would have enjoyed an occasion like this. We Danes don't really go in for formality. We're a rather simple people, you know.'

Morton warmed to him. He felt sure that Larsen would be an ally in the Commission, if he ever needed allies. The man was obviously straightforward, unstuffy.

The Greek, sitting to his left, was a harder nut to crack. He lived, or so it seemed, very much in the past; spoke with passion of events and people, like Venezelos and the battle of Inonu, of which Morton had little understanding. Kafiri was an old man and it showed. He had been Mayor of Pyrgos, not far from Olympia in the Peloponnese, for two decades. Every four years he had driven over to the sacred site and, in a moving little ceremony, kindled the flame which would then be borne across the world to Tokyo, Los Angeles, Montreal or Seoul – wherever the Olympics were being held.

'What is Fitzroy McLean doing now?' Kafiri asked. 'We fought in the mountains of Albania together. He came to see me once in Pyrgos.'

Morton explained that things were rather quiet on the Fitzroy McLean front.

Half-way through the first course Horst Kramer tapped on his glass and rose to his feet. He pushed his chair back and stood there solidly, waiting for them to be silent. He turned first to the Portuguese Commissioner sitting immediately to his right.

'Senhora, let me first of all welcome you as the first woman ever to have been a Commissioner of the European Communities. If my term of office is exceptional in no other respects, it will be remembered for that.'

There was a ripple of laughter around the table. What Kramer had said was perfectly true. The Portuguese had

49

plunged in where the rest had feared to tread by appointing a woman Commissioner. Helena Noguentes. For the first time the thirteenth floor of the Berlaymont building in Brussels was going to be adorned by a female, and not any old female (thought Morton) but a woman – as he had already noted in a brief conversation before dinner – of considerable charm and intelligence. He knew from her biography (which he had finished reading before dinner) that she was thirty-five and had previously been mayor of Oporto. That evening, she was wearing a high-collared cream silk shirt which contrasted sharply with her full shoulder-length black hair; she held her head erect and gazed with a firm level glance at her colleagues around the table. When she heard Kramer's opening remarks, she acknowledged the compliment by a graceful nod of her head.

'Thank you, President,' she said. 'But I'm sure your Commission will be known for many other things besides my presence.'

'Colleagues,' Kramer continued, 'as I stand here today, I am conscious of the long tradition behind me. I am conscious of the illustrious men who have occupied the post which I hold now ... Jean Rey, Walter Hallstein, Mansholt, Malfatti, Ortoli, Roy Jenkins, Gaston Thorn, Jacques Delors. It is a proud tradition and I shall do my best to continue it. Indeed, all of us today are part of that tradition, men – now women' – again he gave a little inclination of his head to the right – 'who have decided to dedicate themselves to the service of Europe. For, of course, we are meeting here for the first time not as national representatives, not as delegates of our individual states, but as servants of the European ideal.' He paused. 'I cannot stress this point too strongly. Sometimes people seem to believe that the Commission is just another branch of the Council, a place where Member States appoint their own men and then expect them to follow their instructions. That will not be the case with my Commission.' He rapped his knuckles on the table for emphasis.

Morton watched the faces of his colleagues as Kramer spoke. How many of them, he wondered, believed what Kramer was saying? Some time in January, as the new Commission started work, they would all troop off to Luxembourg and swear an oath of allegiance in the presence of the august members of the European Court of Justice, but would any of them, in the real world, ever put totally out of their minds the fact that they had been nominated by governments? Though governments could not remove them from office once appointed, there could certainly be second thoughts when the time came round for their mandate to be renewed.

Nevertheless he listened carefully as Kramer spoke and liked what he heard. The idea of being his own man appealed to him. If the Prime Minister thought she had appointed a lap-dog to Brussels, she would have another think coming. There remained the question of the job he was to do. Before he left for Germany the situation had still seemed confused. The Foreign Office continued to maintain that they were pushing strongly through all the appropriate channels (whatever that might mean) for the job he wanted, but nothing definite had as yet emerged.

'Colleagues.' A change in the timbre of Kramer's voice caught Morton's attention. 'I know you must all be waiting for me to talk about the distribution of portfolios in my Commission, so I shall not tantalize you much longer.' He laughed. 'Like my predecessor, Jacques Delors, I want to avoid the rancour and bitterness which have sometimes marked this exercise. If we are to continue as colleagues, we must begin as colleagues. Not for me the Night of the Long Knives, not for me the blood on the floor after an all-night session. Each one of you will find, just in front of you where you are sitting, a sealed envelope with your name on it. I would ask you now to open that envelope, to take out the card, and read what is written on it. You will find an indication of the portfolio, or in some cases portfolios, which I have determined best suit your own particular talents and background. Go ahead,' he urged them. 'And while you do so, I shall be able to get on with my dinner!' Again that guttural laugh.

It was like a party game, Morton thought as he reached for his card. A lucky dip in which the prizes had been pre-assigned. He opened the envelope in front of him, took out a stiff green-coloured card, embossed with the large Greek E which

51

the Community had chosen as the symbol of Europe. There was only one word typed on the card: INDUSTRY. He could, literally, feel the colour drain from his cheeks. The sods, he thought: the incompetent sods! He had had their assurance, near as dammit, that he would get one of the big jobs; that was one of the reasons wasn't it (it was a moment for self-delusion), that he had agreed to come to bloody Europe? What had Evans been playing at? Did Passmore know? He could have shot the lot of them.

He was about to give vent to his anger and bitterness when Kramer once more rose to his feet. 'I hope there are not too many nasty surprises. I've done my best to take all factors into consideration. Obviously, I would prefer not to have any discussion since I do not see that discussion would be helpful. These *are* the dispositions I intend to bring into effect. But of course there may be certain questions of detail. Ah, I see our Spanish colleague has a problem.'

Ariosto Rivera Azul de Balaquentes was waving his napkin in the air to attract the attention of the President of the Commission. 'Si, Senor.' Kramer acknowledged the interruption.

The young Spaniard spoke with cold fury, both hands placed on the table in front of him, fists clenched. 'Information Policy! What is Information Policy? That is not a job for the Spanish Commissioner. I cannot tell my countrymen that Spain, after so many years, has joined the Common Market and that Ariosto Rivera Azul de Balaquentes, scion of the oldest family in the land, has been asked to take charge of Information. I came to Brussels to do, not to talk. For the honour of my country, I formally request a change of assignment. I shall absent myself while you discuss the matter.'

He thrust his chair back, rose to his feet and walked stiff and white-faced from the room. Over four centuries earlier, another Rivera Azul de Balaquentes had captained a ship in the great Spanish Armada and had gone down with his vessel in the seas off Plymouth. The line had worn well. The old sea-dog's descendants were not to be put upon.

Morton watched him depart. What the hell, he thought, if he can do it, so can I. He teetered on the brink of protest, began to slide his chair back, cleared his throat as though about to speak. Three things stopped him. The first was a natural hesitation to draw attention to himself. Unlike the Spaniard, Morton didn't go in for fireworks, didn't on the whole think of himself as an exhibitionist; years of public-schooling had taught him to avoid excess of any kind.

The second factor which gave him pause was the sense that, if he did protest, he might actually end up with a worse job. Kramer was obviously a clever operator; if Morton started complaining about being awarded the Industry portfolio, the President-designate might suggest a straight switch with Information and so the last state could be worse than the first. He couldn't necessarily rely on his colleagues to back him up. Over the years Britain had not made many friends in the Common Market – the hard-bitten tactics of successive governments over the Community budget and the common agricultural policy had seen to that. Nor had there been time for Morton to forge personal alliances which could be relied on at a moment of crisis. In the end the Commission would vote on it and the vote would not necessarily go his way.

The third reason for caution was the fact that Kramer himself, though momentarily taken aback by Rivera's outburst, was once again speaking – this time without rising to his feet. He was clearly using all his powers of persuasion, conscious that, though he needed to assert his authority at the outset, it was also necessary to demonstrate a certain sensitivity – even flexibility. He would rule them not with a rod of iron but with a wand of polyester.

'Colleagues,' he appealed to them in a direct but artful way. 'If nobody else has any problems with his assignment' – he gazed sternly around the table, inviting them to speak while at the same time willing them to be silent – 'I think we should all address ourselves to the question raised by Senor Rivera. I can quite understand,' he continued quickly, 'that our friend from Spain has certain very precise difficulties with the assignment I have suggested. On reflection and, knowing the sensibilities of his countrymen, knowing the historic pride of that Iberian race, I can understand he might consider that having the responsibility for the Community's information policy might not, just by itself, seem to be an adequate challenge. I do not myself accept that assessment, of course. If we are to present ourselves to the outside world, if we are to explain ourselves better to people within the Community, information and communication are crucial. Nevertheless, I can recognize that that is the way Senor Rivera feels and I think we should do something about it.' He paused. 'Perhaps I can make a start myself. As President of the Commission, I have reserved to myself the responsibility for supervising any further enlargement negotiations.' He saw their surprised looks. 'Don't forget, colleagues, that the association agreement with Turkey provides that, by 1995, Turkey will become a full member of the European Community. In the present circumstances, we may all of us consider this an unlikely possibility, nevertheless the commitment exists and negotiations must in due course be pursued. I intend to hand over that dossier to our Spanish colleague.'

Horst Kramer spoke with a straight face, giving no indication at all that his offer was, at best, a hollow gesture and at worst a poisoned chalice. Some of the others, though, were unable to suppress a smile. Dimitrios Kafiri, in particular, found the prospect of Turkish adhesion to the Community more than mildly funny.

'I trust, Mr President, that the position of Greece in this matter is entirely clear. You know that my country will never agree to Turkey's entry into the Common Market.'

'That's not what Greece said during its own accession negotiations,' Kramer reminded him sharply.

Kafiri was too old and wise a bird to be drawn. 'What one says when one is trying to join a club is one thing,' he commented. 'How you behave once you're inside is another thing altogether.'

A general round of laughter greeted this remark. It broke the tension. Kramer knew, then, that he had them where he wanted them. 'Is anybody else prepared to give up a small part of their portfolio?'

Morton had it on the tip of his tongue to say that Ariosto Rivera Azul de Balaquentes could have Industry and jolly good luck to him, but Kramer seemed not to catch his eye. Instead the German looked determinedly towards the other end of the table where the Irish Commissioner, Paddy McGrath, sat next to Pierre Duchesne, the Frenchman.

'Mr McGrath?' Kramer spoke jocularly, but there was an underlying seriousness in his tone. 'How about letting our Spanish friend have the responsibility for Consumer Affairs. After all, you will still have Energy and Forests.'

'There aren't any forests in Ireland,' McGrath replied with some asperity. 'So I don't know why I should have the responsibility for forests, but I suppose I've got it. But, yes, if he wants Consumer Affairs, let him have it. As long as he doesn't start interfering with the way we brew Guinness.' He broke into a broad smile. 'I'll go and get him if you like, and tell him the good news. Information, Consumer Affairs and Enlargement – that sounds a pretty good bag of tricks to be getting along with.'

There was a small ripple of applause. Paddy McGrath, it was clear, enjoyed playing the role of 'good ole boy'. Watching him as he rose to fetch Rivera, Morton couldn't help wondering whether there might not be other sides to McGrath's character.

A few moments later, the Spaniard having rejoined them, all was once more peace and harmony. Morton knew that the opportunity for protest had passed, the moment had come and gone. The deal had been signed and sealed once they let Paddy McGrath leave the room to bring the good news to Spain and when in turn Rivera had indicated his willingness to accept. It had, after all, been a formal protest, a matter of national pride and not much more. Ariosto Rivera Azul de Balaquentes was not a stupid man. He knew the score on Turkey and was no more interested in the role of consumers within the European Community than Paddy McGrath had been. But three portfolios sounded better than one. It would sell in Palomares. As they moved from fish to meat Morton came to terms with the fact that he was the Commissioner for Industry and he had better make the most of it.

After dinner he found himself once more talking to Horst Kramer. They had gone back from the dining room into the

55

salon. Most of the Commissioners were noticeably more relaxed than they had been at the start of the evening. Kramer had a large cigar in his hand, his own private smoke-stack, and he waved it in the air to make the point. 'I'm so glad you were ready to take on the Industry job, Morton. I can tell you in confidence that the British Government was particularly keen. They realize just how important that portfolio is.' He took Morton's arm and steered him in the direction of the large french windows which looked out on to the grounds of the castle. Lowering his voice he added: 'There were others pushing for it, I can tell you, who might not have taken a correct view of the assignment.'

Before Morton had a chance to ask what he meant by a 'correct view' Kramer had moved on, corralling each member of his team for a last brief exchange of words. Morton went to bed that night feeling bemused. Why had the British Government pushed hard for industry without telling him? Why had Kramer agreed? It could hardly be because of his knowledge and experience of industrial problems in Europe. He took off his trousers and hung them over the back of a brocaded armchair, went into the bathroom, washed his face and brushed his teeth. Fuck them all, he thought. Whatever motives, obscure or otherwise, lay behind his present appointment, the fact was he was *en poste* and he intended to do a bloody good job. Quite what that job would involve he didn't know but he was sure he would find out soon enough. He remembered what the pompous old Chaplain used to say in Lower Chapel. 'Sufficient unto the day is the evil thereof. . . .'

He was up early next morning, walking before breakfast in the grounds of the *Schloss*. Coming round the lake in the opposite direction with his coat collar buttoned up against the clear cold morning air and his hat planted firmly on his head was a tall, spare figure whom Morton was unable to place. The man had certainly not been at the dinner the previous evening.

'Good morning,' he said.

'Good morning.' The other man raised his hat. Morton noted the high forehead, leonine profile and the deep-set eyes which, even on that first occasion, spoke of both wisdom and humour. The man held out his hand. 'I am Leopold Brugmann, the Commission's Secretary-General.'

'Ah yes, of course.' Morton held out his own hand. So this was the legendary Brugmann, the man who had served successive presidents of the Commission since the beginning, and who was reputed to know all that there was to know about the way the Community worked; a Belgian aristrocrat who had grown up in the proud school of Henri Spaak and who had, in his own quiet and unassuming way, gone on to rival his master. 'I'm absolutely delighted to meet you,' Morton added. 'I had expected to see you at the dinner last night.'

Brugmann's tired, sad eyes crinkled into a smile. 'Oh no, on the first evening the Commissioners must be by themselves. The Secretary-General knows his place. And I never come to breakfast the next day. That way, if there've been any rows the night before, it is clear that I've had no part in them. The Secretary-General tries to preserve his objectivity.' He laughed. 'But did you have a good evening?'

Morton suspected that the Belgian knew, down to the last detail, everything that had transpired at the previous night's dinner. 'Yes, we did. There was one moment when our Spanish colleague, Senor Rivera, looked less than enchanted with his portfolio, but we sorted that out.'

Again the smile, sensitive, knowledgeable, world-weary almost. 'Ah, Spain. I always knew there would be problems with Spain. The Spanish people are very different. Those of us who come from the Low Countries know that very well. After all, Spain ruled us for centuries. I warned Kramer that just one dossier by itself would not be enough. And you yourself, Mr Morton, are you satisfied with your assignment? It was very much Dr Kramer's own decision. I had no part in it. You must believe me.' Brugmann spoke with considerable earnestness as though trying to convey some coded message or even – perhaps – a warning.

A flight of geese, coming in from Denmark, landed with a good deal of whirring and cackling on the still surface of the lake in front of them. Morton watched the birds hovering, with wings beating and feet flapping, for the last few seconds before touching down. An urge to be frank came over him. 'It's

57

going to be a difficult job for me to do. I'm not sure I know enough about it. I was surprised myself by the appointment.'

Leopold Brugmann – Count Leopold Brugmann to give him his title as it appeared in *High Life*, Belgium's indispensable social compendium – shook his hand a second time. 'Count on me for any help you may need, that's what I'm here for.'

'Thank you.' Morton meant what he said. The Commission itself, he had already realized, would be a cut-throat world. On the surface, they were all colleagues; on paper – and to the outside world – they acted as a 'college'. But there would be real rivalries and real tensions within the house. Weaker men would go to the wall as they always had. It would be good to have as a friend a man who during a lifetime of service had managed to outgrow most, if not all, personal ambitions.

'Let's walk back together,' he said. 'It must be breakfast time by now.'

Brugmann pulled his coat more tightly around his shoulders. 'Brrr, it's cold. I think you're right. Probably, you will even get an English breakfast today, not a continental one, as you call it.'

Morton laughed. 'We may be running out of North Sea oil, but we've still got the great English breakfast!'

Some of the other Commissioners were already in the breakfast room. Like the geese on the lake, Morton thought, there had been a good deal of cackling and whirring as they came in to land, but now they were feeding quietly. Brugmann had excused himself on their return to the castle, saying that he had to consult Kramer before the morning's working session. 'See you later,' Morton had said. He sat down at a table with the Dane and the Greek. Fritz was on duty that morning.

'Good morning, Fritz.'

'Good morning, sir, what would you like for breakfast?'

'Bacon, two fried eggs and the *Financial Times*.' If he was going to be Industry Commissioner he might as well act the part.

The remaining Commissioners trickled in by dribs and drabs. It was extraordinary, Morton thought, how much breakfast revealed about a man's or woman's personality. Some people, of course, didn't appear at all in public so early on in the day – which was an indication perhaps that they didn't much like or trust the face they presented to the world in the early morning. Others were silent to the point of taciturnity; hid behind newspapers; barely replied when addressed. Still others – Morton supposed he counted himself among them – looked forward to the meal with something like enthusiasm. It was a way of getting to grips with the day. He tended to feel good at breakfast. You didn't have to waste time studying the menu and catching the waiter's eye. Over the bacon and the eggs he caught a hint of some expensive perfume and looked up to see Helena Noguentes coming to join them. He rose to his feet, pushing his chair back as he did so.

'Don't move,' she smiled at them. 'I don't come down normally, but it seemed too fine a day to stay in my room.'

An array of cold meats was on the table. This was breakfast German style. Morton offered the plate to his next-door neighbour but Helena declined.

'I'll stick to coffee and croissants.'

Afterwards they got down to work. They met in the library in the east wing of the castle, a sombre room whose leather-bound volumes included, so Morton had learnt, one of three extant copies of the Freiburg Bible as well as the first printed version of Martin Luther's commentary on St Paul's Epistle to the Romans. A collection of Dürer engravings hung on the walls and at the far end of the long room, mounted on a screen and skilfully illuminated, was a triptych of quite outstanding quality. The central panel showed Christ on the cross, while the wings on either side depicted saints and acolytes variously attired but uniformly grief-stricken. Morton, who had more than a passing interest in art, recognized it as German medieval painting at its finest.

'Do you know who did that?' He asked his Italian neighbour, Ippolito Camino, as he took his seat at the long, wide table which filled the centre of the room.

Camino was an Italian of the old school, a man who in the course of a long life had travelled much in the realms of gold. Medieval painting, in Siena, in Arezzo or here in northern Germany was meat and drink to him. People spoke today about European Union as though this was something bold and new, but Camino's mind harked back to a time when Europe had been united by the minds of men, by the intercourse of savants and the exchange of artistic ideas. The Alps, then, had been less of a barrier than they were now.

'An early Schongauer,' he replied, 'a precursor of the famous *retable* at Colmar.'

Morton was impressed.

When they had ranged themselves around the table Horst Kramer called for order. He looked fresh and pink-faced, almost cherubic in fact, thought Morton, although when the light glinted on his glasses in a certain way his eyes could look more sinister than innocent.

'I'm not going to make another speech,' Kramer began, 'certainly not a long one. Perhaps I could begin this morning by saying what I didn't say last night, namely that we must all be grateful to the owner of this splendid place, Ludwig Ritter, for making his home available to us this weekend. Since this is our first official meeting as a Commission, and since we have with us today our Secretary-General, a man who has, as you know, served all my predecessors in the past with distinction' – he turned to nod amiably at Leopold Brugmann sitting beside him – 'I think we should note our appreciation of Mr Ritter's hospitality in the record of this meeting.'

'Who's Ludwig Ritter?' Morton addressed the question to his neighbour, in a whisper.

'The head of Deutsch-Chemie, in Cologne.'

Morton nodded. He remembered the great factory on the banks of the Rhine which he had seen the previous afternoon. And he recalled, when Camino mentioned the name, that he had read an article in some magazine which had described Ritter as the 'boss of the bosses', a shadowy figure who seldom emerged in public; a man of immense wealth whose influence was reputed to extend into the Bundes-Kanzlerei itself.

It was a long day. They broke for coffee and for lunch but, apart from that, Kramer kept their noses to the grindstone. Dinner the previous evening had seen the allocation of portfolios; now it was a matter of structuring the Commission's working methods; of putting flesh on the outline; a moment for identifying the major proposals which would distinguish Kramer's term of office. They concluded their business around five o'clock, in time for Commissioners to catch planes home that night.

'How did it go?' Morton's driver was quick to ask the obvious question as he drove the Commissioner back down to the north German plains.

Morton took the question at its face value. How *had* the meeting gone? Though he was familiar enough with the ways of British politics, he was a novice in these European affairs; hadn't had time to get used to the jargon; he didn't know enough about the background, the working methods, the daily compromises which were forced upon any institution which sought to serve a multiplicity of interests. But looking at the day as objectively as he could manage, he realized he felt uneasy. There had been something in the way Horst Kramer had stage managed the whole thing which had been almost too smooth.

'You know I'm not sure, Gerry,' he replied thoughtfully. 'In some ways, the Commission seems a rum outfit.'

'You can say that again, sir. I've seen some pretty strange things in my time.'

Morton decided it would be prudent not to inquire further. He would find out soon enough what life was like on the thirteenth floor of the Berlaymont.

Chapter Four

'Does it *have* to be Luxembourg?' Isobel sounded peeved. As far as she knew, nothing had ever happened in Luxembourg and nothing was likely to happen. There had been some princess Prince Charles was supposed to have taken a fancy to, or vice versa, but as everyone knew, nothing had come of that.

'The new Commission has to go before the European Court of Justice to take the Oath of Office. I'll drive up from Brussels; you can fly from London.' Morton was ready to be patient with her.

It was their last weekend in England together and they spent it in the country. In the end, they had decided to keep both houses not only because Isobel was still adamant in her refusal to move to the Continent on a full-time basis but also because, with Morton's Commissioner's salary, there was no need for them to let either place to tenants. And it was a way of pretending that nothing had changed. At least nothing fundamental.

They walked up to the gibbet on the hills above Hungerford. She had wrapped a scarf around her head and it held her hair in place against the wind which gusted fiercely at the top of the ridge. Sneaking a glance at her as she strode with her head down, brow jutting forward, Morton couldn't help remembering how often they had walked on these Berkshire Downs when he had first been elected to the House of Commons. He remembered how lucky he had felt himself to be; how envious, it seemed, others were. There had been stories in the press, in the colour supplements, about 'a perfectly matched team', a 'political duet'. But time had moved on. He wondered if things would ever go right again.

'I wonder which of us has changed more,' he said suddenly. 'You or me?'

She turned to him with surprise. On the whole she did not consider him as a man who liked to probe. 'Look, Jimmy. We're both of us in a muddle, let's face it. We may or may not come out of it. Let's not ask profound questions. Let's take one step at a time.'

'Will you come to Luxembourg anyway?'

'Hell, yes, if I have to.'

It was not much of a victory, but it left him feeling good. Besides, she hadn't called him Jimmy in years.

Watching from her seat in the body of the courtroom, Isobel Morton couldn't help thinking what a lot of flummery it all was. She looked at the judges of the European Court sitting up there on the dais in front of her, all dressed up in their finery. Red scarlet robes; white bib and tucker; velvet pants. Great heavens, she thought, they might as well be back in the middle ages!

A woman sitting next to her, another wife she supposed, said: 'They used to wear wigs, you know, but they gave that up a few years ago.'

'Thank God for that; they look ridiculous enough as it is,' Isobel replied. She had never been one for pomp and ceremony. Nor, to be fair to him, had Morton. She leaned forward to catch what the President of the Court, seated in the middle of the line of Justices, was saying.

Professor Cornelius van Rijn, a Dutch lawyer of enormous distinction, who had succeeded to the Presidency of the Court only the previous year, had, it seemed, deliberately chosen to stress the solemn nature of the Oath of Office which members of the Commission would shortly swear.

'The authors of the Treaties' – he gazed sternly around the room, looking not only at the Members of the Commission seated in front of him, but also at the public in the body of the courtroom and the press up in the gallery – 'showed much

63

wisdom in providing this public undertaking or oath. Of course, no one who is familiar with our institutions could doubt the independence of their Members, but it is none the less right that this oath should be taken and that this ceremony should occupy the place it does, coming right at the beginning of the Commission's term. As the guardian of the Treaties, the Commission must ensure that Community law is respected by the Community and by the Member States. . . . '

Isobel's attention began to wander as Van Rijn droned on. She looked around at the paintings and tapestries in the courtroom. She had no idea how many millions of dollars – or whatever it was they used over here – it must have cost to create this European Court of Justice high up on the Plateau de Kirchberg, but she had no doubt at all that, given a similar budget, she could have made a better job of it. Why did justice always have to be so heavy? Could not purposes be serious without the trappings being funereal? If she had her way she would have a courtroom full of light and air, open to the view and to the world, not a place hemmed in by solemnity.

Four rows ahead of her she saw the President of the Commission, a heavy German whom she knew was called Horst Kramer, rise from his seat and step forward to a position immediately in front of the dais. She twiddled the knob at the side of her chair to listen to the English translation since Kramer, as was his right, had elected to take the Oath of Office in his native tongue. She heard a lilting female voice – were there green smiling eyes and brown wavy hair behind it? – say: 'I, Horst Kramer, named President of the Commission of the European Communities by the governments of the Member States of the European Communities, solemnly undertake to exercise my functions in complete independence and in the general interest of the Communities. In the discharge of my duties I undertake not to solicit nor to accept instructions from any government or any other body and to abstain from any act which is incompatible with the character of my duties. I also take note of the undertaking of each Member State to respect this character and not to seek to influence the Members of the Commission in the exercise of their task.'

Morton was eighth man in. Isobel had no idea how the order

of precedence was established but by the time her husband came to take the Oath, she reckoned she already knew it by heart. Since Morton spoke in English, the translator lapsed into silence. Isobel listened through the headphones anyway and realized, with some surprise, that Morton – to judge from the tone of his voice at least – was apparently moved by the occasion. 'Solemnly swear . . . exercise of my functions . . . full independence . . . not to seek nor to accept. . . . ' For her the words were trite formulae, part of the rigmarole which Europeans always seemed to think was so important. But, for Morton, they appeared to matter. She hadn't heard him speak with such feeling since the time – was it really six years ago? – when he had said 'I do' in that freezing church in Newbury. She shifted in her seat to get a better view of the tall familiar figure. Whatever others might think of his Brussels assignment, it was clear that Morton was going to give it a go.

She drove back with him to Brussels. 'Who was that lady I saw you with?' she asked as they entered the Ardennes.

'She's our Portuguese colleague. Some complicated name.'

'I didn't know they let women in.'

'She's the first.'

'She's quite good-looking.'

'Is she?'

Morton's eyes were closed and she couldn't tell whether his lack of interest was genuine or not. Come to think of it, she had never really known whether Morton was interested in other women. 'Keep your paws off her anyway. Big Sister will be watching.'

Morton smiled, still with his eyes shut. 'When the cat's away. . . .' he said.

Gerry McLoughlin knew the road from Luxembourg to Brussels as well as he knew the highway between Cork and Dublin. 'We're just passing Bastogne,' he told them. 'The Germans almost burst through here in 44.'

Morton opened his eyes, looked out at the great sweep of forest and field stretching to the horizon, imagined the panzer divisions rolling through towards Brussels and Paris. There were more ways than one, he thought, of conquering Europe. If you couldn't do it by force of arms, you could try sheer industrial muscle. He thought of that giant complex, Deutsch-Chemie, which he had seen a few days earlier on the banks of the Rhine outside Cologne. Who, in the last analysis, had really won the war, the victor or the vanquished?

They reached Brussels in the early evening and drove straight into the centre of the town. Morton, with the aid of a helpful real-estate agent recommended by Lady Passmore, had found himself a rather grand apartment in the Sablon, one of the few remaining parts of Brussels which retained its medieval prettiness. Apart from the Grand' Place itself, the Sablon and perhaps the Quai aux Briques, most of Brussels had over the last twenty or thirty years fallen prey to the ravages of property developers, especially – or so it seemed – the British who, having done their best to demolish London in a quite spectacular way, were now anxious to export their peculiar skills wherever some sublime architectural heritage looked to be in danger of lasting. It was ironic, thought Morton, that the Allies had liberated Brussels only to destroy it in another way.

But the Sablon, miraculously, had endured. At the last minute a local residents' association had been formed, had enlisted the aid of one or two Cabinet Ministers, had no doubt greased a few palms with the result that at least a hundred buildings of real merit survived around the church of Notre Dame du Sablon, a stone's throw from the Palais Royal.

They parked in the shadow of the church in an area which, on Sunday mornings, would be host to a busy antique market.

'This *is* pretty!' In spite of her determination to be bored by Belgium at all costs, Isobel was impressed.

'Come up and see my etchings.' It was hardly an original remark, but it was all he could think of. Morton was no longer sure of the basis on which his relationship with Isobel was to be conducted, if indeed it was to be conducted on any basis at all. He'd decided to tread warily, make no assumptions. If he had to start from scratch, well, that's what he would do.

'What kind of etchings do you have?' she asked, playing the game.

'Nothing fancy, I'm afraid. Half a dozen workmanlike pieces by some minor masters.'

Looking back, Morton found it one of the stranger experiences of his life. He had after all been married to her for more than half a decade, yet here he was inviting her up, inviting her in, showing her round his apartment as though they had just met for the first time.

They stood by the tall, leaded windows looking out into the floodlit square with drinks in their hands. The smart restaurants directly opposite were getting ready for the evening's business; the antique shops were putting up the shutters.

'Over there is Wittamer, the best chocolate shop in town.' Morton pointed to an elegant facade half-way down the Sablon.

Isobel was not averse to expensive chocolates. 'Perhaps Brussels isn't so bad after all.'

Morton knew that it would take more than chocolates to bring her to Belgium, but it was, he reckoned, a good sign, an indication that – if circumstances were right – Isobel would be prepared to see the good as well as the bad in the situation.

'Can you stay for dinner?' He asked the question diffidently. On the whole he was a self-confident man but Isobel's defection had been a considerable blow to his esteem. He did not wish to expose himself to unnecessary rebuffs.

She smiled at him. 'I'll stay for breakfast too, if you like.'

They walked down to the Grand' Place and had dinner at the Maison du Cygne. The restaurant was in one of the oldest and loveliest houses on the square. The food was excellent; the service impeccable; the bill astronomical.

Morton picked up the paper and put it in his wallet.

'Can you charge it? Am I a legitimate business expense?'

He was offended then, for the first time that day. Her remark caught him on the raw. He had picked up the bill not because he wanted to cheat on his expenses – that was not his way of doing things – but for sentimental reasons. He wanted to remember the evening, remember the occasion. God dammit, he wanted to remember that he had had dinner the day he took his Oath of Office with his lawful and wedded wife and what the hell was wrong with that.

'You know, Isobel' – he sounded cool – 'I'm not sure you *ought* to stay the night.'

'Oh shit, James. Don't get upset. I was only joking.'

They walked back through the streets. It was cold but not unbearable.

'What time is your plane?' he asked.

'Eleven.'

'I'll have to leave long before then. I like to be in the office by nine. But the car will take you.'

'Let's not talk about tomorrow now.' She linked her arm through his and he relented.

She paused in front of Wittamer to look at the offerings in the window. 'Do the Belgians like sex as well?' She turned to him. 'Not separate beds, not tonight Jimmy. I want you tonight.'

Deep down he wanted to tell her to take a long running jump at herself, to get lost, to bloody well clear out of his life and not muck him up when he was trying to get things straight. But of course he said none of that. Instead he cupped his hand under her elbow and steered her firmly away from the chocolates in the direction of his apartment.

Chapter Five

Morton's first few weeks in Brussels passed quickly as he strove to master his brief. Though Peter Simpson, the young man from the Foreign Office whom he had taken on as his Chef de Cabinet, organized his office efficiently and never failed to present him with the right papers to sign at the right time, Morton was reluctant to be merely a cypher. He was a stubborn person and he still nursed the illusion – a dangerous illusion, no doubt, as many would see it – that, having been asked to do a job, he should do it to the best of his ability. Much of the material was unfamiliar to him, but he did his best to keep abreast of the subject.

'What the hell's all this about?' he would ask, confronted around seven o'clock each evening with a pile of papers for his signature. 'Can't I have it in English at least?' But, in practice, he quickly learned that it simply was not realistic to hope to understand every document that was put before him, nor to expect complicated texts, often produced in a tearing hurry somewhere in the bowels of the Berlaymont, to be translated immediately into his own language. The system simply couldn't work if each Commissioner insisted on getting all the documents in his mother tongue all the time, though he might reasonably expect to have some of them some of the time.

But, within these necessary constraints, Morton did his best. Even Peter Simpson, who had a healthy scorn for most of his fellow men, gave occasional signs of his appreciation – if not of the Commissioner's intellectual grasp, then at least of his dogged determination.

'The man knows nothing about industry, domestic or European,' Simpson said to his wife one night on returning from the office, 'but he's intent on learning. That could be dangerous!' he laughed.

Jill Simpson, a sharp, scrawny woman who found her husband's intellectual arrogance often irritating – didn't he know that some people just had to do humdrum jobs like being a wife and mother, for example? – looked at him suspiciously: 'What do you mean by that?'

But Simpson, settling down to a large, late dinner (food in all its forms fascinated him), was not to be drawn.

Isobel's absence was another factor in Morton's dedication to duty. He found it quite easy to scoop up his papers into his briefcase and read quietly through the evening, first at some restaurant in or near the Sablon and then, later, in the wide armchair which he had set beside the now disused fireplace in the sitting room of his apartment. This practice, which he realized after a few weeks was growing into something of a habit, afforded him one small but nevertheless significant satisfaction. Normally, in the Berlaymont, there was a late-evening delivery of mail which would stay in the in-trays until the secretaries arrived early the next morning to sort it out. His Chef de Cabinet had – he knew – established the rule that nothing was to go into the Commissioner without his – Simpson's – visa on it. In general this was a sensible precaution which both enabled the Chef de Cabinet to be informed about what was going on and ensured that the Commissioner was not bothered by a lot of rubbish. But already there'd been one or two occasions when Morton had been miffed, to put it no more strongly than that, to find that Simpson had sat on a document – perhaps a letter or an internal memorandum – which he had been particularly waiting for. So it pleased him to be able to pick up his own pile of incoming correspondence, once or twice a week. That way he could sift quietly through it in the pleasant solitude of his flat, and come in next morning ready to tell Simpson what he, Morton, thought rather than vice-versa.

The external appearance of the manilla envelope which Morton found in his mail one evening in early spring, when the

70

tourists had already begun to thicken in downtown Brussels, was not in itself unusual. The item measured six inches by eight; it had a West German postmark; the address was typewritten. Some trade circular, he decided, and put it on one side for his secretary while he worked his way down to the bottom of the pile. An hour later, when the bells of Notre Dame du Sablon had just struck ten o'clock, Morton finished his reading. He put the papers back into his case and he was about to get ready for bed when he saw the brown envelope lying where he had placed it. Rather than unlock his case again, he picked up the envelope and slit it open, using an ivory paperknife engraved with the head of Queen Nefertiti – an item which he had bought, years ago, in the bazaar in Cairo. Inside the envelope was a letter on a single plain sheet of paper, folded once. There was also a four-page document, stapled in the top left-hand corner. He read the letter first.

'Mr Commissioner,' it began,

> the enclosed memorandum sets out the abuses, and even the crimes, currently being practised by a major European chemical company which the writer considers to be un-acceptable even by the prevailing low standards of the pharmaceutical and chemical industries. The writer wishes to remain anonymous, but if you are interested in learning more, look for an advertisement on the back page of the *International Herald Tribune* advising tulip-lovers to visit the flower fields of Keukenhof.

Morton looked at the letter with distaste. During his time as an MP he had received enough correspondence from cranks, including anonymous cranks, to paper a small room. Some people just couldn't resist putting pen to paper. But there was something about this particular communication which attracted his notice. The letter was not in the usual hand-written scrawl, with heavy underlinings and a liberal use of exclamation marks. It was a neatly typed professional job. It seemed to him that it had been composed on a word processor though he had no idea what kind of word processor was involved. That was a matter for the experts. The paper itself appeared to have no special characteristics, though here again analysis might indicate its provenance. Morton turned his attention to the memorandum which appeared to have been typed on the same machine as the letter.

In spite of his instinctive hesitations Morton found that he spent the next ten minutes totally absorbed. The memorandum began with a general attack on Europe's pharmaceutical and chemical industries:

Pharmaceutical and pesticide companies based in the European Community control the major proportion of the world market for these products. Twenty per cent of world drug sales valued at US $1000,000 million and nearly 50 per cent of the world export market are in the hands of EC-based companies. More than 40 per cent of world pesticide sales valued at US $17,000 million and a staggering 61 per cent of the export market are controlled by EC-based pesticide firms.

European governments benefit from this trade, yet have failed to ensure that the safety standards operated within Europe apply equally to exports. Many products banned, withdrawn, severely restricted or not approved for use in Europe are cleared for export.

The result of the international trade in pharmaceuticals is a distortion of efforts to improve health. WHO has identified some two hundred drugs as being 'essential' for the treatment of most illness. Yet there are somewhere in the region of fifty thousand preparations on the market worldwide. The UN Centre on Transnational Corporations found that, in many countries, the products marketed by transnational pharmaceutical companies 'did not correspond to the major health requirements and priorities of each country'. In Bangladesh an expert committee found that nearly one-third of the money spent on drugs went on 'unnecessary and useless medicines'.

The insecticide dieldrin, described by the World Health Organization as 'extremely hazardous', was banned by the EC in January 1981 – but not for export. Studies in Nigeria found that the chemical killed off many species of 'friendly' insects as well as fish, bats and squirrels, and virtually eliminated one species of monkey. The pesticide industry has in fact encouraged the increased use of pesticides over the past thirty to forty years, claiming they are 'essential' for improved agriculture. However, with that increased use has come a serious threat to health and the environment. Put simply, pesticides are designed to kill. Unfortunately, they don't know when to stop.

Having opened with these broad statements about Europe's chemical and pharmaceutical industry, the writer of the memorandum then proceeded to zero in on one particular company, without naming names, to produce the most damning indictment of the moral, ethical, commercial and industrial practices of a major business corporation that Morton had ever seen in his life – assuming it was true. He came to the last paragraph.

'In the writer's view,' he read, 'the foregoing, horrendous as it may seem, is only part of the story, the tip of the iceberg. The unsound practices, abuses and actual crimes catalogued in this note are all capable of being substantiated.'

The room, Morton observed, seemed suddenly hot and stuffy. He dabbed at his brow with his handkerchief, rose from his chair and strode over to the window, throwing it open. The noise from the Sablon, a few feet below, was immediately doubled in intensity. He stood there looking out at the evening bustle while he tried to decide what to do. He could, he supposed, pass the whole thing over to Peter Simpson in the morning and Simpson, in turn, could get the staff to evaluate the material.

Yes, he thought – that was what he would do. There were hundreds of highly-paid *fonctionnaires* in Brussels sitting around waiting for something to do. Well, they could get off their backsides and do some work. If a Commissioner decided, personally, to investigate all the complaints that were made to him, he wouldn't have time for anything else.

As he turned back into the room he had a brief vision of the bland self-satisfied face of his Chef de Cabinet. The image brought him up short. Hell, he thought, could he really trust

73

Simpson, could he really trust the *fonctionnaires* of the Commission's industrial department, to take the lid off what might in the end be a can of worms? Weren't they much more likely to sit on the lid so as to keep it firmly in place?

Morton surprised himself with the radical nature of his thoughts. The Brussels climate must be getting to him, he supposed. Suddenly he changed his mind. No, he thought; on balance he would keep Simpson out of it – at least for the moment. He would do a little probing himself first, try to assess – so far as he could – the accuracy of the memorandum. That was enough for starters. No doubt there were people about who expected him to treat his job as a well-paid sinecure. If that was the case, he thought, they might end up by being disappointed.

'I see you took your mail home with you last night, Commissioner.' Peter Simpson breezed into his office almost as soon as Morton arrived.

'Couldn't resist it.' Morton hoped he sounded as offhand as he meant to. He put his briefcase on his desk and fished out a bundle of papers. 'I don't think there's anything very urgent.' He passed them over. 'But I'm sure you'll want to have a look at them anyway.'

Simpson appeared to miss the faint note of irony in Morton's voice. 'Could I suggest, Commissioner, with great respect that it's probably best if either I or at least some other member of the Cabinet casts a quick eye on papers before they come up to you. I'm sure it will save trouble in the long run.'

'Of course.' Morton seemed genuinely contrite.

The two men talked for a quarter of an hour, going over the business before them. Since it was Wednesday the Commission would be meeting and, judging by the length of the agenda, Morton reckoned that he would be tied up most of the day. Like others before him, Dr Horst Kramer had determined to make a mark in his first hundred days. He had, moreover, insisted that only the most pressing business should keep Commissioners from attending the weekly sessions. Morton had already experienced the tedium of long and sometimes pointless discussions conducted between colleagues who

74

seemed doggedly determined not to see the other's point of view; he had, nevertheless, respected Kramer's injunction and had been a consistent attender at Commission business. Today, at least, he looked forward to having some extraneous reading matter to occupy him during the duller moments.

'Ask Vivian to come in as you go out, would you, Peter?' Moments later Vivian Perkins, the secretary who had looked after Morton during his fourteen years in the House of Commons and who had followed him to Brussels, entered the room. 'Ah, Vivian!' Morton was always glad to see her. More than most things, he appreciated loyalty. 'How are things today?'

'You took your mail again last night, Commissioner. Mr Simpson seemed quite upset.'

Morton walked over to the large plate-glass window and looked down at the city of Brussels spread out below. What a mess it was, he thought! The combination of mercenary property developers with the growth of European institutions, like the Commission and Council, had been fairly lethal. He could see isolated pockets of traditional architecture, ordinary homes for ordinary people, but they were few and far between, like honest men in politics. He turned to his secretary. 'I don't think you or I need to be *wholly* governed by what Mr Simpson thinks or feels, do we, Vivian?'

Vivian Perkins smiled in a motherly way. Though there was not much difference in their ages – she was only a year or two older than he – Mrs Perkins had always regarded James Morton with something akin to the pride of parenthood. During her years in the House she had had no time for those who suggested that Morton should have gone further, faster. She didn't care for the pushers and the climbers. She liked Morton for what he was: honest, decent, straightforward. He had treated her well; that was why she had come with him to Brussels though she was also intrigued, after so many years in England, by the idea of a foreign posting. As far as she was concerned, Britain's membership of the Common Market in no way changed the status of the Belgian capital. Abroad was abroad. Apart from the fact that the inhabitants didn't eat with chopsticks, Brussels could as well have been Ulan Bator.

'I must say, Commissioner,' (she enjoyed calling him by his new title) 'I rather agree with you. Sometimes those young men from the Foreign Office seem too clever by half.'

He sat down at his desk and went through the diary with her, checking on appointments and engagements. 'I'm going to be in the Commission meeting all morning and we may go on in the afternoon as well since it looks like a fairly heavy agenda. Could you get something from the library for me and have it sent in? I'd like a print-out on the chemical industry. Books and reports, anything relevant, in fact. Tell them I want it quickly.'

'Worldwide, or just Europe?'

'Worldwide, but including Europe, if you see what I mean.'

Vivian Perkins nodded. 'I'll get on to the library straight away.'

Later that morning, while the French Commissioner, Pierre Duchesne, was indulging in verbal pyrotechnics which on the whole left him cold, Morton was handed a brown envelope by one of the uniformed attendants – or *huissiers* as they were called – who had sidled into the Commission meeting for the purpose. He opened it and removed the contents. It was, as he had hoped, a listing of items in the Commission's library which related in some way to the chemical industry.

Quite what he was expecting to find, Morton wasn't really sure. Ever since the previous night, when he had locked the anonymous memorandum in the bottom drawer of his desk in his apartment, he had been mulling over the best way to proceed. The inadvisability of precipitate action was as clear to him that morning as it had been the night before. He was quite prepared to move rapidly and forcefully if he had to, but he liked to have the full dimensions of any problem in his mind before he did. He had the countryman's habit, and knack, of gauging the lie of the land.

As he glanced through the print-out, one item in particular caught his attention. He gave an involuntary grunt of interest which caused the Frenchman to pause momentarily in mid-flow and cast an annoyed glance in his direction.

Wonder Drugs and Corporate Crime: An Investigation into the Practices of the Pharmaceutical Industry. The book,

Morton saw, had been published two years earlier in both the United States and Britain. But what interested him even more than the title was the author's name: F. Murray Lomax. Could there conceivably be another Murray Lomax? He sent a note out with the *huissier* asking his secretary to get the book from the library as soon as she could. That done, he gave his attention to the business on hand.

At precisely ten minutes to one, while the Agriculture Commissioner and the Budget Commissioner were in a seemingly interminable wrangle about what prices to propose for the forthcoming agricultural season, Horst Kramer interrupted rather brutally to say: 'Colleagues, there is one other item which I would like to bring to your attention this morning, before we break for lunch. About an hour ago, the heads of the two largest chemical companies in Europe – United Chemicals in Britain and Deutsch-Chemie in Germany – held a simultaneous press conference and announced their intention to merge. I am glad to say that both gentlemen recognized the need, under the terms of the Treaty of Rome, to seek the agreement of the Commission to such a merger. I have received by telecopier the text of their statements and I shall arrange to have them distributed immediately. The Commission cannot of course give any opinion today. That is entirely out of the question. But I would like us to be able to announce this morning that we are aware of the situation and undertake to give as rapid a response as possible. Could colleagues agree to that?'

It was clear from the look of surprise on Leopold Brugmann's kindly face that Kramer's announcement had caught him entirely unawares. Normally Brugmann, working with the Chefs de Cabinet, prepared the agenda of the Commission meetings meticulously. He knew in advance what the likely outcome of the discussion on any particular item would be; more often than not the conclusions the Commission reached squared neatly with the conclusions which Brugmann wanted them to reach. You didn't have almost thirty years' experience in the same job without learning something about how to manage things. But this morning, as Brugmann recognized, Kramer had outsmarted him, whether intentionally or not he couldn't say. By slipping in the item just before lunch, Kramer had effectively avoided any substantive discussion; he had nevertheless ensured that the minutes of the meeting would record the fact that the Commission was now seized of the merger proposal and would be taking appropriate action. In itself there was nothing wrong with that. What was unusual was that the normal channels had been short-circuited and the time scales radically compressed. One thing puzzled him. Kramer had said that he had first heard of the proposed merger during the course of the Commission meeting itself. But Brugmann, who sat immediately on Kramer's right and who generally kept a close eye on the comings and goings in the Commission's meeting room (he had noted for example that Morton, the British Commissioner, had been given a brown envelope), couldn't recall seeing anything resembling a press communiqué, telecopied or otherwise, being brought in to Kramer. But he let it pass. His attention could have been distracted and it was certainly true that the President had received in the course of the morning's session several messages of one kind or another.

He caught Morton's eye across the circular polished oak table and whispered a word in Kramer's ear. 'Perhaps we should ask the view of our Industry Commissioner?'

Kramer seemed momentarily annoyed. 'There will be plenty of time to study this matter. We do not need to go into it now.'

But Morton raised his hand anyway. 'With your permission, President, I should like it recorded that the accelerated procedure under which the Commission has treated this item this morning in no way prejudges our final position.'

Kramer looked at him sharply. 'Surely, Mr Morton, that goes without saying?'

'I thought it better to say it anyway, President.' Morton spoke calmly but firmly. Like everyone else around the table, he wanted to go to lunch, but he didn't see why he should be bullied.

Before Kramer had a chance to reply, the Italian – Ippolito Camino – intervened on Morton's side. 'These are complex matters, colleagues. It does not do to rush them. I think Mr Morton's reserve should be recorded.'

78

Kramer sensed the small current of sympathy running for Morton in the room. He smiled affably enough, peering over his spectacles. 'The point is already noted. Shall we adjourn?'

Morton walked thoughtfully back along the corridor to his office. He decided to seek the advice of his Chef de Cabinet. Normally Chefs attended Commission meetings only when their respective Commissioners were absent. Wednesday was the one day of the week when the Commissioner was likely to know more about what was going on than his Chef de Cabinet did.

This morning, however, Morton found that Peter Simpson was already well informed about the events of the morning. He was waiting in the Commissioner's office when Morton returned.

'The *Financial Times* was on to us from London about half an hour ago,' Simpson said cheerfully. 'They wanted to know what our view of the proposed merger was likely to be. So I told them that we were studying the dossier but at first sight it didn't seem to present any problems, though that was not for quotation.'

Morton looked at his watch. He was due to attend a lunch given by the Club of 13 in his honour. And since the Club of 13 comprised the heads of Europe's thirteen largest corporations, he had no wish to be late. He put his papers down on the desk and headed for the door. 'I'm sure you're right, Peter; but we had better have our people look at it all the same.' Then he added, casually: 'I made rather a point this morning of wanting to follow this one in person. When our staff have finished their review, make sure I see the papers before anyone else does, won't you?'

'But you're in Portugal next week, Commissioner,' Simpson began to protest. 'It could hold things up. . . . ' He stopped as he realized that Morton had already left the room.

'Shit.' Simpson swore as he walked back across the ante-room towards his own office. Vivian Perkins, still at her desk – she seldom took time off for lunch – looked up severely: 'I beg your pardon.'

'Sorry, Vivian.' Simpson went back into his own office and closed the door with a bang.

79

In the car, en route for his luncheon engagement, Morton wondered whether, by some strange chance, either Deutsch-Chemie or United Chemicals were implicated in the malpractices described in the anonymous communication he had received. Could the Commission launch an investigation on the one hand and approve a merger on the other? Above all, could he – as Industry Commissioner – run with the hare and hunt with the hounds?

The lights at the end of the Rue de la Loi went green for them just at the right moment and they swung left on to the inner ring, doing well over eighty kilometres an hour. A few minutes later they cut down to the right in front of the Palace, followed the tram lines into the Place Royal and began to descend the wide curving street which led towards the centre.

Number 1 Rue Ravenstein, home of the Club of 13, turned out to be a small gem of a building, medieval Flemish architecture at its zenith. It was the kind of house, Morton thought, which you saw in the great paintings by Memling and Breughel. To the right of the heavy oak door was a small brass plaque which read 'Cercle Privé'. Morton told his driver to come back for him at three o'clock; was about to press the bell when the door opened and a liveried old gentleman appeared, looking indeed rather like the warty and blotched characters painted by the Old Masters (almost as though he had stayed untouched over the centuries).

'*Monsieur Morton. Entrez, s'il vous plait.*'

As he followed the man inside, and along a passageway hung with the richest tapestries of the period, Morton patted his inside breast pocket to check that his speech was still there. Though his staff had prepared a first draft, he had worked on that speech himself and was reasonable confident that it struck the right note. When you were talking to the Agnellis of this world you had to choose your words carefully. People like the Agnellis tended to listen. That was one of the reasons they had got to the top. They absorbed information like a combine-harvester.

Morton looked around with some curiosity. From the outside the house seemed to be of modest proportions, but the appearance was deceptive. Though most of the rooms which led off the corridor had their doors firmly closed, Morton noticed two conference areas and a computer centre as well as an indoor swimming pool surrounded by classical statuary. It was clear that the Club of 13 did not lack for money.

At the end of the corridor they turned the corner and climbed a wide stone staircase. Morton had no difficulty in recognizing a Pieter de Hooch and a Vermeer. And on the first landing, confronting him at eye level, was a splendid cityscape which featured Rue Ravenstein as it must have been four centuries earlier.

'*Monsieur le Président a fait acheté ce tableau, il y a deux ans, auprès du Rijksmuseum du Amsterdam,*' Morton's guide informed him with a note of pride in his voice.

'*Et qui est Monsieur le Président?*'

'*Monsieur Ritter.*' The man replied with some surprise. '*Vous ne le saviez pas?*'

Morton shook his head. Somehow, they had failed to tell him that the President of the Club of 13 was none other than Ludwig Ritter himself, head of Deutsch-Chemie – the man who, amongst other things, had been helping to generate the morning's stream of press communiqués.

Morton, having made an effort, lapsed into English. 'Presumably Ritter's not going to be here anyway. I understood he was in Cologne this morning.'

It was clear that the elderly retainer spoke English at least as well as Morton spoke French.

'Oh, no,' he replied, 'Mr Ritter arrived by helicopter a few minutes ago. Of course, the King allows him to land in the courtyard of the Palais Royal.'

'I see.' Morton wasn't really sure that he saw at all.

As they reached the top of the stairs they were greeted by a suave silky-haired, pomaded gentleman who introduced himself as Luciano Rossi.

'I am the Secretary of the Club of 13. It is so good of you to come, Mr Morton. The Members will be delighted to see you.' Rossi took the Commissioner firmly by the elbow and guided him into a magnificent high-ceilinged room. Morton barely had time to observe the splendid array of silver and crystal on the long mahogany table when he found himself grasped vigorously by the hand.

'*Guten Tag, Herr Kommisar,*' said Ludwig Ritter. 'I hope you had no difficulty in finding the way here today. The Club of 13 doesn't advertise its presence. It's not like the Hilton Hotel, though I suspect you may find the food rather better.' He gestured towards the table with a smile.

In many ways Ludwig Ritter resembled Dr Kramer. There was the same fleshy air about both men, the same powerful, almost overbearing demeanour. But whereas there was a pinkish tinge to Kramer, reflected both in his jowls and in the broad bald expanse of his forehead, Ritter's face was of a darker tone; his shoulders were broader and heavier than Kramer's – indeed, thought Morton, this was a man of great physical power. Not at all the kind of chap to encounter in a blind alley on a dark night. He gauged Ritter's age at around sixty-five, give or take a year or two. Looking at him, he realized that the man's features were vaguely familiar. It was as though he had seen Ritter before somewhere though he could not for the moment recall either the place or the occasion.

'Forgive me if I'm a bit late, Mr President.' How easy it was, Morton reflected, to fall into these continental habits. Mr President, Mr Commissioner, Excellency this, Onorevole that. The unctuous phrases tripped off the tongue; after only a few weeks in Brussels he found himself falling almost unconsciously into the habit. 'As you may know, the Commission meets on Wednesday mornings and things sometimes run on.'

As he spoke Morton caught a quick exchange of looks between Ritter and the Club of 13's Italian secretary, Luciano Rossi. Was there a faint smirk on Rossi's face? Were the gentlemen of the Club of 13 already apprised not only of the Commission's agenda but also of the results of their discussions?

'Ah yes, of course. I hope your discussions were fruitful.'

There was more than a hint of interrogation in Ritter's voice. Morton felt convinced that the man knew perfectly well that the proposed merger between United Chemicals and Deutsch-Chemie had been raised at the Commission's meeting that morning, but he decided to let the question, if indeed it was a question, go unanswered. There was a time and a place for everything. As far as he was concerned the matter was *sub judice*.

Ritter marched his guest rapidly round the room, as a jockey might parade his mount in the paddock before a race. Morton met, in quick succession, the captains and commandants of European industry. Like Ritter himself, the members of the Club of 13 had a solid, substantial air about them. Being successful was a weighty business in every sense of the word. Some of the names were familiar; some of the faces were familiar. Sometimes familiar names matched familiar faces. The traditional sectors of European industry were represented – steel, ship-building, automobiles, chemicals. People might talk about 'comparative advantage', about leaving the dirty work to Japan and Korea and Singapore and other so-called newly industrial countries; but the reality as they all knew was that Europe could never survive if the classic wealth-producing sectors sank beneath the waves of international competition. The newer industries were there as well – tele-communications, bio-technology, computers. Morton knew that when he had time he would have to study the dossiers in detail, match the faces with the men and the men with the jobs.

Down at the far end of the room he saw someone he recognized.

'I believe you know Sir Gordon Cartwright.' Kramer eased him down the straight.

Morton greeted the tall British industrialist whom he had last seen on the occasion of that Sunday lunch at Chequers – what a long time ago it seemed now! 'Did you drop in by helicopter too?'

'Company jet, actually. I'm going back after lunch; do you want a lift? Plenty of room.'

Looking back at that lunch later in the day, Morton had the firm impression that he had very much been on show, almost on trial. When finally they had sat down at a table he had found himself between Ritter and Cartwright. Though both men had touched on the subject of the proposed merger, Morton had refrained from comment except to indicate that the Commission was studying the matter and would give its reply in due course. He had sensed a certain disappointment, almost as though his interlocutors were hoping that he would give some indication of a likely favourable outcome to the Commission's deliberations.

'It's going to be good for Britain,' Cartwright assured him somewhere between the cheese and the fruit. 'Good for Europe too. Certainly good for us in United Chemicals. We have to create industrial units in Europe with the size and complexity to take on the Americans and the Japanese. That's what Ludwig and I are trying to do, aren't we, Ludwig?'

He leaned forward in front of the Commissioner to address the Club of 13's President.

'Exactly so.' Ritter had no hesitation in agreeing with his British homologue.

But Morton would not be drawn any further, and both men, seeing this, dropped the subject, not without some reluctance.

Later, when the plates had been cleared and coffee and liqueurs were being served, Ritter tapped with a fork on the rim of a glass and called for silence.

'Gentlemen.' He read his speech from typewritten notes: 'Today we honour Europe's new Commissioner for Industry. This is our first meeting, Commissioner, of 1989 and we felt it right that you should be present. Congratulations on your appointment!' He leaned forward, picked up his glass, raised it and invited all present to do the same.

Remaining seated while the brandy fumes and cigar smoke wafted over his head, Morton couldn't help wondering what these good gentlemen who seemed today so full of bonhomie might not be like if they were crossed. Individually each member of the Club of 13 wielded a lot of power. Taken together, they represented an almost overwhelming force.

After Ritter had sat down, Morton himself responded. He spoke with care, conscious that he was – in some sense – setting out his own philosophy, his own approach to the job as he saw it in these early days.

'We must indeed ensure,' he told them, 'that Europe possesses the industrial clout, the necessary sinews, to take on the growing competition from America and Asia. That means, of course, that the structures must be apt for the task.'

There were some murmured 'hear, hears' around the table. They weren't exactly sure what he meant – Morton himself wasn't exactly sure what he meant – but the words seemed to strike the right note.

'At the same time,' Morton continued, 'we must seek to maintain, and indeed increase, the element of free and fair competition within Europe. It is competition that brings unit prices down, competition that ensures consumer choice and ultimately product quality.'

This time the response was markedly less enthusiastic. These were men who had spent most of their lives believing that bigness was next to godliness and they weren't going to change their way of thinking in a hurry. But Morton, though he recognized the dangers, stuck to his text. 'During my term of office as Commissioner I shall seek to be guided by those principles: the reform of industrial structures and the maintenance of fair competition.'

When he sat down, Ludwig Ritter congratulated him somewhat perfunctorily. 'Of course, competition is very important, Commissioner. I know it's a basic principle of the Treaty of Rome but we have to recognize that the world is very different from what it was when the Treaty of Rome was signed.'

After the meal Morton found himself alone for a few minutes with Gordon Cartwright. The industrialist took his elbow and steered him confidentially into a corner of the room.

'I saw the PM the other day, James. We spoke of you, actually. Wasn't it that weekend we were both at Chequers that she asked you to be the next British Commissioner?'

Morton was surprised at the question. Looking back on that strange Sunday he had decided that Cartwright's presence at Chequers had been more than coincidental. All those questions he had asked about his, Morton's, views on industry. It was almost as though even then Britain had decided to go for the industrial portfolio, with Cartwright being designated to check out his suitability. So why was Cartwright pretending not to remember the circumstances of the meeting?

'Indeed it was,' he replied drily. 'I'm afraid it all came as a bit of a surprise.'

Cartwright lowered his voice. 'I just wanted to tell you that the PM is delighted at the way you've settled in. I know you couldn't say much at lunch but I'm sure you realize how much the PM wants this merger to go ahead. This time at least she believes in the *European* solution.'

Morton was amazed at the persistence of the man. He felt a hard angry knot forming at the pit of his stomach. Deliberately forcing himself to be affable, he said: 'Of course, I'd love to help, Gordon. Both you and the PM must know that. But I've already discovered that the Commission's a strange institution. Procedures count for a lot. It's not always easy to cut corners.' He paused and added lightly, as his anger mounted: 'Even if you wanted to cut corners. And I'm not sure I do.'

Shortly after that fairly frigid exchange Morton's visit came to an end. Since the Club of 13 had, apparently, further business to conduct, Morton took his leave with another series of handshakes all round. Luciano Rossi escorted him all the way to the front door. As they walked down the long corridor, Morton asked: 'What happens when the Club isn't meeting? Is this building still used?'

Luciano Rossi seemed to hesitate. 'I'm here all the time, of course, since the club needs a permanent Secretary. And we have some central facilities for research and documentation.'

On one of the closed doors which Morton had observed earlier that day, he noticed a sign saying '*Action Industriel*'.

'What's *Action Industriel*?'

'That's French for Industrial Action.'

'I know that,' Morton replied impatiently. He had begun to take a strenuous dislike to this foppish Italian. 'I mean, what does it do?'

Rossi was again evasive. 'Sometimes the members of the Club of 13 decide that, rather than operate individually in some particular area, they will take a joint initiative.'

Morton let it go at that. It was clear that the man did not wish to explain any further and in any case, Morton thought, it was none of his business as long as they stuck to the rules.

Action Industriel was, he imagined, a public relations operation of some kind.

Driving back to his office, Morton felt suddenly tired. For some reason he had found his meeting with the Club of 13 a rather tense experience. He had the feeling that he was being used and he was not actually sure that he cared for the idea.

Chapter Six

'What does the F stand for?'

Morton kept his eye on the road as he asked the question. He had given Gerry, his chauffeur, the weekend off and was enjoying putting the Jaguar through its paces. Ever since they left Brussels the speedometer had been hovering around 140 kilometres per hour. With the motorway crammed with Saturday morning traffic as the *Bruxellois* headed for the coast on this first fine day of spring, it paid to be careful.

'Federico, actually.' Murray Lomax laughed. 'We lived in Edinburgh but my mother was going through an Italian phase!'

The two men hadn't met, except in passing, for several months – in fact not since that luncheon at the British Ambassador's residence the previous November. Had anyone asked him, Lomax would have admitted that he had been somewhat surprised to receive the Commissioner's telephone call, half-way through the week, suggesting a meeting. Not, of course, that it was unusual for Commissioners to ring up journalists, particularly the correspondents of renowned and reputable newspapers like *The Times*. Commissioners were as anxious as anyone else to ensure that their ideas were faithfully reported and informal briefings, particularly of the press of their own country, were very much part of the tradition. What had surprised Lomax was that Morton had suggested not half an hour in his office which was the usual formula, but – rather more imaginatively – an excursion to Bruges. 'I haven't been there for years,' Morton had said. 'I rather wanted to look in at the Groeninge Museum. We could talk on the way and have a spot of lunch as well.'

In the event, it wasn't until they were half-way down the motorway and savouring the delicate aroma of the chemical plants around Ghent that Morton indicated what was on his mind.

'I wanted to pick your brains, Murray, about the European chemical industry. I saw you'd written a book about it. How did it do? *Wonder Drugs and Corporate Crime*. That's a pretty snappy title.'

Lomax looked at the Commissioner sharply. 'Books don't sell on titles, Commissioner. Somebody has to be behind them. The publishers let this one drop like the proverbial hot potato. We sold two thousand copies altogether as far as I remember. They remaindered the rest and let it go out of print after eight months.'

'Why didn't they push it?'

Lomax didn't reply immediately. He concentrated instead on the passing countryside. With Ghent behind them the air had become purer. He rolled down his window again.

'I've often thought about the answer to that question,' he said at last. 'My own view is that someone leaned on them, almost certainly the industry itself. They didn't like the book. They threatened to sue, not only the publishers but the distributors as well. They were too late to stop the book coming out but they killed the chance of a paperback sale.'

They had turned off the motorway. Bruges lay only ten kilometres ahead of them. In the distance they could already see the outline of the famous belfry rising over the fields of Flanders.

Twenty minutes later they parked the car and set off on foot down the narrow streets and along the banks of the canals where the first boatloads of tourists were already appearing like the daffodils of spring. They paused to examine the carvings and bas-reliefs on the ancient buildings; to admire the delicate, intricate architecture of the period; to absorb the sights and sounds of this well-preserved remnant of European history.

'Don't get me wrong,' Lomax said as they stood in front of the harmonious courtyard of the Beguinage, 'I recognize the role of industry and its right to generate wealth and profits. Without the wool trade of Flanders we would never have had Bruges. What I'm against is industry's abuse of power. That's what I tried to expose in my book.'

Over lunch, after they had seen the Memlings in the Hospital of St John and the Breughels and the Bosch in the Groeninge Museum, after they had trudged up to the top of the Belfry to gaze out towards the sea, now over fifteen kilometres away but once the source of Bruges' power and fame, Lomax returned to his theme.

'If you're interested in bribery, negligence or fraud, in unsafe manufacturing practices, anti-trust violations, or blatant and dishonest promotion of ineffective or dangerous drugs, particularly in Third World countries, you'll find that the pharmaceutical companies have done it. What's more, they are still doing it.'

'What about the chemical industry proper? Is that as bad as the pharmaceutical industry?'

'In its own way it is. Take pesticides. That's as good an example as any. In 1972 the World Health Organization estimated that there were some 500,000 cases of pesticide poisoning annually, 9,200 of them fatal. Oxfam estimates that by now that figure has risen to almost a million cases, with over 15,000 deaths a year. Approximately half the cases and three-quarters of the deaths occur in developing countries. In 1980, Shell was reported to have earned 7 per cent of its annual profits from the sale of three pesticides – aldrin, dieldrin and endrin – which have been banned or severely restricted in the European Community. Yet there is no evidence that such highly toxic chemicals provide more benefit than those with a moderate or low degree of toxicity.'

Morton listened with close attention as Lomax expanded on his subject. Much of what the journalist was saying tended to confirm the thrust of the memorandum which he had read a few days earlier. He tried to bring the conversation to a sharper focus.

'Did you have a chance to look at, say' – he made the

question sound as casual as he could – 'Deutsch-Chemie or United Chemicals? How do they rate on the ethical score card?'

Murray Lomax, a careful Scotsman under most circumstances in spite of his one Italian forename, weighed his words with special care as he replied. 'I wish I'd been able to look at the chemical industry itself in greater detail. The German chemical industry in particular is fascinating and I would have liked to have written about it. But I was running out of time and money for that matter. *The Times* gave me leave for six months to do the research and some of the writing, but it was unpaid leave. That's Murdoch for you!' he laughed.

Again as casually as he could, Morton brought him back to the subject in hand. 'What, in particular, interested you about the German chemical industry?'

Lomax, warming to his subject, poured himself another glass of wine. 'Take I.G. Farben, for example, Commissioner. Before the war I.G. Farben represented what was probably the single largest concentration of industrial power anywhere in the world. After the war, the Allies pursued their policy of decentralization and split it just as they split up Krupp. But if you look at the remnants of the Farben empire today, you find that each part of it, whether it's Hoechst or BASF or Bayer or Deutsch-Chemie, is much bigger than I.G. Farben ever was. A company like Deutsch-Chemie, for example, has an annual turnover that exceeds sixty billion Deutsche Mark. Or again, take the people who run the companies. Before the war you had men like Duisberg who was a giant in his own way, I admit. Certainly he was a public personality, more public anyway than the present leaders of the German chemical industry. But if you look at their *real* influence and power then even Duisberg can't hold a candle to someone like Ludwig Ritter. You don't hear much about Ritter; he's a fairly shadowy figure but in terms of influence he's a colossus. Did you know that Ritter's brother is Ernst Ritter, West Germany's Minister of the Interior?'

Morton suddenly realized why Ludwig Ritter's face had seemed familiar when he met him that day at the Club of 13's headquarters in Rue Ravenstein. There was a strong family resemblance between the industry magnate and the politician.

'I suppose Ludwig Ritter finds the relationship a convenient one.'

'I think they both do.'

Towards the end of the meal Lomax said: 'Forgive me asking, Commissioner, but do you have – how shall I put it? – an ulterior motive in asking all this?' He gestured expansively at the plush decor of the expensive canal-side restaurant to which Morton had invited him. 'I mean, I'm delighted to be able to sing for my lunch, as it were, in such agreeable circumstances, but could I possibly know the reason?'

Morton looked at the man's red face, the slightly bulbous nose, the sharp but friendly eyes.

'What I'm going to tell you,' he said, 'can't be used in any way. Not yet. You mustn't talk about it to anyone. But I want you to know and give me your advice if you feel able to.'

Lomax knew when it was time to concentrate. He pushed the wine bottle out of reach. 'Go ahead,' he instructed.

Fifteen minutes later Morton had said all that he wished to say. 'Well?' he asked, expectantly: 'What do you make of it?'

Lomax pulled the wine bottle back towards him and poured himself another glass. When, finally, he spoke he chose his words with care.

'As I told you, I know more about pharmaceuticals than chemicals, but everything you tell me, everything the man says – whoever he is – strikes me as having a ring of truth about it. I don't know which particular company he's referring to and I'm not prepared to speculate. It might be a British company; it might be a French one; it could be a German one. Judging by the fact that the letter was posted in Germany, perhaps it *is* a German one. But I'm convinced about one thing, Commissioner, the memorandum you have received is written by someone who knows what he's talking about. And I'll tell you something else' – Lomax lowered his voice – 'whoever wrote that note is a very brave man. If he's still working for his firm, then he's risking his career. In fact, he may be risking more than his career.'

Morton felt a sudden chill. 'What do you mean?'

But Lomax would not be drawn except to say: 'These people

can play it rough if they want to. I discovered that, as I told you.'

They drove back to Brussels on a winding, circuitous route which took them through the quiet villages of Flanders. It was a bright, sunny afternoon and the countryside, having woken from its long winter sleep, gladdened the eye and the heart.

'Thanks,' Morton said, as he dropped the journalist off at his office. 'I've learned a lot.'

Lomax took Morton's hand through the car window. 'We could do with some spice, Commissioner.' He spoke wistfully. From a journalistic point of view Brussels was important but not exactly exciting.

Morton smiled. 'If there's a story, Murray, you'll be the first to know.'

Chapter Seven

Hans Kunig was a precise, tidy man. As an upper-echelon executive in Deutsch-Chemie, he had demonstrated that a love of hard work combined with a rigorously methodical approach both to intellectual problems and to the day-to-day organization of his life could bring substantial dividends. Since his arrival from America four years earlier he had risen rapidly in the company hierarchy. Whether the fact that he had quite early on come to the notice of Ludwig Ritter himself had been an element in his rapid promotion, Hans Kunig wasn't quite sure.

As he prepared to leave his office for the day Kunig recalled the occasion of that first meeting. He had had a message that Ritter wanted to see him – not in his suite at company headquarters outside Cologne (the great man seldom appeared at the plant) – but at his country castle, forty kilometres outside the city. Kunig had driven up there in some trepidation. Apart from glimpses of Deutsch-Chemie's President at the annual Christmas party and one pep-talk which Ritter had given to employees on the occasion of the company's fortieth anniversary, Kunig had had very little contact with the man.

'I hope he's not going to fire me,' he had said to his wife half-jokingly. 'Perhaps he's going to promote me.'

Helga Kunig, a thin, nervous woman who had never really wished to return to Germany from the United States where she considered that the life she led was in most respects ideal, had sounded concerned.

'Stick to the laboratory, Hans. That's what you're good at. As an executive, you can fall as fast as you rise. Then what would we do? We have children to think of.'

In the event, the meeting with Ritter had gone well. Kunig had arrived early at the *Schloss*, had spent ten nervous minutes driving around in the surrounding countryside, had at last summoned up the courage to ring the bell at the outer gate. To his relief the butler had allowed a certain warmth to seep through into his manner as he opened the door.

'Ah yes, Mr Kunig! Herr President is expecting you.'

Ritter had been waiting for him in the library and had greeted him affably enough. He had a paper in his hand which Kunig recognized at once as a photocopy of an article he had recently written in the journal of the German Chemical Society.

'Most interesting. Most interesting, indeed.' Ritter had tapped the document with the middle finger of his left hand. 'You're sure of the equations, are you?'

'As sure as I can be. And colleagues of mine who are still working on these problems have indicated their general agreement with my line of argument.'

'Yes, one of them brought the article to my notice. Most thoughtful of him.'

At this point Kunig still wasn't sure which way the interview was going to turn out. He was beginning to think that his poor beloved wife who for some reason found life so difficult (a fact which often exasperated and saddened him) had on this occasion at least good grounds for her pessimistic view of his excursion to Schloss Ritter. He had cleared the article through the proper channels but if Ritter had decided to get rid of him, that wouldn't make a Pfennig's worth of difference. The man was an autocrat, always had been, always would be.

He had only been reassured when Ritter, handing the paper back to him, had asked: 'Is that what happened at Bhopal?'

'Something like that. Nobody knows for certain. The people who might have been able to explain what happened died as a result of the accident.'

'Terrible, terrible.' Ritter had shaken his head. 'How many people were killed altogether?'

'At least three thousand at the time and people are still dying, even today, from the after-effects.' And he had added: 'Of course, the special circumstances contributed to the possibility of accident.'

'What do you mean by that?' Beneath Ritter's overtly accommodating manner was a harsh questioning note. Kunig had hastened to explain: 'The quantities of methyl-isocyanate being stored were considerable. Far greater quantities than would ever be permitted in Europe. Here there are stringent regulations.'

'And the phosgene? That was a factor too, wasn't it?'

Funny, thought Kunig, how phosgene – which had been at the base of the mustard-gas used in World War One to such deadly effect – should have resurfaced so many decades later as a necessary ingredient in the production of agricultural pesticides.

'Yes, phosgene almost certainly was a factor, although, as I say, no one is sure of the precise interactions. What we do know is that the tank overheated, the cooling systems failed to work, the liquid vaporized and was vented as a poisonous cloud in the environment. I was merely suggesting in my paper that similar reactions could occur in other chemical processes involving chemicals with analogous molecular structures.'

'Such as?' Again the harsh inquisitive note.

Kunig had hesitated. 'Nothing that is currently manufactured, sir, as far as I know anywhere in the world. But you remember Agent Orange or 2-4-5-T, the defoliant which the Americans used at the time of the Vietnam War?'

'Of course I remember.' Ritter nodded curtly.

'Well, it seemed to me' – there was still a note of uncertainty in Kunig's voice – 'that this class of compounds might pose similar problems and dangers in manufacture under certain circumstances unless adequate precautions were taken. My paper was, I admit, predictive, based on computer analysis of chemical structures.'

Ritter had seemed to lose interest in the subject. 'Thanks for coming. It's been most interesting.'

Kunig had driven back home feeling puzzled. He was not clear why Ritter had wished to see him in the first place nor, indeed, what the point of the interview had been. He had never spoken of that particular matter with Deutsch-Chemie's President again. He had, on the other hand, found that his career within the company advanced more rapidly after the interview than it had before. Though he sometimes regretted that his transfer and rapid promotion on the executive side in effect precluded him from pursuing his interests in scientific research, including the kind of research he had been writing about in the learned journal which Ritter had got hold of, there were other rewards. Helga, for example, had begun to re-adapt to life in Germany. She didn't like it. She still dreamt of being able to drive out to the Safeway to fill the back of her huge Chevrolet station-wagon with a dozen large cartons of groceries; she still missed the friends she had made among the mothers at the children's school. But she recognized that things were going well for Hans and if they were going well for him, she supposed, they must be going well for her.

She had asked him once, not long after they had arrived back in Europe, why he had left America. 'You had your immigration papers; you had your green card, Hans,' she had protested. 'The children were American; they could have stayed American.'

'It's not as simple as that,' he had replied. 'I never knew my parents; I don't think I ever saw them; they were taken away and I went to America. But I knew that they were German. I knew that one day I had to come back to the place where they lived, to the country where they died.'

She didn't really understand him, either then or since. It seemed to her that people from Europe had for decades been emigrating to America and few, if any, felt an overwhelming compulsion to return to their home country. It was useless to try to change his mind. The funny thing was that even though Kunig had left his old firm – Ponting Chemicals – she knew he still kept in touch. At least once a month letters were delivered which she felt sure came from Kunig's old employer. And on their quarterly telephone bill, where long-distance calls were itemized, she recognized the Delaware number of Ponting's US headquarters.

Kunig looked at his watch. It was only five o'clock but his

secretary had already gone home. As in many other industrial enterprises in Germany, office working hours were eight in the morning to four in the afternoon. Executives of course tended to stay longer but even they, by late afternoon, had packed things in. It was very much the German spirit. Start early, leave early, above all, go to bed early so you can be fresh for the next day's work. Naturally, things were different down at the plant. There a shift system operated – weekends included – which ensured that the capital investment of Deutsch-Chemie's shareholders, spread as they were throughout Germany and the world, was not for one moment left idle and unproductive.

Before leaving, Kunig walked down the corridor to the photocopy machine where he spent two or three minutes. He came back to his office, put some papers in his briefcase, gave one last quick look round as though to check that everything was tidy and in good order, then walked to the lift, rode down to the ground floor and went out to the company car park. As an executive he had a BMW of the 600 series. Other colleagues went in for Mercedes but he himself had always found it a heavy, somewhat flashy, car. The BMW, he thought, reflected his own personality better. Fast. Efficient. Practical. Possibly dangerous?

Deutsch-Chemie's plant on the banks of the Rhine above Cologne was more like a town than a factory. The chemical works themselves were the nucleus around which was grouped a constellation of other buildings, including houses and apartments, sports complexes, civic centres, libraries, medical facilities and churches of several denominations – all of them lending substance to Deutsch-Chemie's proud boast that it looked after its workers from the cradle to the grave and even beyond. The Kunigs, like other executives, lived on the outskirts of the complex, away from the river and core area, in an agreeable suburb where each house had its lawn – almost as though, Helga Kunig sometimes thought wistfully, they were back in America. On that fine May evening the two Kunig children were out playing at the front of the house when their father's car pulled up and Kunig got out. The two children ran to the car.

'Poppa!' they cried.

Kunig hugged them. The girl – Wilhelmina – was the fairer of the two, nine years old and already a surprisingly mature and thoughtful person; the boy – Gunter – was two years younger, tousle-headed, lovable and massively untidy.

A few minutes later they all sat down to supper together, like a million other German families across the land. As they ate Helga watched her children with a fierce and passionate pride. They gave her more joy than anything else she knew; at the same time they caused her, sometimes, unbearable pain. She had a deep, irrational fear that something would happen to them, or to her, or – worst of all – to Hans.

'Eat up now!' If she had said it once, she had said it a hundred times.

Wilhelmina did as her mother asked; the boy ran off into the road only to be retrieved and scolded with mock severity by his father.

Later, when the children were asleep and they were sitting together in the comfortable drawing room of their home, she sensed that something was bothering him. She knew him well enough to realize that he could not, would not be pressed. Either he would tell her in his own good time or not at all. She looked at him with affection as well as love. When she had met him, ten years earlier, she had had been on the brink of a breakdown. She had finished school, had dropped out of university – the pressures were too great – and was deeply unhappy in a boring law firm in Bonn, when Kunig, appearing as if by magic like the proverbial knight on a white charger, met her and carried her off with him back to America. He had rescued her from a mediocre clerical career. More important, he had rescued her from herself. In America she had suffered two bouts of depression, one of them prolonged, but Helga knew that without the framework, the stability that Hans provided, her depression could have turned into something very much worse. How much Hans understood all this she didn't really know. Sometimes she wondered whether she understood it herself. Her moods could frighten her so much that she found herself wanting to cry out, aching for reassurance. Having the children was a help but, in the darkest

99

moments, even that wasn't enough. She could find herself trembling in the kitchen and only the sound of the car drawing up in front of the house could bring her to pull herself together.

'What is it, Hans?'

She looked at the tidy face, the heavy black spectacles, the slightly pointed ears, the white even teeth. She wouldn't, she thought, be much good at describing him to the Missing Persons Bureau but, when she closed her eyes, she could see his features as clearly as she could see her own. 'I wish you'd tell me what it is,' she added. Whatever worried him, worried her much more.

He smiled. 'Nothing's bothering me, Helga.'

She knew that he was lying – or, if not lying, at least dissembling. 'For the last six months you've been nervous, anxious. It's not like you.'

'Nervous? Anxious?' He tried to laugh it off.

'You bring papers home,' she said, pointing to the briefcase which stood beside his chair. 'You never used to do that.'

'I'm an executive now, Helga. I can't always stop work just because the factory has closed.' He laughed again, uneasily, or so it seemed to her.

They went to bed early. She wanted him to make love to her but he turned on his side, facing away. She was not sure whether or not he was asleep. Later, when she heard his quiet breathing, she slipped out of bed disappointed, almost angry. She felt the budding of panic inside her but fought it back.

Much later, when she returned, he was awake. As she got back into bed, he said: 'We will go back to America, Helga, one day. I promise you that.'

'When?'

'Soon. Sooner than you think. There are things I have to finish here first.'

They heard the boy stirring in the next room. 'Ssshh!' He pulled her towards him.

As he made love to her, she felt the blackness, the panic recede. Perhaps, after all, things would be all right.

Chapter Eight

When he told her, in the margin of one of the Commission's meetings, that he would be visiting Oporto, she had been delighted. 'How splendid! I shall be there myself as it happens. If you can stay on for the weekend, we could do some sight-seeing.'

Helena Noguentes had been as good as her word. She picked him up early on Saturday morning from the hotel where he was staying.

'I want to show you the port lodges on the banks of the Douro. All the great houses have cellars there – Cockburn, Sandeman, Taylor. As you know, the British' – she turned to him as she drove – 'invented the port wine trade. At least half the houses today are still British-owned.'

'Port kept the clubs of St James's going. Still does.' Morton laughed. He was in a good mood. Two days of intensive meetings with government and industry in Lisbon and Oporto had gone well.

Portugal's integration into the economy of the Common Market was proceeding more or less as planned. His staff had flown back to Brussels the previous evening; he was glad to be on his own for a while. Peter Simpson was a competent young man, as he was the first to recognize, but Morton found himself increasingly irritated by his Chef de Cabinet's super-vision. 'No, Peter,' he had told him firmly. 'I shall manage perfectly well on my own. I'm not going to make any speeches; you can be sure of that!'

In the event, he had had to make one little speech. The

venerable Masters of the Port Wine Institute of Oporto had heard that not one, but two, European Commissioners were coming to visit them that Saturday morning and had laid on a guided tour of one of the lodges. After they had led their guests through the vaults and cellars, redolent of the grape, the local grandees had arranged a small wine-tasting ceremony. Some gracious words of welcome had to be replied to in kind.

Morton raised his glass of tawny port and held it up against the light which streamed in through the windows of the ancient lodge. A few yards below, the river Douro flowed on its last short journey to the sea.

'I drink to your city, your country. I drink to your famous wine. I'm honoured to be here today with my fellow Commissioner Senhora Noguentes. I want to tell you how fortunate we all consider ourselves to be to have such a capable colleague. Indeed it is the first time that a woman has joined the Commission, so I must congratulate you on that as well!'

There was a solid round of applause. Morton wasn't sure that the crusty old men who were present that morning were enthusiastic feminists. He rather doubted it. But it was clear from the way they treated her that they had a good deal of time for Helena as a person.

When, half an hour later, they had left the city to head for the hills, he asked her about her experience as Mayor of Oporto.

'They liked me most of all, I think,' she explained, 'because I cleaned up the Douro. Those dear old gentlemen we saw this morning were some of the worst polluters. I took them all on – and won.' She smiled. 'There are people who swim in the Douro now, though that's not for me. I'm glad Dr Kramer decided to give Portugal the environment job in his Commission. I feel I know what I'm talking about some of the time at least.'

The day had begun well and it continued in the same way. After a couple of hours they turned off the main road, stopped briefly for lunch at a wayside café, then took a series of minor roads leading into the high interior of the country. She had brought binoculars and passed them to him so that he could survey the mountains and the sky.

102

'You may see a golden eagle, or a white-tailed eagle. There are several pairs up here.'

The road had become narrow and rocky as it climbed. She pulled into the side and they both got out of the car. Morton put the field glasses to his eyes.

He saw it almost immediately, hovering high above a crag, body and wings silhouetted against the bright cloudless blue of the sky.

She saw what he was looking at and took the glasses from him. 'Yes, that's your golden eagle. *Aquila chrysaëtos*. The king of birds.'

'We have a few in Scotland. They're protected but still the farmers shoot at them. They say they take the lambs.'

'Farmers are the same everywhere. People are the same everywhere. Sometimes I wonder if we shall ever win.'

Up till then Morton had thought of her as a clever politician who had parlayed a provincial reputation into nationwide recognition. Now he saw there was substance as well as form.

They left the car and climbed up a track between two mountains until they reached a vantage point where they could look over into Spain and the high sierra beyond.

'You need a mule to cross the border here,' she told him, 'and it would take you several days.'

'I'd like to do that.' Standing there, Morton couldn't help thinking how remote his previous life was beginning to seem. How could one compare those endless hours in the House of Commons, picking at the minutiae of legislation, with this great empty land in which the birds of prey soared and swooped with the air-currents that rose from the mountains? It seemed to him that he had spent so much of his life going down one set of tracks, tracks that had been programmed right from the beginning – all those ties hanging in the cupboard – yet here he was shooting off in another direction altogether. Was he becoming in the process a different person?

As they picked their way back down he asked her whether she was a biologist by training. 'You were pretty quick with that Latin name.'

'I have the basics, enough to tell a hawk from a handsaw, as they say; but my doctorate was in chemistry. Having a scientific discipline helps when you're dealing with environmental matters. I may not know the answers, but I know how to ask the questions.'

As she spoke an idea formed at the back of Morton's mind. Some time, perhaps soon, he would need allies in the Commission if he was to do what he knew now he might have to do. Helena's support could be very valuable. And if he could line up the Greek and Dane as well, others might join in.

When they reached the car, hot and thirsty, Helena pulled out a picnic box from the boot. 'Vinho Verde, try it.' She poured him a glass and he drained it at a gulp.

'Better than Sandeman's best and that's saying something!' He laughed.

'James, don't you want to kiss me?'

It sounded so formal, so precise, so absolutely right. He looked at himself from a great height as though, by some peculiar transposition, he had changed places with that huge circling eagle they had seen earlier in the day.

'By Jove, I think I do.'

She roared with laughter, tossing her black hair back and turning up her face to his. 'You're so absurdly English, James.'

He had forgotten what it was like to kiss someone for the first time.

As they had dinner that night in Oporto in a one-time Moorish palace which had been cunningly converted into a restaurant, she talked to him of her childhood and youth in the hills above the Douro. 'My parents were rich, one of the largest land-owning families in Portugal. We had three thousand hectares of vines. The peasants still trod the grapes with their feet. My brother is running the estate now.'

'Do you see much of him?'

'Not really. He doesn't approve of my political opinions.' She smiled.

What a handsome woman she was, Morton thought. There was something exotic about her, some Moorish strain which lent a special magic to her face. He was enough of a male chauvinist to believe that marriage was the right and proper fate of women, especially handsome women, so he asked: 'Were you — are you — married?'

Clearly, the question didn't bother her in the least. 'Once. To a count who had an estate not far from ours. My parents pushed me into it. They had an idea that this would be a great union of land-owning families and I was too young at the time to resist. But it didn't last long. He was not a bad man, but all he cared about was hunting. After we separated, I moved into town and went into politics.'

She spoke simply, encapsulating a lifetime in a few sentences. If wedlock had left her with any scars, they were not visible on the surface.

'How about you?' she asked. 'Mrs Morton doesn't seem to come to Brussels much, does she?'

Under any other circumstances Morton would have huffed and puffed in an attempt to turn the question. His whole upbringing, his whole attitude to life, had taught him to avoid intimacy at all costs, to shy away from giving direct answers to direct questions, above all questions which aimed to elicit information about his personal life. Others had pried and probed, but Morton had never given the faintest indication that his marriage to Isobel was in any way shaky, not to say foundering, not to say utterly and completely on the rocks.

He looked at her across the table. 'Isobel and I are going through a sticky patch at the moment.' It was as close as he had ever come to a confession.

She drove him back to his hotel, took his arm as they walked into the lobby. The doorman knew her, greeted her and she responded warmly.

'They still think of me as the Mayor here.'

'And what would they think,' Morton asked, 'if the Mayor of Oporto spent the night with the gentleman from England?'

'Of course I'm going to spend the night here. My room is next to yours on the fifth floor. My bags were brought round earlier today. If I had stayed out in the country, I could never have got to the airport tomorrow morning in time to catch the plane to Brussels!'

It was his turn to laugh then. 'I'm sorry. All this is a bit new to me.' Then he thought, how would Isobel know anyway?

And, even if she did know, would she care?

'I'm not much of a catch,' he said as they went upstairs together. 'Failed Tory politician, middle-aged, balding. You could do better, you know.'

She didn't bother to go to her room but followed him into his, clung to him passionately as soon as they were through the door.

'I wanted you as soon as I saw you that first day,' she whispered to him as she pulled him on to the bed. 'Didn't you realize?'

'Look,' he protested but the note of conviction was lacking. 'Do you really think this is wise? We're colleagues after all.'

She was genuinely cross with him then. 'What will people say? What will people think? That's all you British seem to care about. And anyway, why should the others know anything? I'm not going to move in with you back in Brussels.'

But Morton was concentrating more on the present than the future. He unbuttoned her blouse and drew it off her.

At the sight of her lean, firm body, and her small olive-coloured breasts peeping out from the folds of the garment, he felt suddenly, intolerably cheerful.

They flew back to Brussels the next day, lovers now as well as colleagues. Sitting in his seat next to her and leafing contentedly through the pages of the *International Herald Tribune*, Morton found three items which interested him. Except for the fact that they appeared in the same edition of the paper, there seemed to be no connection between them.

'Fascinating article here,' he confided, tapping the page with his middle finger. 'The suggestion is that the Americans are using defoliants in Central America just as they did in Vietnam. Agent Orange or the equivalent.'

She took the paper from him and studied the article carefully. When she'd finished she said: 'If the report is true, who's manufacturing it? Agent Orange has been banned worldwide – for over a decade. If anybody's making it, they're breaking the law – to say the least.'

Helena returned to her reading. Morton, still thinking about toxic defoliants and the particular puzzle posed by their

106

apparent presence in Central America, gazed out of the window of the plane. They were, he noted, flying across northwest Spain. Down below he recognized the features of the Basque country and could, on this clear day, even make out the towns along the coast. As they crossed into France he remembered with a twinge of guilt that he had spent his honeymoon in Biarritz with Isobel. That was before she got her business going in London, before those damned Japanese girls made her life so successful, before – the thought still gave him pain – she decided that he was too old, too boring, and too undynamic to be a long-term prospect for her. Looking down, he could see the great pink bulk of the Hôtel du Palais – favoured by the rich, royal, and famous – set right by the water's edge. He remembered how once, when he had been swimming off the rocks beneath the hotel while the red flag was flying, the guards had blown their whistles at him and he had had to come in reluctantly from the surf. Some minutes later they had pulled in a man who had drowned.

He sighed. It all seemed all so far away now. Turning again to the paper, he noted a small item: TORIES NAME NEW CHAIRMAN. 'Mr Kegan,' he read, 'has risen rapidly in the ranks of the Conservative Party. He takes over as Chairman at a time when morale at Central Office is low and, perhaps even more important, coffers are severely depleted. Tim Kegan will devote himself to fund-raising, especially among the large industrial corporations whose contributions to Party finances have been falling off in recent years.' *Tiens*, thought Morton, that nasty young man had come a long way already and no doubt would go further still. He wondered how Kegan would get on with men like Gordon Cartwright. Would he persuade Cartwright that United Chemicals' future was safer with the Conservatives than with, say, the Alliance whose leaders had recently been making all the right noises about creating an acceptable framework for industry and enterprise?

Thinking about industry, he found himself going over once again, as he had so often in the last few days, his conversation with Murray Lomax. He had attempted to check and double-check the accuracy of the information Lomax had supplied, while taking care – of course – not to arouse the suspicions of the industry in question. This had not been easy since he had decided, from instinct as much as from anything else, that he would continue to keep Peter Simpson in the dark. However efficient his Chef de Cabinet might be at arranging the day-to-day routine of his Commisioner's life, Morton sensed that he would be reluctant to pursue an elusive quarry through the tangled thickets of Europe's industrial undergrowth.

'Surely not our problem, Commissioner,' he could hear Simpson say in his bland but determined way. 'Our job is to support European industry, not to make trouble for it.'

So Morton, with the bit between his teeth, had unusually by-passed his own people. He had instead turned to the head of the Commission's legal department, Laurent Guimard, a cool elegant Frenchman in his early forties who, unlike so many other graduates of France's prestigious Ecole Nationale d'Administration, had somehow managed to prevent his evident intellectual abilities from swamping his common humanity.

'Of course I shall help,' he had told Morton, 'that's what I'm here for. If the Commission is the guardian of the Treaties, the Commission's legal service must act both as the spear and the shield. If we act together, we shall be much more effective than if we act apart. Of course, we shall be objective. The Commission's legal services are always objective, *n'est-ce pas*? But that doesn't mean we shall not enjoy the pursuit of our quarry.' And the Frenchman had sniffed the air like an old *chasseur* testing the wind in the forests of the Loire.

A few days later Guimard had slipped quietly into Morton's office. What the Frenchman had told him about the results of some carefully conducted preliminary investigations had been enough to persuade Morton that whatever might be the nature of the beast he was chasing, it was almost certainly not a wild goose.

It wasn't until the plane was actually landing at Zaventem, Brussels' national airport, that his eye fell on the third, and most crucial, item in that day's *International Herald Tribune*. It was in the small ads on the back page, right at the bottom of the column. 'Tulip-Fanciers Meet Keukenhof Main Gates Next Saturday Noon' he read.

'Ah!' he exclaimed.

Helena looked up. 'Found something interesting?'

'In a manner of speaking.'

They said goodbye to each other as they came out of the arrivals building. The relationship seemed suddenly formal, certainly more formal than it had been a few hours earlier when they were lying side by side naked, with the morning sun streaming on to the bed. Morton wanted to say something more to her but he wasn't sure how to put it. He sensed shoals ahead but, with other things on his mind, decided to ignore them.

Chapter Nine

Hans Kunig followed the left bank of the Rhine and crossed into Holland at Arnhem. The famous bridge, rebuilt since the war, showed few signs of the furious struggle of September 1944. How beautiful, how peaceful the countryside looked now he thought as he drove on down towards the flower fields of the coast. It was hard today to imagine what it must have been like then, hard to reconcile the evident order and prosperity with the grim facts of war. The Dutch knew how build and to rebuild, he reflected. No nation better. They worked every inch of their tiny country, turned natural disadvantages into unnatural advantages. Take the Rhine, for example. As he drove he glanced over to the great river running parallel with the road on his left. The Germans treated the Rhine as a kind of industrial sewer but the Dutch, having no alternative sources of supply apart from underground water-tables which were themselves replenished largely from the Rhine, had no choice but to purify the water when it reached them, treating it chemically as well as biologically, so that finally the honest Dutch peasant working in the fields on reclaimed polder land, or the sophisticated city-dweller going to his office in Rotterdam or Amsterdam, might have an early-morning cup of tea or coffee before starting his day. He shuddered to think how the water drunk by the good burghers of Arnhem had possibly begun its life as a chemical effluent from Deutsch-Chemie's giant works a few miles further up the river on the German side of the border.

It was a hot day. Spring had turned suddenly into summer.

He fished out a handkerchief and wiped his brow. He felt tense as well as warm. He recognized that he had taken a first step, more than a first step, along a dangerous road. If Morton kept the rendezvous, took and acted upon the documents, the flak might start to fly around Deutsch-Chemie's headquarters as intensely as it had on that fateful occasion at Arnhem. He didn't expect the finger of suspicion ever to point at him but in any case, as he had told Helga not so long ago, they would soon be returning to the States. A frown crossed his face. Risking his own neck was one thing; risking his family's health and happiness was something else. He wiped his forehead again. The road sign, high up above the motorway, told him that Den Haag – the Hague – was only eighty kilometres away. He looked at his watch; he had plenty of time.

Take the Chelsea Flower Show, multiply it a thousand times, add some windmills and ornamental lakes and rabbits running on lawns, throw in a gentle breeze wafting up from the North Sea to bend the heads of several million tulips and you would, Morton supposed, come somewhere near giving an accurate description of the Keukenhof flower fields in Holland in the early summer. Even the visiting crowds somehow managed to be absorbed in the scenery. What would Wordsworth – dear boring old Wordsworth whose heart leapt up when he beheld a daffodil – have made of Keukenhof?

Morton sat on a bench outside the main gates like any other flower-fan or tulip-fancier. He had dispensed with Gerry's services for the weekend and had enjoyed his rapid drive in the Jaguar from Brussels to Antwerp and on to the Hague. That was the thing about Europe, Morton thought. Once you were across the Channel with four fast wheels beneath you, almost anything was in striking distance. Being on the Continent was more than a geographical fact; it changed the way you looked at things. If you could drive to Paris for lunch or Amsterdam for tea, national frontiers began to seem pretty insignificant.

He watched the people arriving at the gates of the gardens, some on foot, some on bicycles, some by car, some by the great air-conditioned coaches which had transformed long-distance

111

travelling in Europe. He had no idea what kind of man or woman he was looking for.

'I shall have to take your word,' the man sitting next to him on the bench said. 'I know I can't expect written guarantees that my confidence will be respected.'

Morton looked up in surprise. He had been so busy keeping his eye on the entrance that he had failed to notice his neighbour.

'You *are* Mr Morton, aren't you?' asked the tidy, dark-haired man with heavy black spectacles, who held a briefcase firmly on his lap. 'Can we talk? My name is Hans Kunig.'

'You're a brave man, Mr Kunig.' Morton found himself instinctively echoing the words which Murrary Lomax had spoken a few days earlier.

They joined the crowds and passed through the gates into the gardens. Once they were inside the pressure of people eased as the tourists spread out in different directions seeking their own routes through the abundant foliage.

'I was glad of the trip anyway,' Morton said. 'I've never been here before.'

'Nor have I, but it seemed a good place to meet.'

Kunig seemed nervous and Morton tried to put him at his ease. 'Of course, you can have my word and I speak for the Commission as a whole, I can assure you of that. Anything you say, anything you give me, will be treated with the utmost discretion. If the Commission decides to pursue this case, no one will ever know of your involvement.'

They were standing together at the far end of one of the giant greenhouses for which Keukenhof was famous. There was nobody near them. Most of the people seemed to prefer to stay outside enjoying the breezes from the sea.

Kunig looked at the tall, bluff man in front of him.

'I believe you,' he said simply.

'You'll have to do more than that. I want to know why you're doing this. Why are you taking these risks?'

Kunig sighed, once more pulling out his handkerchief and wiping the sweat from his face. 'It's a long story and it's too hot to stay here. Shall we go to Scheveningen? I know a little restaurant by the sea where we can talk.'

Two hours later, after a long and careful interrogation of the man, Morton knew that he had enough, more than enough, to build his case provided the documents were there to back it up.

'I've been with Deutsch-Chemie for the last four years,' Kunig had told him. 'I was working in America before then.'

'Who did you work for in the States?'

'Ponting Chemicals.'

Morton was surprised. 'So you joined the opposition when you came to Deutsch-Chemie? Ponting couldn't have wanted to let you go. Deutsch-Chemie is their main competitor in some key areas, isn't it?'

Kunig shrugged as though unwilling to go into past history. 'Oh, it was all very amicable.'

After a while Morton had changed his line of questioning. 'What made you first suspect that all was not right at Deutsch-Chemie?'

'One of the first things I noticed was the consistent falsification of test results.'

'What kind of tests?'

Kunig tapped the briefcase which he had placed on a chair next to him. 'It's all in here. EEC rules require that any new product, before it is put on the market, should be subjected to a whole battery of tests. The rules are laid down from Brussels in the so-called Sixth Amendment to the EEC Directive on Dangerous Substances. But there was much more than that.' He had gone through the list of Deutsch-Chemie malpractices, citing chapter and verse wherever he could.

From his conversations with Murray Lomax, and from his reading of the memorandum which Kunig had sent, Morton had had more than an inkling of what to expect. But even so, the litany of wrongdoing took him by surprise. The falsification of test results was only a start. Worse still was the deliberate use of human guinea-pigs – people of all kinds, young and old – who were persuaded, through financial incentives, to participate in various experimental programmes – sometimes causing irreversible damage to their health and even loss of life. And at a more technical level, Kunig demonstrated convincingly how Deutsch-Chemie had abused its dominant position in the market, fixing prices and rigging contracts and indulging in every kind of monopolistic and monopsonistic practice.

There was one area where, no matter how reluctant Kunig might be to answer, Morton knew he had to probe and to keep on probing until he was satisfied with the response. He looked at the man across the table. Looked him straight in the eyes, held Kunig's gaze with his own, willed him to give an honest, accurate reply.

'Why are you telling me all this? You have a good job in the company, as I understand it. You're putting it at risk and maybe more than that as well.'

A shadow passed over Kunig's face, to be succeeded by intense sorrow, even anguish.

'Can we go outside – on to the beach? I'd like to walk.'

'Of course.' Morton wondered whether the man was going to faint.

They went outside and walked along the beach towards the great expanse of dunes and sand which somehow had miraculously managed to survive the pressures of the nearby conurbations. The beach was empty except for the occasional afternoon stroller out with his dog, and a group of small children looking through the flotsam and jetsam. The gulls, sweeping in from the North Sea en route for the rubbish tips inland, flapped overhead in a leisurely confident way.

For a time they progressed in silence. Morton preferred not to press the man. Let him reply in his own way and in his own time. The tone could be as important as the substance.

'I'll give you an answer to your question,' Kunig finally said, 'but it will take time, I have to go back into history. How much do you know about the origins of the German chemical industry?'

'Not enough, it seems.'

Kunig paused to collect his thoughts. 'We must really start at the turn of the century,' he began. 'At that time there were three German companies who dominated the world's production of dyestuffs. You probably know the names. BASF, which stood for Badische Analin Soda Fabrik of Ludwigshafen; Bayer of Leverkusen; and Hoechst which was named after the town Hoechst am Main.'

Morton listened intently, Murray Lomax, that day in Bruges, had already whetted his appetite.

'The fight for overseas markets,' Kunig continued, 'had been achieved on the basis of cut-throat competition at home. Kickbacks, price fixing, bribery, patent disputes – all this was the stuff of the game in those early days and it wasn't until Karl Duisberg, who had been the general manager of Bayer, brought the companies together in what he called a "Community of Interests" that some order emerged out of the chaos. Duisberg actually made his proposal at the height of the Battle of the Somme in July 1916. The big three, that is BASF, Bayer and Hoechst, joined up with five others to form the Interessen Gemeinschaft der Deutschen Teerfarbenindustrie. Later on, this structure can simply to be known as I.G. and the individual members as the I.G. Companies. This was the origin of I.G. Farben. It's worth remembering that I.G. Companies, in particular BASF, were behind the use of poison gas in World War One.'

Kunig paused. 'I'm giving you the background,' he said, 'because it's important if you're to understand the present situation and my own motivation. But let's move on from World War One to the second. I.G. Farben was deeply implicated, almost from the start, in the rise of the Nazi movement. By 1937, almost all of the members of the I.G. managing board had joined the Nazi Party, including Karl Krauch, Fritz Ter Meer, von Schnitzler, Max Ilgner, Otto Ambros and others – you'll understand in a moment why I remember the names so well. I.G.'s factories and laboratories were by then working overtime in preparing for Hitler's attack on the world. If you actually look at the products which I.G. produced, you see that almost everything necessary for Hitler's war effort was there: synthetic oil, synthetic rubber, poison gases, magnesium, lubricating oil, explosives, methanol, sera, plasticizers, dyestuffs, nickel and thousands of other items. The moving spirit behind it all was Karl Krauch. In fact Krauch became the symbol of I.G.'s contribution to Germany's military strength. When the Wehrmacht overran Europe, Hitler himself gave Krauch the decoration of Knight of the Iron Cross which was usually reserved for military heroes. Hitler called him "one who won marvellous victories on the battlefield of German industry." '

There was a bench set at the end of the long sweep of sand, facing out to the sea.

'Why don't we stop for a moment?' Morton suggested.

They sat down side by side, with Kunig's briefcase between them. 'I come to the most difficult part of my story,' Kunig continued, 'and that is the involvement of I.G. Farben in Hitler's programme to eliminate the Jews. Have you ever heard of Zyklon B?'

'No.' Morton shook his head. But he could guess what was coming.

'Zyklon B was the lethal gas manufactured by an I.G. company and made for use at Auschwitz and other death camps. When the Germans conquered Poland, Himmler organized special SS squads to begin the mass slaughter. The first extermination centre was set up at Chelmno, in Poland, in the fall of 1939. At that stage they were using carbon monoxide from the exhausts of mobile gas vans. This was a pretty primitive and inefficient instrument, but even so they managed to attain a killing rate of one thousand a day.'

Morton shuddered as Kunig, more determined than ever now to reach the end of his story, went on: 'In August 1941, using five hundred Russian prisoners of war as an experimental group, Hoess, who was the Commandant at Auschwitz, introduced into the air-tight chambers there a new asphyxiating agent, Zyklon B, whose generic name was actually prussic acid. Zyklon B, as I said, was manufactured by an I.G. company and its use revolutionized the programme for the "Final Solution of the Jewish Question". There is absolutely no question that the management of I.G. Farben knew what the product was being used for; they knew all about the concentration camp. But their involvement went far beyond that. There was a special section at Auschwitz known as I.G. Auschwitz. This was a production plant for chemicals which relied on slave labour from the concentration camp. From the records we have, three hundred thousand concentration camp workers passed through I.G. Auschwitz of whom at least

116

twenty-five thousand were worked to death. The plants, when completed, were so enormous that they used more electricity than the entire city of Berlin.'

Kunig leant back on the bench and stared blankly out to sea. He seemed exhausted by the effort of telling his story.

'What happened to men like Krauch after the war?' Morton asked.

Kunig smiled grimly. 'Oh, that was a scandal all right! By the time the Nuremberg trials had turned their attention from the military war criminals to the industrial war criminals, everyone was beginning to bother about the Soviet menace. The Cold War had intervened and the Russians, who had been with the Allies during the war, were now seen as a major threat. Industrialists in America, who had always maintained links with their counterparts in Germany, raised questions in Congress about the war trials, particularly the war trials of businessmen, so that when the actual verdicts were handed down, the steam had gone out of the whole affair and the sentences were ludicrously light.

'Take the verdict on Karl Krauch, for example. The court found him guilty of slavery and mass murder, but he was sentenced to imprisonment for a mere six years and he didn't serve all of that.'

Then Kunig turned to him and added in a simple and matter-of-fact way: 'Both my parents died at Auschwitz in the I.G. Farben camp. What's more, I believe that Ludwig Ritter, directly or indirectly, was instrumental in their deaths.' He pulled a set of photographs from his pocket. 'Take a look at these.' He went through them one by one. 'Here's a picture of the members of the I.G. managing board in 1937. There's Schmitz, Kuehne, Krauch himself, Ter Meer, Hermann Abs and so on. And that young man, in the background, is Ludwig Ritter who at the time was acting as personal assistant, a kind of aide-de-camp, to Krauch.' He turned to another photograph. 'This is a picture of Himmler visiting the I.G. plant at Auschwitz in March 1941. Again, you can see Krauch in the picture and other I.G. representatives and you also see Ritter walking just behind Himmler.'

Morton whistled. Even now, so many years later, he

117

thought he could see the resemblance between the man he had met the other day in Brussels and this youthful figure walking in the footsteps of one of Hitler's henchmen. But it was hard to be sure.

Kunig went through the rest of the photographs. 'That's Krauch being sentenced at the Nuremberg trials. See the look on his face. Even in court, he praised the efficiency of the Auschwitz solution of the labour problem.'

Morton saw that there were tears streaming down the other man's cheeks. He felt moved beyond words, wanted to put a steadying arm across the German's heaving shoulders, but pulled back from some inbred reticence.

'I think I see now,' he said slowly. 'It's revenge, isn't it? Even now, revenge is the key.'

Kunig fought back his tears, wiping his eyes with the back of his hand and then blowing his nose fiercely into a handker-chief.

'Yes, of course it's revenge. But it's more than that. I see these people still doing what they've always been doing, lying and cheating. Poison gas in World War One, Auschwitz in the second. The old habits die hard.'

They sat there in silence, on the bench looking out to sea, both of them wrapped in their own thoughts. After about ten minutes Morton made up his mind.

'I think we should go now.' He spoke gently but firmly. 'I'll take this if you like.'

They walked back together the way they had come. This time Morton held the briefcase.

From time to time as they walked Morton glanced at the man beside him. Kunig, he thought, seemed younger than his years. If his parents had died at Auschwitz, he must have been born during the war if not before. For a moment he was puzzled, tried to sort out the dates, then put the problem from his mind. Some men, he supposed, simply wore better than others.

They came back towards the Scheveningen end of the beach. 'You see,' Kunig suddenly broke the long silence, 'Deutsch-Chemie is, of course, the direct lineal descendant of I.G. Farben. The allies broke up the company at the end of the war

118

into several parts: Hoechst, Bayer, Deutsch-Chemie and so on, and now each one of those parts is larger than the parents. Ritter was never even prosecuted after the war, let alone sentenced. If the top management of I.G. Farben escaped virtually unscathed, what was the point of the prosecutors going after young men like Ritter who had only just embarked upon their careers?'

Morton felt if was time to change the subject. In spite of their walk, Kunig still looked pale and strained.

'Tell me about your children.'

Kunig's face broke into a smile for the first time that day. 'I have two. A boy and a girl. The boy wanted to come with me today to see the big barges on the Rhine.'

'I'd like to meet them one day.'

He wondered, as he spoke, how much he and Isobel had missed by not having a family. Would things have gone better for them if there had been a couple of kids around the place? He brought his mind back to the business on hand. It was too late to think about that now.

When they reached the cars Morton held out his right hand, still keeping hold of the briefcase in his left.

'Goodbye,' he said. 'And thank you.'

Kunig left first, jumping into his BMW saloon and accelerating rapidly away. Morton followed after five minutes. He drove at a leisurely pace since he was in no hurry to get back to Brussels. It was not every day that he came to Holland. He had seen the tulip fields and the coast, had walked along the dunes at Scheveningen. There was still time for a rapid visit to the Port of Rotterdam itself. You could hardly be Commissioner for Industry without having visited Rotterdam.

Less than an hour later Morton was standing at the quayside of Europe's newest and largest industrial port, observing the comings and goings which had made Rotterdam one of the fastest-growing centres of world trade. From where he stood he could see at least twenty boats in the process of loading and unloading and that was only part of the story.

He was intrigued to see how the Rhine barges, those great long, bulky boats whose slow but steady passage through the countryside he had observed that morning on his way to

119

Keukenhof, came right down into the port itself to rendezvous with the giant container-ships.

He strode over to a pair of capstans where a small group of stevedores were celebrating the end of the afternoon with a bottle of schnapps. His Dutch consisted of a few words of Flemish picked up in Brussels, but one of the dockers came to his rescue by indicating that he could speak in English if he wanted to. He even conjured up a glass and offered Morton a drink. 'Gezondheid!' Morton said, and received a half-mocking round of applause.

He pointed to a passing barge which was carrying a consignment of metal drums. Each drum bore a code symbol and number.

'Where does that stuff come from?' He asked the question casually.

'Germany, for sure,' one of the Dutchmen replied. 'Chemicals for export. Two or three shipments a week are coming down the Rhine, these days.'

'Who checks the consignment?'

'The customs, I suppose.' The man shrugged. 'That's not our business; we just do the loading.'

'*Dank U wel.*' After a few minutes Morton put his empty glass with the others on the capstan and walked back to his car. How easy it would be, he thought, to change the labels. What customs officer, confronted with that sinister hazchem warning and the skull and crossbones symbol, was ever going to run tests to see if the substance those drums contained was the substance they were meant to contain?

Half-way back to Brussels, he swung off the motorway into the countryside. He stopped the car in the middle of a bridge which crossed a small canal, took all the papers from Kunig's briefcase and, after giving them a quick glance, locked them in the boot of his car. As he did so he knocked over a can of oil. He righted it and stowed it to one side, noticing as he did so that a small oil smear had appeared on one of the papers. Morton walked to the edge of the bridge, glanced left and right to see that no one was coming, and dropped the case into the canal. He waited till it sank beneath the scummy waters, then he straightened and walked back to the car.

Half a mile away, Peter Simpson watched through binoculars. For some while he had had a sense that Morton was pursuing some game of his own, some game his Chef de Cabinet was not privy to. There had been that time when Morton had taken papers to his apartment one evening and had failed to bring them all back the next day. There had been the half day spent with Murray Lomax. What on earth had that been about? There had been the discarded copy of the *International Herald Tribune* with the pencilled cross against the small ad. In the end, Simpson had decided to let his curiosity get the better of him. And it wasn't, he reflected, just curiosity. He had a job to do as well.

Chapter Ten

It seemed to Morton that Isobel had been more than a little cross when he rang to say that, for the second weekend in succession, he would be unable to get home to England.

'Can't you make an effort? I haven't seen you in ages.'

It had been on the tip of Morton's tongue to say that the problem was of her making, not his, but he restrained himself. In his experience, women seldom forgave you for pointing out the truth. He wasn't, in any case, sure that he wanted to see Isobel just at the moment, whether in England or Belgium. By deciding not to follow him to Brussels she had forced a change in their relationship. At first Morton had refused to recognize that anything was happening, had sought to maintain to himself, as much as to the outside world, that it was all a matter of logistics. But he was not a stupid or naïve man. When he looked at the calendar and saw that, apart from her brief flying visit to Luxembourg for the Commission's inauguration before the European Court, Isobel had resolutely stayed her side of the English Channel, Morton realized that things could hardly be said to be looking up. He might, at one stage, have cared a great deal, but since that weekend in Portugal with Helena, matters had begun to appear in a rather different light. Helena had made a powerful impression on him. He enjoyed her mind; he enjoyed her personality; he had enjoyed going to bed with her as well. Indeed, as far as that side of things was concerned, the night they had spent together in Oporto – and the continuing liaison which had grown out of it – reminded Morton of the earlier, balmier days of his marriage where both vigour and inventiveness had been in order.

There was something else that made him less than anxious to see Isobel for the time being. Morton had never had much time for gossip; it was not something that appealed to him; on the whole he preferred not to know, even when other people seemed to be determined to tell him. But not even Morton could in the end ignore the persistent rumours which reached him on the grapevine about Isobel's relationship with the newly-appointed Chairman of the Conservative Party, Tim Kegan. Had it been merely a matter of doormen's tittle-tattle, Morton would have turned a deaf ear. But it was more than that. The whips, of course, had a very good nose for these things. It seemed that, up there in Birmingham or wherever it was she lived, Mrs Kegan had begun to kick up a fuss and the whole little pot was steaming so merrily that they weren't sure they could keep the lid on. Could Morton just possibly, the Chief Whip had suggested as delicately as he could over the telephone to Brussels, rein his wife in a bit? 'Not trying to get involved in your personal affairs, old boy, of course. Far be it from me. But this is a Party matter, you know. Wouldn't look good to have a matrimonial scandal involving Kegan just at the moment, not now he's taken over as Chairman.'

Morton found it surprising that the Party hierarchy should see the affair mainly in terms of damage limitations, the damage of course being assessed not in terms of its impact on the lives of people involved, including himself, but in a purely political context.

'I hear what you say, Harry,' he had told the Chief Whip frostily at the end of their conversation. 'I'll think about it.'

In the event, Morton had said nothing to Isobel. This was not the kind of conversation you had over the telephone – and, anyway, Morton wasn't sure he wanted to have the conversation at all. He had sometimes wondered, in the course of his marriage, whether Isobel hadn't perhaps had the occasional fling. 'A bit of a goer' was the expression that came to mind, the kind of thing men said to each other, only half-joking, late at night in the bars of the House of Commons. But he had come to terms with all of that, taking Isobel for what she was.

But in one respect at least, Harry Braithwaite's thinly-veiled allusions came as a relief. If Isobel had been, was being unfaithful, then surely he could be too? Fidelity was a two-way street, *n'est-ce pas?* They would one day have to sort things out, but in the meantime he was glad to know that his peccadillos, if that was the right word, were more than matched by hers.

'No, darling,' he repeated, 'I'm afraid I can't get over, not this weekend. The Commission has decided to go into retreat at some watering place outside Paris. *Le weekend de reflexion,* they call it. The idea is to do some long-term thinking.'

'Perhaps we should do some of that ourselves.' After Isobel had rung off, Morton stared at the receiver in surprise. Did she really care what was happening to them? Or was it just that things weren't going too well for her at the moment? Isobel, he reflected with a mixture of bitterness and admiration, had a knack of sizing up a situation to determine with considerable accuracy precisely where her own advantage lay.

Le weekend de reflexion was not a figment of Morton's imagination. The idea had been mooted almost as soon as the new Commission took office but the operative date had been constantly postponed owing to the pressure of day-to-day business. It was only now, in mid-May, that the twelve members of the Commission had finally found a time which suited them all. They had made their way singly or in groups to what had once been a Benedictine convent on the outskirts of Paris but had now been converted to an up-market conference centre. They had met, in informal and wide-ranging sessions, from Friday night to Sunday morning. They had discussed most of the subjects which, as Horst Kramer put it, 'were relevant to the construction of a united Europe', and a good many that were not. The sessions ended at noon on the last day.

'*Frei Zeit*! Now, freetime yes?' Kramer had closed the 'weekend' with a heavy joke.

Morton had been delighted when Helena suggested at the end of the meeting that they should drive back to Brussels together.

'What a good idea! We can stop in Paris for lunch.'

124

They ate at some expensively unpretentious little restaurant on the Left Bank, in the shadow of Notre Dame. It was a perfect day. Bright, clear skies; trees blossoming; birds chirruping and children playing in the sand-pit in the little recreational park which the once and future Mayor of Paris had imaginatively provided in the shadow of the Cathedral.

Morton watched a barge making its way downriver between the Left Bank and the Ile de la Cité. A line of washing had been hung out on deck and he caught a glimpse of people having a meal in the sun-filled cabin.

'I wouldn't mind living on a barge,' he said. 'I'm sure one would fall into the rhythm. Those people probably spend their whole lives on the waterways of Europe.' As he spoke Morton had a mental picture of himself as an older, wiser man – politics and passion spent – chugging peacefully towards oblivion.

'Don't kid yourself,' she interrupted his reverie. 'You're much too ambitious to spend ten weeks like that, let alone ten years.' She looked at him across the table. 'I was listening to you this weekend, James. You throw up a good smoke-screen, that bluff British manner of yours, but in my estimate you're one of the sharpest of the bunch. If Kramer was to disappear for any reason, you could easily find yourself in his place.'

'You flatter me.' Below them, the barge followed the bend of the river and was lost from view. Morton gazed after it, watching the ripples subside.

He turned to her. 'Certainly, there are still things I want to do. I suppose you can call that ambition.'

When they had finished their meal they walked across the bridge to the Cathedral. Helena pointed to the front of the building. 'Look there, the stone is still corroding. The smoke and the smog may have gone from Paris, but the acids are still in the air. In less than half a century we have destroyed the work of a thousand years.' She spoke with passion, with conviction, just as she had that afternoon in the high sierra.

That was the moment, as they stood outside the front of Notre Dame, gazing up at the magnificent rose-shaped stained-glass windows which came as close to achieving artistic perfection as anything else Morton had seen in his life, that

125

he decided he had to tell her.

'Helena.' He took her arm as they walked on. 'There's something I have to tell you, something important, something that has to stay between us for the moment. . . . Nothing personal,' he added, when he saw her raised eyebrows.

As they drove from Paris to Brussels on the motorway later that afternoon he told her everything, without of course revealing his sources of information. (There was no need for Helena to know about Kunig; no need for anyone to know.)

'I want to haul Deutsch-Chemie before the European Court of Justice,' he concluded. 'I want to blast the whole thing wide open. I'm convinced I have enough material for the Commission to make and win its case but I'll need help.'

'You'll need more than me. You're playing with fire. Do you know what you're up against? Anyway, why do you suppose that the Commission will back you? It's not a radical Commission, you know that. Not with Kramer running it.'

They were skirting Mons. In the distance Morton could see the great spoil-heaps which marked Mons' mining past. As they drove further into Belgium the weather changed perceptibly. The day, which had begun so brilliantly, now was dull and overcast. Morton's own mood reflected the change in the weather. His spirits, having once risen like the pinnacles and spires of Notre Dame, now sank. 'Are you sure?' he asked gloomily.

Helena turned to him as he drove and smiled. 'Cheer up, James. There are ways of changing the odds.'

'Such as?'

'Oh, come on.' She sounded impatient. 'You're a politician, aren't you? You know how the game is played. Go public! You'll never get the Commission to back you if you ask them first. Can you see Kramer agreeing to an attack on German industry? Can you see a man like Duchesne supporting you? No, the only way to do this is to get the public on your side. Shoot first and explain later!'

Twenty kilometres from Brussels a sign pointed off the motorway. *Waterloo – Champs de Bataille*. Looking at that

126

sign, listening to her words, Morton came to a decision. Helena was right. Before he could take Deutsch-Chemie to the European Court of Justice in Luxembourg and blow them out of the water, he first had to win his battle inside the house.

Helena brought him back to the present: 'Come and have dinner at my place. I love to cook and I don't get enough chance nowadays.'

Morton looked at her with surprise. It seemed to him that she had been deliberately keeping the conversation at an impersonal level. Women didn't talk, for example, about air pollution, however riveting a topic it might be, when they had other more private things to say.

'Are you sure?'

'Yes, of course I'm sure.'

Later, as they sat at the candle-lit dining-table in her flat overlooking the Cinquantenaire park, mellow with food and wine (a simple steak and salad with a bottle of Château Margaux to wash it down) she explained it to him. 'Of course, I want you, James. I've been thinking about it ever since we came back from Oporto. But I know you're married, know you care for your wife. If you tell me that Portugal is one thing, but Brussels is another, I'd mind; but I would understand as well.'

When he took her hand across the table, knowing he was being drawn down a road which he did not really wish to take, she added: 'No need for a car to fetch you in the morning, James. You can just step across the street from here.'

So he stayed the night, sharing her toothbrush and sleeping with her in her big double bed. There was an urgency, a crude vigour, in their lovemaking as though sheer physical activity could compensate for the uncertainties of the situation.

Chapter Eleven

'I don't think we can go on meeting like this,' he said.

Isobel, naked, for a moment thought that he was joking. Nobody, surely, actually said that nowadays except in jest. But then she remembered that Tim, not of course through any fault of his own, poor darling, lacked some of the finer social graces such as knowing how to fight off the cliché when it reared its ugly head (ugh – there was one!) She raised herself on one elbow, long blonde hair spreading out over the pink satin pillow. (For once they were meeting in her place, not his.) She looked at him sadly as he lay on his back, hands behind his head with the sheet draped decorously around his nether regions, like some piece of classical statuary. The Dying Gaul, perhaps?

'You really mean that, don't you? What's the matter?'

'Nothing and everything,' Kegan replied. 'Phyllis suspects something and I think Central Office does too. I was in Smith Square the other day and your name cropped up. Our relationship clearly isn't as secret as we thought.'

'As secret as you hoped!' She spoke bitterly; why couldn't men ever have the courage of their convictions? 'Okay, so we had lunch at Wheeler's once or twice. That doesn't prove that we're having a torrid affair, does it? Anyway, why did my name crop up?'

He sighed. He loved going to bed with Isobel, was besotted with the woman in fact, but she talked too much. There was no doubt about it.

'Tell me.'

'It wasn't so much *your* name,' Kegan replied wearily, 'It was your husband's. He's not quite living up to expectations – at least as far as the Party is concerned.'

'What do you mean?'

Kegan was reluctant to be drawn but Isobel pressed him. Finally he said: 'Quite a lot of people were rather hoping Morton would look favourably on the proposed merger between Deutsch-Chemie and United Chemicals, or at least be prepared to recommend it to the Commission.'

Isobel jumped angrily out of bed and wrapped a robe around her. 'God, you're all so cynical! I suppose you're wondering how much Gordon Cartwright will chip in to Party funds, if James takes the right decision. Was that why you sent him to Brussels as Industry Commissioner in the first place?' She stormed into the bathroom and slammed the door.

In Dolphin Square, Kegan reflected, half the floor would have heard the argument, but that was not really the point. What was the point then? He lay staring at the ceiling, trying to work things out.

A few minutes later Isobel emerged from the bathroom, fully dressed and in a conciliatory frame of mind. She needed a man in her life and Kegan still seemed a solid bet. But she realized, as she made her apologies for her sudden outburst, that her defence of the absent Morton had been both spontaneous and heartfelt. If you lived with a man long enough, the roots grew down deep whether you liked it or not.

'Why did you get dressed?' he asked. 'I'm the one who has to leave, not you.' He pulled her roughly on to the bed beside him. Clichés came in many shapes and sizes. They could be what you said or they could be what you did. Making love after a quarrel was a cliché but it was one which Kegan found impossible to resist.

After he had gone it was Isobel's turn to lie in bed thinking about her life. What Kegan had said had shocked her more than she could ever have imagined. When a man started talking about 'not going on meeting like this', the writing – as she knew from her considerable experience – was on the wall. It was obvious that Kegan was running scared.

Carefully, Isobel set about reconstructing her game-plan.

From what Kegan had said it looked as though Morton was taking a surprisingly activist role in his job in Brussels. There had been more than a hint of grudging admiration in the way Kegan had described Morton's unwillingness to toe the Party line. Maybe, thought Isobel, she had misjudged her husband after all these years. She knew he was honest and decent but was he finally headed for glory over there the other side of the Channel? Hell, if that was the case, the situation could be very different, particularly if Kegan was wobbling.

She reached for the telephone beside her bed. It was Sunday evening so she felt sure that Morton would be at home. She let the phone ring a long time but there was no reply.

She tried again two hours later, still with no success. Puzzled and more than a little annoyed, Isobel replaced the receiver. Where the hell was he, then, at this time of night?

Chapter Twelve

O n the Tuesday following the Commission's *weekend de reflexion* Morton woke early in his flat in the Sablon, looked at his watch and reached for the telephone. Had he been asked, he would not have been able to say at what precise point he had decided to seek the direct assistance of Murray Lomax. For some time now, in fact ever since he'd had a chance to examine in detail the material which Kunig had supplied, he had been aware that he needed allies, reliable allies, not just in the Commission itself but also outside. Turning to the press for help was not something that Morton did instinctively. Like many politicians he had an ambivalent relationship with journalists, recognition of the usefulness of their role being tempered by a natural suspicion of their motives. But over the last several days he had become increasingly aware that the media would play a vital part in his strategy. Indeed, after that long conversation with Helena on the way back from Paris, he had concluded that his only hope of winning the battle inside the Commission was to win it outside first.

'Murray Lomax? James Morton speaking.'

The voice at the other end sounded sleepy. Once or twice a week Lomax played bridge into the small hours with colleagues in the international press corps.

'Hello, Commissioner, what can I do for you?'

'Are you free for lunch? I hope so. I need your help.'

'Name the time and the place.' In his mind, Lomax had already cancelled the game of tennis that he had arranged with his colleagues at the Castle Club, a superior establishment in one of Brussels' leafy suburbs where both journalists and bureaucrats tended to spend their long lunch hours taking off weight on the courts before putting it back on at the table.

Around four o'clock that afternoon Morton returned to his office with a smug, contented look.

'Good lunch?' Vivian Perkins knew the signs. She had spent years watching members of the House of Commons roll up for Prime Minister's Questions at half-past two.

'Very good, thank you, Vivian.'

Half-way through what remained of the afternoon, Peter Simpson arrived in Morton's office in a considerable hurry. Dispensing with the normal civilities, he held up a cardboard folder interspersed with sheets of pink blotting paper, an item known within the Berlaymont as a '*signataire*'.

'I'm afraid you didn't sign these papers, Commissioner, before you left on Friday for your weekend of "reflection".' There was a faintly sneering tone in Simpson's voice as though he entertained considerable doubts about the intellectual powers of the college and about the value of bringing its members together for prolonged informal deliberations. 'They've just been sent back to us.'

'I'm so sorry.' Though Simpson could rile him at times, this afternoon Morton felt in a friendly mood. He took the file from his Chef de Cabinet, took out his pen and prepared to sign. Then a frown crossed his face and he pushed the *signataire* away.

'No, this is too soon, Peter. I'm not prepared to approve the merger, or rather recommend that the Commission approve it, merely because the staff have written a paper saying that *a priori* they don't see any problems. I think we have to take it a little deeper than that. I didn't sign those documents on Friday because I didn't *want* to sign them, not because I missed them.'

Simpson began to protest, his plump face flushing with annoyance, but Morton cut him short. 'Oh yes, I know very well that the point is on the Commission's agenda for the next meeting, but all it says is that I'm going to make a statement. Well, I *will*.'

132

*

The Commission's press room on the first floor of the Berlaymont was packed. Murray Lomax had clearly done his stuff with 'the lads'. Journalists from all twelve countries who were members of the European Community were present as well as other members of the international press corps such as the Americans and Japanese. In fact, thought Morton as he strode into the room at precisely twelve noon, there were probably more foreign correspondents gathered together than you would find on any other occasion except, perhaps, for a White House press conference. He caught sight of Lomax sitting in his usual position, two rows from the front on the left-hand side of the room. Lomax gave a quick thumbs-up sign and the Commissioner nodded almost imperceptibly in return.

'Ladies and gentlemen' – Morton went straight to the heart of the matter – 'as you may know the Commission has been seized with a request to approve a merger between two of Europe's largest chemical companies, Deutsch-Chemie and United Chemicals. I shall, however, be recommending that the Commission suspend any action on that request until it has completed an investigation into the affairs of one of the companies involved. Allegations of misconduct have been made of a serious nature which I cannot of course disclose today but which, if substantiated, could materially affect the Commission's judgement.'

At least a dozen of those who listened to James Morton that morning had been alerted by Lomax that the Commissioner for Industry was planning to make a major announcement which would certainly not be to the liking of at least one major component of the European chemical industry. But very few of them actually anticipated the bombshell which Morton delivered.

'Is that definitive, Commissioner?' The question had a sharply inquisitive ring about it. Morton recognized the man behind the voice. He was Konrad Gruber, the representative of one of the German wire-services, Deutsche Press Agentur. What Gruber wrote appeared next day in over a hundred newspapers and radio stations up and down Germany.

'It is,' Morton replied firmly. Why did people always say 'definitive' when they meant 'definite'? 'The Commission is now examining the evidence available to it and will not be considering the merger application until that process is complete.' He turned to take the next question and saw Lomax's upraised hand. 'Yes, Mr Lomax?'

'Can you indicate, Commissioner, which of the two companies is under investigation?'

'I can tell you that it is not United Chemicals.'

'In other words, it's Deutsch-Chemie?'

That particular exchange, uncomplicated though it was, was something that Morton and Lomax had discussed carefully in the course of their most recent lunch. Morton at first had been hesitant about naming names but Lomax, once he had grasped the point of the press conference, was emphatic.

'You have to pin the tail on the donkey, otherwise they won't run it, or at least not the way you want them to run it.'

'You are right, Mr Lomax,' Morton now replied. 'I shall be recommending tomorrow that, using the powers available to it under the relevant articles of the treaty, the Commission will be investigating Deutsch-Chemie and will, if necessary, take appropriate action.'

This time the penny dropped in a big way. There was an audible gasp in the room. The Commission had not sought a full-frontal confrontation with European industry in well over a decade – in fact not since the battles with Hoffman-Laroche and Ciba-Geigy over Librium and Valium. What made the story even more surprising was that here was the Commissioner for Industry, a man most people would assume to be close to if not actually in bed with the multi-nationals, making the running.

Morton took one last question amid the growing uproar. Again it was a German, a striking blonde woman from *Die Zeit*, Germany's most prestigious weekly. Morton remembered meeting her at some cocktail party. What was her name? Barbara something-or-other?

'Are you sure the Commission will back you at the meeting tomorrow?'

He was prepared for that question too. 'The Commission is

the guardian of the Treaty, madam.' He looked round the room. There was a brief, sudden hush, a pregnant pause before the inevitable stampede to telephones and telexes. 'Thank you, ladies and gentlemen. That is all.'

Five minutes later, when he returned to his office, all the telephones were ringing and his secretary was looking seriously harassed.

'I've got Sir Oliver Passmore on one line and the President of the Commission on another. They both sound rather cross. In fact extremely cross.' Vivian Perkins could not keep the note of concern from her voice. She hoped that Morton knew what he was doing. 'What shall I tell them?'

'Tell them that I'm out to lunch, Vivian, and that I won't be back for the rest of the day. No, I mean that. Unavailable. Incommunicado. Vamoosed. Bolted. Gone to ground.'

Morton was as good as his word. He spent the afternoon walking in the Forêt de Soignes, allowing the beauty and quiet of the woods to work their customary magic. Outwardly James Morton might have seemed calm. To those around him, such as his secretary, his behaviour that morning after the press conference had a nonchalance that bordered on bravado. The reality was far different. Morton knew that he had that day crossed some personal Rubicon and that things would never be the same again. He also knew that what he had done that morning was not an aberration, but a deliberate and premeditated action, something – he realized now – that he had been mentally preparing for months if not years.

'Fuck them all,' he said to no one in particular as he strode energetically through the trees.

He returned to his flat in time to see the seven o'clock news. It was gratifying to note that, as far as Belgian television was concerned, both French and Flemish-language channels had items about the morning's press conference and had even managed to dig up a photo of the British Commissioner from their archives. He ran through the other channels. The Germans, it seemed, had gone to town in a big way, including footage of Deutsch-Chemie's plant on the banks of the Rhine as well as a brief interview with an indignant Ludwig Ritter.

135

The same, to a greater or lesser extent, went for the Dutch and French stations. As far as Morton could tell, most of the coverage seemed to be favourable. One pretty girl on Antenne I, who was the anchor-person on the nightly news show, even went so far as to comment that the Commissioner's actions had 'introduced a new dynamism into the dialogue between the social partners'. Morton wasn't quite sure what she meant – the French had a way of wrapping things up in fine-sounding phrases – but it seemed to him to be a compliment rather than the reverse. The BBC, he noted, catching the tail end of the six o'clock news (Britain, as always, was an hour behind Europe) played the story straight down the middle without any kind of editorializing. Morton suspected that a gentle steer could well have been provided from the Downing Street press office. It would have been too much to expect the BBC, which the Prime Minister regarded as a dangerously radical body, to oppose Morton's actions but at least they could, under pressure, be expected to remain relatively neutral in the matter. He fared better with ITV, being the subject of an enthusiastic commentary from Independent Television News's political correspondent: 'Nobody heard much of James Morton during his years in the House of Commons.' The reporter was harsh, but fair. 'But tonight that situation has certainly changed. Britain's Industry Commissioner has rocked the boat in no uncertain way. It is clear now that the proposed merger between Deutsch-Chemie and United Chemicals, one of the largest ever mooted in Europe, cannot go ahead in the near future at least. Tonight the City is taking stock of the situation but already several million pounds have been wiped off the value of United Chemical shares. There will be more on this story in our Ten O'clock News later tonight. . . .'

Morton turned the television off as the telephone rang. It was Isobel. Her voice sounded strange; there was some note in it that wasn't quite right.

'Hello, darling. Everyone's talking about you here tonight. Apparently Gordon Cartwright has already been on to the Party chiefs. It seems he's rather cross.'

'Hold on.' There was a distinctly steely note in Morton's voice. 'How do you know all this?' He thought he knew the answer to the question but he wanted to hear what Isobel had to say.

Isobel took it in her stride. 'I went to Patricia's this afternoon to have my hair done. Amanda Braithwaite had been in earlier. Apparently Harry was fit to burst when he heard about your press conference.'

It sounded plausible enough but then, Morton reflected, Isobel had always been quick on her feet.

'Where are you now?'

'At home,' she replied quickly, and added, before he had time to speak: 'I mean it, James. I'm impressed. Where did you get the evidence?'

Isobel's question seemed natural enough but Morton was taking no chances. He knew those sods back home and he wouldn't have put it past them to use Isobel to get at him.

'You must understand I can't tell you that. Not even you.'

Isobel laughed lightly down the line, as though the matter was of no importance to her.

'Oath of office, huh?'

'Call it what you like.' The steel was still there.

She changed the subject. 'I tried to reach you Sunday night but you weren't answering.'

'Our *weekend de reflexion* ran on. We didn't get back till Monday morning.' Even bluff, decent men could be devious if they had to.

He didn't know whether Isobel believed him or not and, as he put the receiver down, he realized he didn't care.

Half an hour later the telephone rang again. This time the voice was one which James couldn't place immediately. Midlands accent, Birmingham perhaps? Not that he had ever been to Birmingham.

'Forgive me for calling you at home.' Kegan came straight to the point. 'I don't want to beat around the bush and I'm sure you wouldn't expect me to. The Party's furious; so, of course, is the Prime Minister. Can't you unscramble this before it's too late? This is going to do us a lot of damage with our friends.'

'Which particular friends?'

'The ones who count. The ones who put up the funds so we

137

can win the next election.'

'I'm only making a recommendation. The Commission is entitled not to follow me.' Morton was suddenly angry. 'I don't know how you got my private number, but this conversation is out of order anyway. Read the rule book, Kegan.'

As he slammed the instrument down, breathing heavily, Morton had an intuitive feeling that it was Isobel who had given Kegan his number. Had Kegan asked Isobel to call and then later, when Isobel got nowhere, decided to call himself? Were the two of them working together on this? He dialled Isobel's number in London, but there was no reply.

Morton sat there for a long time that night, glass in hand, television turned to a faint burble, contemplating the wreckage of both his marriage and his career.

But when the next day he bought the newspapers at his local newsagent in the Sablon, he knew he was right. Most of the papers carried the story on the front page. What was more important, they had gone beyond the bare facts of his announcement at the press conference to present, already, the broad outline of the charges against Deutsch-Chemie. How exactly Lomax had spread the word Morton didn't know, but there was no doubting the man's efficiency. *The Times*, of course, had more than any other paper – both in terms of news and background; but that, given the circumstances, was only right and proper.

Two hours later, as Morton made his (deliberately late) entrance to the Commission's Wednesday morning meeting, he could see immediately, from the angry glance that Dr Horst Kramer shot him, that the session would not be without its fireworks. As he sat down there was a momentary pause in the proceedings and he heard the French Commissioner, Pierre Duchesne, say in clear and hostile tones: '*Il ne faut pas exagérer quandmême.*' And then the man continued, speaking English for Morton's benefit, 'Could I suggest, Mr President, now that Mr Morton has graced us with his presence, that we interrupt the order of the proceedings and deal immediately with yesterday's events.'

Kramer, as though anticipating Duchesne's suggestion, re-

138

sponded immediately: 'I consider that to be an excellent idea.'

But Morton was not going to be bullied. Helena was clearly on his side since she had given him a covert wave when he arrived. Morton nodded a greeting to her. It was ironic that, at this crucial moment, he should be looking to his mistress rather than his wife for support. And he noted, as he shuffled his papers, that there were one or two other encouraging smiles around the table. The Greek and the Italian seemed to be with him too. Morton decided he would push it to a vote if he had to.

'Excuse me, Chairman; forgive me if I'm wrong – I was regrettably delayed at the start of this meeting – but would I be correct in supposing that you did in fact approve the agenda at the beginning of today's meeting?'

'*Ja*, that is correct.' Kramer sounded gruffly suspicious. What was Morton up to now?

'In that case,' Morton continued sweetly, 'I see no reason to depart from the order of business which you yourselves have just established. You will see that the item on industrial policy – Communication from the Commissioner Responsible – is inscribed at point nine on the agenda. But I'm quite happy to have a vote on this if you would like to.'

Kramer backed down with bad grace. He wasn't prepared to run the risk of being defeated on a procedural motion. There were Commissioners present who might be with him on substance, but who would nevertheless uphold Morton's right to insist that the Commission stick to the agenda which it had itself established.

For Morton it was a small but significant victory. Not for the first time, he had given a clear warning that he was not to be pushed around.

When, finally, they got to item nine around midday, much of the heat seemed to have gone out of the issue. All present had received during the course of the morning the Commission's daily résumé of overnight press commentary, including photocopies of relevant articles from all major European newspapers. And they had been able to appreciate for themselves the general acclaim that had greeted Morton's initiative. Inevitably, each Commissioner tended to look first at the press

139

of his own country. If they were applauding in Rome and Madrid, then it would be safe to applaud in Brussels too. Even Paddy McGrath, the Irish Commissioner, who was hardly the closest of Morton's allies (what Irishman ever made common cause with a Briton if he could avoid it?) had to recognize that the *Irish Times* and the *Irish Independent* had struck a note of welcome and he moderated his own attitude accordingly.

'Now that we've reached this point on the agenda at last, Mr President,' McGrath said, 'perhaps Mr Morton would be so good as to inform us why he felt it necessary to go public, as it were, with his recommendation before colleagues had had the chance to hear it for themselves.'

There were one or two rumbles of assent as McGrath spoke, but Morton decided to face them down.

'Each of us must take his own responsibilities. I took mine. Perhaps colleagues would now like to hear my report in detail. I am quite sure I shall be able to answer any concerns they may have. . . .'

In the end they didn't vote on it, though Kramer would have forced one if he had thought he could win it. But it was obvious that a large majority of the Commission had already decided that their best course of action, as prudent politicans, lay in approving what Morton had already done. By the end of the morning the Commission had decided to suspend all further consideration of the merger between Deutsch-Chemie and United Chemicals until such time as relevant inquiries had been undertaken. Some of the Commissioners, in particular McGrath and Duchesne and, of course, Kramer himself, had wanted to press Morton about the source of his information. But Morton had remained adamant.

'I'm sure you will understand, colleagues, that it would not be right for me to divulge anything of the kind even within these four walls.' When Morton used the term 'even within these four walls', he meant, of course, 'especially within these four walls', but he was tactful enough not to say so. As they all knew very well, most of the leaks in the Berlaymont came from the thirteenth floor itself.

The Commission also decided that morning to charge Morton with the responsibility for conducting the necessary investigations and for preparing, in conjunction with the legal services of the Commission, the appropriate legal actions if these seemed to be indicated.

They broke for lunch shortly before 1 p.m. As Morton gathered up his papers and prepared to leave the room, the President of the Commission approached him. Morton had seldom seen a man look so angry. There were pink flushes on both cheeks and he was breathing heavily as though controlling himself with great effort.

'Please follow me,' he hissed.

Kramer stormed off down the carpeted corridor without waiting for Morton to speak.

Premiers and prime ministers, heads of state and heads of government, even the pope had been received over the years in the office of the President of the European Commission; policies and budgets had been formulated there; ambitious strategies devised to promote the 'construction of Europe', a concept which of course meant something different to each successive occupant. But from a strictly historical viewpoint, that afternoon's spectacle was not particularly edifying.

'Your behaviour was not correct, Mr Morton.' Kramer stood with his back to the desk, facing Morton as the latter entered the room. 'You know it and I know it. You may have got away with it once, but you will not be able to bounce the Commission a second time.' Before Morton could reply, Kramer continued: 'Your own Government will never back you. I shall never back you. You are wrong on procedure; you are wrong on substance as well. I do not know where you got your information, but I can assure you you are making a big mistake.'

For a moment Morton felt overwhelmed by the almost physical nature of Kramer's attack, to such an extent that for several seconds he found himself forced onto the defensive. Could Kramer be right? Had he been wrong not only in the way he had bulldozed the Commission, but on the facts as well?

But then, as he stood there, he remembered the walk he had taken on the beach with Kunig, remembered the anguish on the man's face as he had spoken of the death of his parents, remembered the talks he had had with Lomax and the dossier which Laurent Guimard had provided for him.

'Mr President' – he found the words at last – 'whether or not my Government backs me is of no concern. I serve the Commission, not the British Government. Whether or not *you* back me is, however, of considerable importance not just to me but, I would suggest, to Europe as a whole. In due course I hope to convince you that I am right and you are wrong.'

For a moment Morton thought that Kramer was going to strike him.

'Never, never, never.' He spat out the words. 'Be sure of that, Mr Morton.'

Without waiting for Morton to respond, Kramer stormed from the room.

Chapter Thirteen

He had tickets for the opera that Friday – a more than passable performance of *Don Giovanni*. (The Brussels Opera wasn't Milan or Covent Garden, but it was coming up in the world and rumour had it that aficionados with *abonnements* even came from as far afield as Paris for the evening.) Morton invited Helena to go with him.

'The Belgians make rather a do of first nights, I'm told,' he said apologetically. 'I've got to dig out my dinner jacket.'

At the end of a long day in the office he went back home to change. He had arranged that Helena would come to his apartment and they would go on together. What an odd turn life was taking, he thought, as he dressed. Here he was putting on his old but still serviceable dinner jacket, a garment he had worn regularly over the last thirty years – beginning with a Commem Ball at Oxford and including occasions like that memorable evening at Glyndebourne when Isobel had thrown a tantrum because the champagne wasn't cold – and yet, even though the clothes remained the same, the man inside them had certainly changed. He sensed within himself a purposeful edge which he had not been properly aware of before.

Since he was ready in good time he went over to the window and waited for Helena to arrive. She had been a great help the other day at the Commission meeting, had spoken out clearly and emphatically in favour of Morton's approach, had indeed swayed some of the others. It was odd how a man could slip into a relationship without really thinking about it. Had Isobel come to Brussels in the first place, he was sure he would never have begun an affair with Helena. He was not a philanderer at heart, never had been, never would be. But men were creatures of habit and comfort. Sitting by himself in the evening, reading his papers, had been all right in the beginning. He had been learning the job; being alone had been a relatively novel experience, particularly after all that camaraderie in the House of Commons. But in the long run he knew he was not built for solitude.

He saw her car pull up behind a large brown Citroen parked immediately underneath his window. He noted, idly, that the Citroen had German number plates. Some tourists, he supposed, enjoying an expensive meal at the Ecayer Royal. It didn't surprise him that people drove from Germany to Belgium to eat. One could have altogether too much *kartoffel* and *knockwurst*.

At the opera itself he enjoyed the sensation of being at least a minor celebrity. Brussels had its own rhythms and priorities and making a success of the Common Market was not necessarily one of them. But *les Belges* were nevertheless quite aware that they owed a good deal to the presence of international organizations in their midst. The ripples created by Morton's sensational press conference had spread far and wide but some of them had lapped the nearer shores as well. Count Armand de Grote, for example, whose grandfather had founded Belgium's steel industry, greeted him with what seemed to Morton to be a faintly mocking smile. 'Ah! the hero of the hour!' The Count was an elderly man, tall as a lamp post, and decorated with a white walrus moustache which quivered as he spoke. 'We are all trembling in our shoes wondering who will be next.' The Count laughed lightly as he moved on, but there was a hint of warning in his voice.

Amid the crush of people heading for the bar at the first interval, Morton saw a figure whom he recognized but for a moment had difficulty in placing. The man was impeccably, almost fussily, dressed. Silver hair, every strand in order, contrasted with bronzed features, the whole being admirably set off by a dark-blue velvet dinner jacket evidently purchased at one of Europe's finer establishments of haute couture. He

144

saw the man glance in his direction and finally remembered where he had seen him before. It had been the day he had addressed the Club of 13, that strange occasion in the old house on Rue Ravenstein when Europe's leading industrialists had gathered together mainly – or so it appeared – for the purpose of giving him lunch. What was the man's name? Rizzi? Rossi? Yes, Luciano Rossi. He sighed inwardly as he saw that Rossi, having refilled his glass, was heading determindedly towards him.

'Mr Morton! How very good to see you here!'

Helena, who had made a brief sortie to talk to the Portuguese Ambassador and his wife in another part of the room, had now rejoined him and Morton presented her to the Italian.

Luciano Rossi bent over Helena's hand, raising it towards, but not actually to, his lips. It was the traditional gesture of high society but somehow the Italian made it seem foppish. He turned to Morton once again. 'And how is your apartment in the Sablon? Not too noisy I hope.'

With a wave and a smile and a whiff of expensive cologne, the Italian was gone.

'How did he know you lived in the Sablon?' Helena asked.

'I suppose I must have told him the day I went to talk to the Club of 13.' Morton was mildly puzzled – he couldn't remember having a conversation about his living arrangements with Luciano Rossi. But then the bell rang for the second act of *Don Giovanni* and he put the matter out of his mind.

After the opera they went on to a party thrown by one of Belgium's biggest banks. This *par excellence* was a country, Morton realized, where business, finance and high society were inextricably mingled. Of course there was plenty of old blood around but some of the most prominent members of *Le High-Life* were from families whose fortunes had been made in the last century or in the early years of the present one and whose titles – *comte* or *baron* or whatever – had followed their wealth as the plough follows the tractor. It was almost midnight before Morton and Helena were able to leave.

145

He drove her back to her apartment and was going to drop her at the door but she turned to him and said: 'Tomorrow's Saturday. Why don't you stay? We can sleep late and then we could go to the country. I am sure you could do with a break. I certainly could.'

'I don't have any clothes. I'm not going to go around in my penguin suit all tomorrow.'

She laughed. 'Go and get some then. It will only take you twenty minutes.'

Deep down Morton recognized that he didn't really want to spend the night at Helena's place. He had done it once and had decided then that it shouldn't become a habit. He had no idea where things stood between him and Isobel (they hadn't spoken in days); he doubted whether matters could continue the way they were. But that didn't mean he was ready to exchange one imperfect relationship for another. He was powerfully attracted to Helena but was that enough? He sighed as he drove back to his apartment, surrendering after all to pressure. How was it that suddenly his life had become so complicated?

As he entered the building he noted that the brown Citroen with the German number plates hadn't been moved. If the driver of the car was still in a restaurant somewhere, then he was certainly making a meal of it, Morton thought. He changed quickly into casual clothes, put a toothbrush and a razor in his pocket and turned out the lights of his apartment.

The man sitting watching in his car fifty yards away across the square saw the lights go out and grunted with satisfaction. He started his engine and drove quickly off past the church, turned left on the Rue de la Régence and continued until he reached the Place Royale. The first telephone kiosk he came to was out of order. The man swore angrily at the work of nameless vandals and got back into his car to find another one. When he did at last find an instrument that was working, his conversation was brief and to the point. 'He's back.'

In the event, Morton decided not to take his own car back to Helena's. His large white Jaguar was inevitably conspicuous and he had no wish to leave it parked outside Helena's building all night. He got into a late-night taxi which was cruising through the Sablon in search of stragglers, leaned forward and told the driver to take him to the Cinquantenaire.

When the man who had been watching came back from the telephone, he saw that the white Jaguar was still in front of Morton's apartment. He backed his own car – a blue Renault 5 – into a side street where he could still see Morton's building, then looked at his watch. Three a.m., the boss had said. Well, if that's what the boss wanted, that's what the boss would get.

It was a magical sunlit day. They slept late, breakfasted on Helena's terrace, then drove out towards the Ardennes.

'It's not the wilderness, but it's splendid all the same, isn't it?' They were standing on one of the high points of the land, looking at the vast panorama of pine. It wasn't his country, but still Morton felt he wanted to defend it. Too many people thought it was funny to take a poke at Belgium without realizing how much the country had to offer.

They had lunch – the traditional *moules et frites* – in a small Ardennes town, a cluster of grey stone houses bisected by a fast-flowing river. Afterwards Morton, with an uneasy feeling that he had been playing hookey for too long, told her that he had to get back.

She insisted on driving him to the Sablon. The first thing they both noticed, as they entered the square, was that there were no stained-glass windows in the church.

'What the hell . . . ?' Morton began to exclaim, but then he saw that not only were there no windows in the church; the pretty medieval building in which his apartment was situated had a gaping hole in its side. The whole area had been cordoned off and policemen were holding back a crowd of sight-seers behind a barrier of trestles.

It was impossible to get closer to the scene so Helena parked the car at a distance. They saw there was no point in rushing. Whatever damage there was had been done several hours earlier. What they were witnessing now was a mopping-up operation. Morton noticed the television cameras just outside the cordoned-off area. Trust the ghouls, he thought.

With Helena a step behind him he walked to the barrier, thrusting his way through the crowd. When he reached the trestles he tapped a policeman on the shoulder and the man turned round. 'What happened?' Morton asked.

The man seemed surprised that anyone should still be in ignorance. 'A car bomb exploded here last night. Around 3 a.m.' And he added, as though this was the most tragic aspect of the event. 'They destroyed Wittamers. No more chocolates.'

Morton was filled with a sense of dread as he asked: 'Anyone killed?'

'Yes,' the man replied laconically. 'The British EEC Commissioner, apparently. His apartment was on the first floor; his car was parked outside. Look.' The man pointed to some debris which had been cleared away to one side; Morton recognized some mangled remnants of what had once been his white Jaguar. He had a brief vision of a brown Citroen parked in front of the building the night before. 'They're digging him out now.'

'Oh my God!' Morton exclaimed. He could almost feel the force of the blast, the shattering impact.

The policeman, who had seen worse things in his time – he had been present in the Heysel stadium the night Liverpool played Juventus – shrugged. 'Terrorists. Belgium is full of them nowadays. Apparently the Communists have already claimed responsibility for the attack. So have the Flemish nationalists. I guess the Commissioner just happened to live in the wrong place.'

Morton realized there was no getting out of it. 'I *am* the Commissioner,' he said. Three feet away from him a woman turned in his direction. She had been watching intently as the rescue teams sifted through the rubble of the building, but when Morton said 'I am the Commissioner' his voice penetrated her consciousness and she turned round. Morton's stomach gave a great churning movement as he recognized the tear-stained face in front of him.

'Isobel?' he exclaimed. 'What on earth are you doing here?'

'Oh, Jimmy!' She flung herself into his arms. 'It's been so dreadful. I heard it on the news and caught the first plane.

148

Thank God you're alive.' And then, with unerring instinct, her eye fell on Helena.

Shit! Morton thought gloomily, wondering whether it might not after all have been better to have been blown up in the explosion. He said rather formally: 'Isobel, I think you've met Helena Noguentes. Helena, this is Isobel.' Then he thought: James Morton, you've really screwed it up this time, haven't you?

Isobel, who still hadn't fully taken in the significance of Helena's presence, burst into tears. I thought you were in there, buried in the rubble.'

Morton took a deep breath. There were times when a man could lie or bluster his way out of things, but he was not sure that this would be one of them.

'No, Isobel.' He spoke quietly, conscious of the boom-microphones which were thrusting in his direction. 'I wasn't here last night.' He half-turned only to realize that Helena had already slipped quietly away.

Chapter Fourteen

She took Brussels by storm. She took *him* by storm. Morton had forgotten during the months of separation just how determined Isobel could be. While he had been still genuinely shocked by the closeness of his escape, Isobel reorganized his life from top to bottom by the practical expedient of moving back into it. The bombing, it seemed, had forced her to decide where and how she wanted to live. Isobel's viewpoint was simple. If Morton was important enough for someone to want to assassinate him, then, hell, that meant he was important, period, so maybe she'd misjudged him the last few years.

They stayed in the Hôtel Amigo, near the Grand' Place, while Isobel looked for a house. There were security men in the corridor outside the room and in the lobby of the hotel, and they followed him wherever he went. Even if Morton had wanted to see Helena, it would not have been easy. He would have trailed a squad of goons in his wake. And Isobel in any case would have none of it.

Once she said to him, as they hurried off to inspect a house in the suburbs which she had her eye on, 'We both screwed up. You've had your fling, but I don't want you to think that I'm Simon-pure.' She put her hand on his knee as she drove aggressively through the traffic on the Chaussée de Waterloo, much as she used to drive through Knightsbridge to her shop in Beauchamp Place. 'I'm not saying that what you did is the same as what I did or vice-versa, but at least it helps to balance up the scale.'

Morton laughed. Isobel took such a refreshingly down-to-earth view of things. 'I don't want to know about you and Kegan, as long as it's over. It is over, isn't it?'

She overtook a bus on the wrong side. 'Hell, yes,' realizing somewhat to her surprise that she meant what she said. 'Even without the bomb, it would have been over. I didn't like the way he'd been leaning on you, the way they all were. Frankly, that nauseated me.'

'You knew about that? You were there, weren't you? I must say, I wondered at the time. First you rang, then half an hour later, Kegan rang. It all seemed so pat. You can be pretty rough, you know.' He said it lightly but he could still taste the bitterness.

Isobel put her hand back on the wheel so that she was free to hoot violently at a rash pedestrian who was trying to cross the Chaussée without waiting for the lights. 'What about Helena?'

'Let *me* deal with that.' As he spoke, Morton remembered the note Helena had sent him in the aftermath of the bombing: 'Please let me know, *both of you*, if there is anything I can do to help.' Later, Morton had had a quick conversation with her in the corridor on the thirteenth floor.

'She's your wife, James. I saw the look in her eyes when she discovered you were still alive, not buried there under the house. We can still work together; we *have* to work together. But, now that I've met her, I'm not going to mess all that up. How could I?'

She tried to smooth the way for him and Morton was grateful for that.

But still it hurt. She had meant more to him than he cared to admit. He found himself at moments almost resenting Isobel's melodramatic return.

The house they finally found was an old villa in Rhode St Genèse, one of the southern suburbs of Brussels. It was large, full of light and – this was what appealed to them specially – surrounded on all sides by a magnificent mature garden on which the previous occupants, an elderly Belgian couple who had departed to find something smaller and more manageable, had lavished every care. When they saw it the azaleas were in full bloom and even though those particular splendours would

151

shortly fade, there were rhododendrons and fruit trees — apples, pears, peaches, cherries — enough to supply a regiment.

'What's more, you can go jogging in the forest each morning,' Isobel had joked. 'Work off your unnatural urges!'

It was a suggestion which Morton politely declined — jogging had always seemed to him a fairly pointless exercise — but, like Isobel, he fell in love with the place. He had liked particularly the look of the old tennis court, shaded by trees and climbing plants, at the far end of the garden. 'I'll certainly play tennis. We can both play.'

'We'll give tennis parties.' Isobel suddenly saw the possibilities of her new role as a *châtelaine*, gliding gracefully among her guests on sunlit lawns.

One consequence of the bombing in the Sablon was that the Belgian authorities insisted on permanent police protection and placed a kind of sentry-box in the street outside. They warned Morton to change his route each day as he was driven to the office, something that was easier said than done. As time passed, however, and as the normal rhythm of life resumed, the images of violence faded. Morton began to think that the destruction of his flat had been purely coincidental — there had been explosions in the centre of Brussels before and they had not been directed at EEC Commissioners. It seemed as though the police were tending to that opinion as well. Regional conflict — the Walloons versus the Flemish — was, they suggested, regrettably endemic in Belgium and sometimes innocent bystanders got caught in the middle. Or perhaps Wittamer had indeed been the target. A bizarre ecological protest against conspicuous consumption?

But one evening as Isobel and he sat on the terrace contemplating the surrounding vegetation, Morton said: 'A funny thing happened today at the office.'

'What?' Isobel, thinking about whether the garden could take a swimming pool as well as a tennis court, was listening with only half an ear.

'A Belgian policeman, the inspector who is in charge of investigating the Sablon incident, came to see me. He said that since they suspected the bomb had been exploded through a

152

remote-control device, they were checking on whether any cars or people had been noticed in the vicinity at the time.'

'And?' Isobel decided that a swimming pool would be a lot of work and would spoil the look of the garden. If she and Morton had had children it might have been a different matter. She concentrated on what her husband was saying.

'Apparently a Renault was seen parked for several hours that night in a side-street. Someone happened to make a note of the registration number and the police have traced it back to a chap called Luciano Rossi. They made inquiries, and of course it turns out that there's a perfectly good explanation. Rossi was at the opera that evening – I actually met him there – and his driver was waiting to pick him up after a late-night supper.'

As he spoke Morton remembered his first encounter with Luciano Rossi the day he had visited the Club of 13's headquarters in the Rue de Ravenstein. He recalled the closed doors along the corridor and the discreet plaque saying 'Industrial Action'. Could Rossi or his paymasters in industry conceivably have organized an attempt on his life on the ground that he, as Commissioner, was threatening their interests? Or, more precisely, Ludwig Ritter's interests. The more he thought about it, the more plausible the idea seemed to be.

The following day he made an appointment to see the Belgian Minister of the Interior, Hugo van Reder, an ebullient and popular politician who doubled as the Mayor of one of the city's Flemish communes.

'Leave it to me,' Van Reder said confidently after Morton had finished outlining his suspicions.

A week later the Minister returned the compliment by visiting Morton at the Commission's headquarters.

'Thanks for the suggestion,' he said. 'It turned out my people were already thinking along the same lines. We visited the Club of 13 but found nothing unusual. Actually we didn't expect to. But we talked to Mr Rossi too – in the friendliest possible way. I think he understood the message and will no doubt convey it to his superiors. Of course, he probably knows we don't have any proof but he also knows that we don't need proof to make life difficult and unpleasant. We don't like people exploding bombs in our city. If your suspicions are correct, I doubt whether you will have any more trouble from that quarter. The illustrious members of the Club of 13 have too much at stake in other areas. And if your suspicions are not correct, why then' – he smiled disarmingly – 'what have we lost except a few hours of our time? Even so, I think we shall keep the guards in place, don't you agree?'

So the *gendarmes* stayed in their box at the end of the drive as an additional precaution. But on the whole Morton felt reassured. Hugo van Reder was as tough as nails and would have left Rossi *et al* in no doubt at all as to the consequences which would attend any further freelance initiatives by *Action Industriel*. And the very fact that the Commission as an institution was now irrevocably committed to pursuing the case against Deutsch-Chemie meant that his own position was less exposed. Even if they get me, Morton thought in his more pessimistic moments, there are others who will pick up this particular baton and run with it.

That weekend Isobel went shopping in the centre of Brussels.

'*Deux grandes boites s'il vous plait.*' Her view was that, now that Wittamer had reopened, you might as well be hung for a sheep as a lamb. Belgian chocolates were slightly more expensive than gold, measured ounce for ounce, but they certainly tasted better than a Hershey Bar.

As she left the shop with the elegantly-wrapped purchases in her hand, she saw Helena Noguentes on the pavement outside, looking at the display of cakes and sweetmeats in the window. Behind her, on the other side of the Sablon, Isobel could see the huge tarpaulin which had been hung over the facade of the building which had once contained Morton's flat.

She felt the wave of bitter, vindictive anger rising, like fire, inside her. Here she was in bloody Belgium, leaving behind many good things such as her job, her hairdresser and her lover in order to set up house and home like any good housewife amid the alien corn with her dearly beloved husband, and what happens? The said husband, instead of being truly and properly grateful for all the adjustments his better half has to make, and all the hard work she has to do, like arranging for cooks and cleaning ladies and getting hold of electricians to

154

change all the ghastly lamp fittings in the house, quite clearly sinks into a gloom, looks before and after and pines for what is not, all because he's had it off a couple of times with some foreign bitch who probably dropped her knickers right in front of him in order to get him into bed.

Life, she felt, would have been easier if Morton's fling with Helena had merely been one of many affairs. At least the man would know how to handle things, instead of going around like a wounded beast with a look of silent suffering on his face.

'Senhora Noguentes, isn't it? How good to see you!' She spoke with glacial charm.

'Ah, Mrs Morton. How do you do?' Helena smiled at her uncertainly.

Isobel regarded her coolly, appreciating – in spite of herself – Helena's dark beauty, her raven hair contrasting with her olive skin. 'Do you like chocolates too?' The sarcasm in the question was almost palpable.

For a moment Helena didn't quite take her meaning, but then when she finally grasped what Isobel was driving at, she replied with a quiet dignity: 'Your husband must make up his own mind, Mrs Morton. I have already made my position clear.'

She brushed coolly past and entered the shop.

Isobel, bested for once in her life, thought of all the rotten things she could say about Helena and then added a few more. She considered hurling the chocolates into the street but decided against it. It never helped to throw good money after bad.

It was funny, she thought. There she was after all these years ready to tread the straight and narrow; determined to 'make a go of it', as they said; prepared to love the man warts and all, and yet he was slipping through her fingers. Isobel realized that for possibly the first time in her life other influences apart from the force of her personality were liable to determine events. If only she could have had a baby! In the role of proud father, Morton would be a pushover.

Chapter Fifteen

'Photocopies of photocopies?' Dr Horst Kramer, President of the European Commission, sounded sceptical. 'How are they going to tell anything from that?'

'No, sir,' Peter Simpson replied quietly but firmly. 'These are the original copies, not copies of copies if you see what I mean. I substituted one set for the other. If you let Ritter have these, he can bring in the experts and they will probably be able to discover by internal evidence precisely what photocopying machine was used and that in turn will help identify the source. Any machine,' he continued, 'will have its own set of characteristics and peculiarities, however minute these may be. A scratch on the glass will show up on the copy and that particular blemish can identify the machine just as surely as a serial number.'

As he spoke, Simpson found himself being grateful for his early exposure to the darker side of diplomatic life. ('An intensive training in clandestine techniques,' that old queen at Magdalen had said.) Following Morton to Holland; opening the safe in the Commissioner's office, removing and copying the papers – all this had, he prided himself, come as naturally to him as to a full-time professional.

The two men had met late one night – long after everyone else had gone home – in Kramer's office in the Berlaymont. The initiative for the encounter had come originally from Simpson, but Kramer had not been slow to respond. Indeed, he had taken a certain malicious pleasure from the fact that it was one of Morton's own personal staff who was blowing the gaffe.

'Thank God there are still some people around with their head screwed on the right way,' Kramer had commented gruffly when Simpson had finished outlining what he knew. 'Morton bulldozed this thing through the Commission and, unless we stop him, he will bulldoze it through the European Court as well.' He lit a large thick cigar, puffed at it for a few seconds, then said: 'Let me summarize. The car registration number has been traced to a man called Kunig who apparently works for Deutsch-Chemie; you saw Kunig hand over a briefcase to Morton; later you saw Morton throw the briefcase into a canal in Holland; you discovered a set of papers dealing with Deutsch-Chemie's activities in Morton's safe in his office; you suspect that these papers were originally copied by Kunig at Deutsch-Chemie's headquarters outside Cologne, though this is something that we shall allow the company itself to establish. Am I correct? Is the circle closed?'

'Correct.'

Simpson felt that he had done all that he could do. What happened next was surely up to Kramer.

The large German had one more question: 'Why are you doing this, Simpson? This is slightly unusual behaviour, is it not, for a Chef de Cabinet?'

For a second Simpson wondered whether he should tell Kramer the truth; that he was a place-man put in by Passmore and the people behind him to make sure – *entre autres* – that Morton did what he was supposed to do and to take appropriate remedial action if he didn't. But he realized that this wouldn't do. Not for Kramer anyway. He looked the other man squarely in the eye.

'I'm doing it because I think it is right. Right for the Commission and right for Europe. I see no other course of action. Just don't tell anyone about my part in this.'

It was the kind of language Kramer understood. He rose to his feet and held out his hand. 'You can rely on me.'

After Simpson had gone Dr Horst Kramer sat down at his desk, picked up the telephone on his private line and dialled a number in Germany. When at last the call was answered, Kramer said: 'I want to talk to Dr Ritter, please.'

'May I say who is calling?' The butler, recognized the

157

voice immediately. Quite apart from that early encounter in the German *Schloss* over which Ritter had presided, he had – over the last weeks – taken several calls from the President of the European Commission. Though it was none of his business, he could see that Ritter and Kramer had remained on close personal terms in spite of the brouhaha involving Deutsch-Chemie.

He was surprised that on this occasion Kramer didn't give his name. But that, again, was nothing to do with him.

'Just say it's important,' Kramer urged him.

'Of course.' The butler laid the receiver on the marble table in the hall and went in search of his master.

If Simpson felt any trace of remorse as he drove home that night, he showed no sign of it. On the contrary, his wife remarked that his appetite was even healthier than usual. As he shovelled in a plateful of re-heated lasagna Simpson reflected that loyalty came in many shapes and sizes. One could be loyal to one's immediate superior, in this case Morton. Or one could be loyal to some wider concept of duty, to a political party for example, or to the government of the day. Or, most usefully of all, to one's own interests. Good old self-interest. There was nothing quite like it.

Passing his plate up for a second helping he comforted himself with the thought that most actions, his own included, were capable of various interpretations and that ambiguity was often the secret of survival.

Alone in his study later on, he called Sir Oliver Passmore at home. As soon as he heard the Ambassador's parched tones at the other end of the line he came straight to the point.

'I've done what you suggested, sir. I'm fairly sure Kramer will have taken the hint.'

Sir Oliver was clearly pleased. The dry, brittle laugh was unmistakable.

'Excellent, Simpson. I suggest you keep your head down for the time being.'

Simpson replaced the telephone with a certain feeling that, however furiously flak might start to fly in the immediate vicinity, his long-term career prospects had certainly been improved. *Sir* Peter Simpson? It sounded good. Even though they were cutting back on the Ks (some quite senior ambassadors were missing out nowadays), he was sure that when his turn to be considered for a knighthood came round, there would be no doubts or hesitations.

For Morton the next few days were some of the busiest of his life. Working closely with Laurent Guimard, he concentrated on preparing the case for the European Court. Once or twice Guimard had questioned Morton about his sources of information, indicating that the Commission's case would certainly benefit from personal testimony were that to be available. But Morton had been firm on this point; he had given his word to Kunig that there was no question of his identity being revealed at any stage and he had stuck rigorously to that promise.

'So we must do out best with what we have, then.' The Frenchman had set about organizing the Commission's dossier as efficiently as possible, reluctantly recognizing that the star witness (whoever he or she might be) would never be able to perform. Presenting documents in court was one thing but presenting credible personal testimony, testimony that stood up to cross-examination, was something else again.

'We're going in there with one hand tied behind our back,' Guimard had told him.

Morton had shrugged. There was nothing he could do about it.

If Morton's time was fully occupied, so – it seemed – was Isobel's. At last installed in Brussels, she had immediately conjured up, Morton noticed, a large circle of intimate friends with whom she lunched at frequent intervals in expensive Brussels restaurants.

'No point in letting all that good money pile up in the bank,' she told him.

Besides developing an active social life, Isobel had taken steps to open a branch of her business here in Brussels.

'Have you seen their houses?' She was genuinely amazed. 'The decor in some of them is positively Victorian. Chiko and

159

the girls will have a field day once I get them over here.'

She had taken a lease on an elegant old building near the Place St Catherine – an up and coming area – not far from the centre of Brussels, and was already making preparations for the grand opening of *Isobel de Bruxelles*.

'But don't expect me to invite your ex-mistress, darling,' she had told him in honeyed tones. 'I can't stop you seeing her in the office, I suppose. But that's as far as it goes, huh?' She had wagged a reproving finger at him. No doubt Morton had heard about that little fraught episode outside Wittamer's. If so, so much the better. He should know how things stood.

Morton had said nothing. If Isobel chose to taunt him, well – that was Isobel and her way of doing things. He had wanted to say to her, in a voice of sweet reasonableness, that one day this particular worm might turn, but he had bitten back the remark. He had enough on his plate as it was without precipitating a domestic crisis.

He met Helena one evening for a drink in her apartment.

'Does Isobel know you are here?' she asked.

'No, of course not.'

'Why *are* you here? I told you I won't come between you and your wife.' Then she relented as she saw the look of suffering on Morton's face. 'You're not in love with me, James. You're tied to Isobel and you always will be. The more she wounds you, the closer you will stick to her. I know you public-school Englishmen. The strain of masochism runs deep.'

He took her in his arms as though to deny the force of her remarks and she raised her mouth to his as she had done that first night in Oporto, standing on tiptoe to reach him.

'I do miss you, James. You must know that.'

'Isobel's in London tonight,' he murmured. 'She's bound to call. But we can be together for a few hours at least.'

'I wish you *could* stay all night. I'd like to wake up with you beside me again. Of course, I'll come between you and Isobel if you give me half a chance!'

Morton laughed lightly, turning the topic aside. 'I don't know what you see in me.'

'You're a real human being, James. That's what I see in you. There are so few of them around.'

In the end he stayed till midnight. They made love with a passion which Morton at least had never experienced before. In his heart he knew it might be the last time. But he could not bear to say so, or even think it.

Chapter Sixteen

There were four police cars altogether and the men in them, all members of Germany's *Verfassungsschutz* – the internal security force – knew their job. They had picked the hour before dawn, when the body's diurnal cycle is at its lowest ebb, when reactions are slow and resistance weak. They surrounded the house in the quiet suburb of Cologne, taking care that all escape routes were closed; then, as the sky began to lighten above the lime trees which fringed the garden, the two men from the leading car walked up the drive and banged on the front door.

They gave him time to dress, but no more than that. When Kunig protested at the intrusion, one of the men flashed some papers at him which bore the stamp and seal of Germany's Ministry of the Interior, the body responsible – amongst other things – for the security of the State. And when he asked to be able to call a lawyer, they told him roughly that there would be plenty of time for that later but that for now their instructions were clear; he was to leave with them at once.

'And my wife? My children?' Kunig was distraught as Helga and the children, roused by the commotion, huddled miserably at the top of the stairs, recognizing instinctively that the very sheet-anchor of their existence was being torn away from them.

Helga had thrown a shawl over her thin nightdress. She followed him down the stairs as they took him away; pleading with them. The tears stained her cheeks and her shoulders shook uncontrollably as she realized what was happening.

'Don't take him! Let him go. It's all a mistake, it has to be! Tell them, Hans, that it's a mistake.'

But the men gave her a withering look and one of them said mockingly: 'Twenty years. Twenty-five maybe. You'll be an old lady by the time he comes out, Mrs Kunig. You won't even be able to visit him where he's going.'

Kunig had wanted to speak, to reassure her beyond doubt that it was indeed an error and that he would be back to have breakfast with them before the children went off to school; but in the end the words stuck in his throat and a numbing terror descended on him.

'Can I say goodbye at least?' he asked. But the two police-men seemed not to hear him; they marched him off to the waiting car while others began to search. The last sound Kunig heard from his house was the heart-rending sobbing of his wife.

He shut his ears against the sound as the car sped away. There was not time now to think about Helga and the children. He had to think about himself. Above all, he knew, he had to deny every charge. He must not allow himself to be forced into a confession. They had nothing to go on, surely; he had taken every precaution.

'On what grounds are you arresting me?' He spoke with a calm which he did not feel.

The driver turned his head round to the back where Kunig was sitting handcuffed to the door.

'Under State Security Ordnance number fourteen. You are going to be charged with the betrayal of commercial secrets. In Germany, as you may know, that is a crime not merely against the company concerned but also against the State itself. It carries a maximum penalty of life imprisonment.'

Kunig felt the blood drain from his cheeks. He closed his eyes. What on earth was happening? How had it all gone wrong. 'I once again demand to see my lawyer.'

'Oh, you'll be able to see your lawyer all right,' the police-man said. 'But it won't help. They've got all the evidence they need. And they'll find more. Make no mistake about that.'

When they had finished searching the house, the three policemen came into the kitchen where Helga was waiting dazed and trembling.

'You're not to leave this house, do you understand? Not till you hear from us. For all we know, you may be implicated too.'

Then one of them, kinder than the others, took pity on her. 'You just picked the wrong man, didn't you? Bad luck, it can happen to anyone.'

It took two days for the news of Kunig's arrest to reach Brussels. Morton was just preparing to go into the Wednesday morning Commission meeting when Peter Simpson came into his office.

'Oh, by the way, Commissioner,' he said casually after they had got rid of one or two routine items, 'did you see that the Germans have arrested a chap in Cologne? Apparently, he's an employee of Deutsch-Chemie, called Hans Kunig. Seems to be a fairly senior executive.'

Morton felt as though he had taken a blow to the stomach. 'Kunig? Never heard of him,' he parried. 'What's the charge?'

'Passing information to the Commission.'

Morton took a deep breath. His best hope was to bluff it out, both now and in the future. There was no evidence that Kunig had been in touch with the Commission and without evidence the Germans could never prove their case. The only thing that could nail Kunig would be if he, Morton, revealed his relationship with the man.

He spoke casually. 'Even if it were true, I don't see what it has to do with the German Government. Is it a federal crime to inform public authorities about an employer's misdeeds?'

Simpson looked at Morton curiously. He knew, because he had witnessed the event, that Morton had been in contact with Kunig; indeed, since he had had the opportunity to inspect the documents which Morton had brought back from Holland, Simpson was aware that the Commission's case against Deutsch-Chemie rested heavily on the evidence that Kunig had supplied.

'Actually, in Germany it is,' he said. 'The Germans are rather like the Swiss. Short of murder, and treason, betraying commercial secrets is about the most heinous crime you can commit.'

Morton picked up his papers from the desk, preparing to go to his meeting. He looked his Chef de Cabinet straight in the eye. 'I've no idea who Kunig is or what he has done, if anything. I can't imagine it can affect the Commission's case against Deutsch-Chemie one way or the other, but keep me posted if you hear anything, won't you?'

When Morton had left Simpson went through to the outer office. 'Vivian, can you ask our press people to put out a statement? Tell them that the Commissioner has no knowledge of Kunig – that's the man who has just been arrested in Germany on charges of industrial espionage – and will have no comment to make on any allegations that may be made.'

Simpson walked across to his own room, smiling with quiet satisfaction. In its way it was like a hi-jacking, a classic hostage situation. He had told Kramer, and Kramer in turn must have told Ritter, of Morton's contacts with Kunig. Ritter had obviously decided to involve his brother, Ernst, the West German Minister of the Interior. And the Germans, it was clear, had now come down on Kunig like the proverbial ton of bricks. The charges would be brought by the Federal Government's Director of Public Prosecutions, but Deutsch-Chemie would write the ticket and make sure that the DPP knew precisely what to say. Morton must surely know by now that if the Commission pursued the case against Deutsch-Chemie through the European Court, Kunig's prospects of escaping with anything less than a very long sentence would be slim indeed.

When he came home that evening, Morton felt as near despair as he had ever been. He sat on the terrace with a glass of whisky in his hand and said to Isobel: 'The truth of the matter is that I was gung-ho for action, wanted to make a name for myself, I suppose, didn't want people to say, "There's old Morton packed off to Brussels, dead-end job for an end-of-the-road politician." Pride, personal vanity – that's what it was.' He swung round to face her. 'And who pays the price? Not me. I sit here in my garden drinking whisky, surrounded by rhododendrons and loving wife.' He smiled wrily. 'And the man who gets it in the neck is poor old Kunig. First he loses both his parents in a concentration camp, now he'll probably spend the rest of his life behind bars.'

Before Isobel could reply, they heard the sound of car tyres on the gravel drive, saw a long black Mercedes pull up to the house, and a tall weather-beaten figure get out and walk towards them.

'Leopold!' Morton held out his hand. 'What a pleasure to see you! Come and have a drink? Do you know my wife?' Suddenly Morton felt his spirits rise. Ever since their first meeting at the *Schloss* in the German countryside, he had become increasingly aware that Leopold Brugmann was the solid foundation, the bedrock as it were, on which successive Commissions built their castles in the air.

'Forgive me for intruding, James, on such a scene of domestic tranquillity' – Brugmann smiled with perhaps just a trace of irony – 'but I thought it best to talk to you here, rather than in the office. Walls have ears, as they say, particularly in the Berlaymont.'

Morton braced himself for what was coming. 'Tell me the worst.'

'Kramer is going to try to get you thrown out. The German Government is furious and they're leaning hard on him. Kramer's furious too, by the way. He's never forgiven you for the way you bounced him and the Commission into bringing the case against Deutsch-Chemie.'

'It was the only way to get things moving.'

Brugmann sighed. 'You've ruffled too many feathers, James. Kramer could force colleagues to a vote and this time you might not win.'

For the second time that day Morton felt as though someone had punched him in the solar plexus.

'And what happens to the case against Deutsch-Chemie if the Commission sacks me?' he asked.

'The Commission will drop it like a shot, I'm afraid.' Brugmann shook his grey head. 'One or two of them might want to continue but most of them will lack the stomach for the fight.'

'So I run home with my tail between my legs, having achieved precisely nothing. What do you say, Isobel?'

166

'Why don't you listen to Brugmann,' Isobel replied quietly. She turned to the Secretary-General. You didn't come here this evening just to tell my husband he was going to be sacked, did you?'

The Count smiled once more, that same faint flickering smile. 'No, of course not. I came to offer my help. You see' – he spread his hands in rather a charming way, fluttering the fingertips towards the rose bushes which surrounded them – 'I rather admire what your husband has been trying to do and I've had an idea which I think could be of some help.' He turned back to Morton. 'A man was arrested in Germany a couple of days ago and charged with handing over commercial secrets to the Commission. His name is Hans Kunig. Your office put out a statement this morning saying that you had no knowledge of him and no dealings with him. That statement was false, wasn't it?'

When Morton didn't answer, Brugmann continued: 'It doesn't matter. You don't have to say anything. I know from my own sources that the West German Government are aware of your contacts with Kunig; they know that he has sent or given you internal Deutsch-Chemie documents and they can pinpoint the key elements of your relationship with considerable accuracy.'

Morton sat there open-mouthed while Brugmann talked.

'They have no possible means of knowing anything,' he protested finally. 'Certainly not of proving anything.'

Brugmann rebuked him in the mildest possible tones: 'Someone has fished a briefcase out of a canal in Holland. The case belonged to Kunig. Apparently you were observed throwing it into the water. And there is other evidence.'

'What kind of evidence?' Morton was still stunned.

'Enough.'

Brugmann leaned forward in his seat and a note of urgency came into his voice. 'You *must* admit your links with Kunig. If you're going to save your position at the Commission and go on to win the case against Deutsch-Chemie, you must make a statement *now* indicating that Hans Kunig is the man who supplied you with evidence and, what is more, the Commission proposes to subpoena him before the European Court in Luxembourg as your star witness!'

Morton felt suddenly angry. 'And what happens to Kunig? Do the Germans drop the charges against him just because he has appeared as a witness in the European Court? Every word Kunig speaks in that court will be used later in evidence against him at his own trial. He'll refuse to testify. He'd be damning himself if he did.'

'Do you seriously think' – the ghost of a smile crossed Brugmann's face – 'that a man who is being held incommunicado in a German prison is going to say "no" to the opportunity of paying a visit to the Grand Duchy of Luxembourg, if only for the purpose of testifying before the court? Particularly if, in reality, the German prosecutor already has all the evidence he needs.'

Morton looked at Isobel and then they both looked at Brugmann.

'You mean . . .' Morton began.

Brugmann raised a warning finger to his lips.

When Brugmann had gone Isobel said to Morton: 'Count me in on this one, darling. We've been making a hash of things recently and that's probably my fault as much as anything. But I want to help you fight these bastards, and I can be quite energetic, as you know!'

Morton looked at her in surprise. 'We may not win.'

'We can try.'

That brief exchange left Morton happier than he had felt for a long time. Isobel, he knew, could be a most effective ally. What's more, when all was said and done, the bloody woman was still his wife.

'We'd better have some champagne.' He opened a bottle. 'Although I'm not sure we should be celebrating with Kunig languishing in prison.'

'Let's drink to his release.'

As he raised his glass Morton thought how odd it was that so much of his life, including – if what Brugmann said was right – his own personal future was now bound up with a middle-aged German industrial executive whom he had met just once. Who the hell had revealed Kunig's links with the

Commission? Someone in Deutsch-Chemie? A neighbour or a 'friend'? And how in heaven's name had they traced the briefcase? Even Kunig had not seen him dump it in the canal. Who else could have? Who else could even have known he was in Holland that day?

'Isobel,' he said suddenly, 'I've got to go back to the office now.'

'What on earth for?'

'I've got to see whether all the papers are still in the safe.'

Morton was surprised to find his secretary still at work.

'I thought you'd gone home hours ago.'

'Just catching up.' Vivian Perkins was often the last to leave, staying far later than most of the Commissioner's staff.

'Who knows the combination of the safe besides you and me?' Morton came straight to the point. 'Does Simpson?'

'Indeed no. This is something I've always kept to myself.'

'Could he have found out?'

'Well, I suppose it's possible,' she replied cautiously. 'I know he sent Mrs Morton flowers on her birthday. He asked me to arrange it.' Vivian thought for a moment. 'Since he knew the date of her birthday, he could have guessed the combination number. We chose Mrs Morton's birthday because you said that's the only date you can remember. You said you were too scared to forget it!' Vivian reminded him.

'I should have known better,' Morton commented grimly.

They went into the office together and opened the safe. To his surprise Morton saw that the papers Kunig had given him were still there. Somehow he had expected them not to be. He took them out and examined them carefully. As far as he knew, they had never left his office. Even Laurent Guimard, trusted lieutenant though he was, had to consult them *sur place*.

Then, as he studied them with his secretary sitting by his side, Morton realized that these were not in fact the documents that Kunig had handed over.

'Where's the oil-stain? Look through them carefully, Vivian; see if you can find a mark on one of these pages.'

She didn't understand the basis of the request – how could she? – but she did as she was told. (She would even have eaten frogs' legs if Morton had asked her to.)

'Nothing on any of these.' She handed the pile back to him.

He remembered the morning in Sir Oliver Passmore's office, the way Peter Simpson had been handed to him on a plate pre-packed and oven-ready, a Chef de Cabinet in waiting.

'Damn him!' he said out loud. 'Damn both of them!' He thrust the papers back inside and shut the safe with a bang.

Chapter Seventeen

'Why?' Morton asked furiously. 'In God's name, why?'
For once in his life Simpson appeared shaken. The
vigour of Morton's attack, launched as soon as he came into
the office (Morton had arrived early so as to be ready and
waiting) took him by surprise. He stood stiffly in front of the
Commissioner's wide desk, like an errant schoolboy summoned by his headmaster.

'I did what I thought was right. What you were doing, what
you *are* doing, is in my view not in the Commission's interest
nor in HMG's interest. You may be able to ignore such
considerations. I cannot. You were not ready to listen to
reason, insisted on pressing the case against Deutsch-Chemie
to the detriment, as I saw it, both of Britain and Europe – and
you did this as Commissioner for Industry, a position which
our Government had expended considerable effort to obtain.
Finally, as I say, I did what I had to do. As you surmise, I
followed you to Holland, opened the safe, read the documents
and, yes, informed the President of the Commission.'

Morton found it hard to contain the anger which boiled up
inside him.

'And Kunig? Did you think of the consequences for him?'

Simpson held his ground. 'I'm sorry about Kunig, Commissioner, but I believe that there are other more important
aspects to this question.' Simpson's lips tightened as he spoke.
He knew that he would live to fight another day. They had
assured him of that.

Morton waited until he was certain that his rage had quite
subsided.

'I want you out of here by lunchtime,' he said finally. He couldn't resist adding: 'Go back to Passmore, Simpson. Perhaps you can help him polish his ceremonial swords. There's no place for you here. I believe in what I'm doing and I need people around me who will help, not hinder.'

When Simpson had gone, Morton rang Kramer's office and asked for an immediate interview, only to be told that the President of the Commission did not intend to see the Commissioner for Industry either that morning or at any time in the foreseeable future.

Well, thought Morton, the battle lines were being drawn in no uncertain way.

'What do you propose to do now?' Vivian Perkins, hovering discreetly, had no wish to push Morton into unnecessary disclosures, but she could see that the Commissioner was in a mood for confidences.

By way of reply Morton pulled a piece of paper out of his pocket. 'Could you type this out for me, Vivian, then send it down to the press room for the twelve o'clock briefing.' As he spoke, he remembered the famous lines from *Macbeth*: 'If it were done when t'is done, then t'were well/ It were done quickly. . . .'

Vivian read the paper as she began to type: 'James Morton, the Commissioner for Industry, today announced that the Commission intends to call Hans Kunig, the Deutsch-Chemie employee now under arrest in West Germany, as a witness in the case which the Commission is bringing before the European Court in Luxembourg. . . .'

She was half-way through when Morton, who had gone back into his office, poked his head round the door again. 'I shall need a car from the pool.'

Vivian looked up from her machine in surprise. 'Where are you going?'

'I'm not going anywhere, not today. I have to be here when the balloon goes up, as they used to say. But Mrs Morton will be taking a little trip. Official business.'

'May I ask where? They will need to know in the pool.'

But Morton had already had another idea. 'On second thoughts, Vivian, I'll send Gerry with Isobel. He was complaining the other day that he hasn't had enough long-distance trips recently, too much running around town. And anyway, Isobel may need help the other end. I'd prefer Gerry to go. I can have a pool car myself.'

Vivian Perkins turned back to her typewriter with a distinct sense of exhilaration. It was obviously going to be one of those days.

Later that morning, soon after he had finished interviewing two possible internal candidates (this time he was determined to resist any outside pressures) for the job of Chef de Cabinet in succession to Peter Simpson, he heard a soft knock on the side door which led into his office directly from the corridor of the thirteenth floor. The etiquette was that only Commissioners themselves entered another colleague's office without passing through the ante-room. He looked up to see Helena Noguentes.

'Do I disturb you?' She gave him a dazzling smile, showing no sign of embarrassment or confusion.

'No, not at all.' Morton could not disguise the note of hesitation in his voice. The champagne which he and Isobel had consumed the previous night, and the atmosphere of shared purpose which had accompanied it, had left him ill-prepared for an unexpected encounter with his mistress. Morton reckoned that he was learning to handle life's little complexities fast but not, perhaps, that fast.

The smell of her perfume wafted across to him, making him wonder for a brief moment whether in fact he was as firm of purpose as he supposed. 'How nice to see you!' He rose from his desk, kissed her on the cheek, then steered her firmly in the direction of the large leather sofa at the far end of his room.

She sensed his uneasiness. 'Don't worry, James, this is a business call.' She was amused to see him relax. How bad the English were at handling personal relationships! But then she decided that perhaps she was being too hard on him. After all, the man had a wife, wanted – for a reason best known to himself – to keep her, so what else could he do except give her a frosty peck, especially with that old dragon of a secretary in the outer office?

She smiled at him anyway. 'Remember, when we were in

173

Oporto, I told you I'd cleaned up the Douro. Well, when I came to Brussels as Environment Commissioner, I had an inventory made of water quality on all the major rivers of Europe, to see how much still needed to be done here.'

Morton nodded. He wasn't quite sure what Helena was driving at, but at least it was clear she wasn't about to make a scene or seduce him on the office floor.

'How could I forget Oporto!'

Helena smiled, acknowledging his stab at gallantry. 'I should explain,' she continued, 'that our monitoring programme pays particular attention to the frontier regions. After all, the EEC is a supra-national grouping, so we have to be concerned with the quality of water as it passes from one country to another. We've been looking at the Rhine downstream of Cologne because this is the water which passes into Holland; this is what the Dutch have to drink and if that water is contaminated you could find that Dutch supplies of water are jeopardized on a very large scale indeed.'

'Go on.' Morton was beginning to understand why Helena was telling him all this.

She needed no urging. 'I don't want to become too technical; perhaps it's enough for me to say that there have been several occasions in recent weeks when the Dutch have had to close down their water intakes because of upstream pollution. In other words, they've had to stop taking Rhine water for periods ranging from twenty-four hours to forty-eight hours until such time as water quality has returned to acceptable levels. The Dutch, of course, have been rather angry and they've been on to us.'

'Where's the pollution coming from?'

'We're not sure. Possibly from some industrial discharge on a stretch of the Rhine between, say, Cologne and Düsseldorf. What worries us and the Dutch most of all is the nature of the pollution. On all three occasions when the Dutch have had to close down their intakes, it's been because unacceptable levels of highly toxic chemicals have been found.'

'What kind of chemicals?'

'PCBs and PCTs, for a start. Also' – she paused, to let the point sink in – '2,4,5,T and other compounds normally associated with the manufacture of Agent Orange.'

Helena rose to her feet, smiling. 'We're taking it up with the German authorities but, as you can imagine, we're not getting much cooperation. The German Minister of the Interior, in case you didn't know, is responsible not only for State Security but also for environmental matters. In fact, when we tried to ask them about that stretch of the Rhine, they told us to get lost on the ground that the nature of industrial discharges was confidential, like all other aspects of industrial processes in Germany! I just thought you would like to know.'

She paused by the door. 'There's something else I have to say, James. I know whatever there was between us is over, has to be over. But I want you to know that I shall always care for you.'

Morton was grateful to her for making it easy. He knew it had to end. But, unlike her, he could never have found the words to say what had to be said. He walked over to her and placed his hands lightly on her shoulders.

'Thank you, Helena. Thank you for everything.'

Then he kissed her goodbye.

When she had gone Morton stood by the window for several minutes, looking down over the ravaged heart of Brussels and trying to fit the pieces of the jigsaw – personal and professional – together.

When Isobel returned to Brussels from Germany late that night she was in an ebullient mood in spite of the exertions of the day.

She came to sit on the sofa with Morton as he watched the news on television. 'The children are being looked after by Helga's sister,' she explained. 'Helga herself seems to have had some kind of nervous breakdown and is in hospital. The strain of Kunig's arrest was too much for her. But she's expected home at the weekend.'

'Did you talk to the children?'

'Yes. Fortunately they both spoke English. Apparently Helga hoped that they would all go back to America one day, so they kept it up at home. The sister told me she couldn't

175

understand why Kunig left his job at Ponting's in the first place.'

'I'm not sure I really understand that now either,' Morton said, 'not if you look at the mess he's in. Was the sister helpful?'

'Yes. She took a very dim view of Kunig's chances otherwise.' Isobel closed her eyes and leaned back. A quiet, satisfied smile appeared on her unblemished face. 'I'm pregnant, by the way,' she said. When she saw him looking at her in openmouthed amazement, she added quickly: 'Oh don't worry, darling, it's your baby, no one else's. A big bouncing Morton boy to inherit all those lovely acres. It was the night we moved into the Amigo after the bombing. I'm sure of it.'

So it's all going to be all right after all, then, is it? Morton thought. He could feel the tears pricking at his eyelids. They'd consulted doctors and quacks up and down the country to no avail; they'd given up hope years ago, and then after all the fruitless time and effort she goes and pulls the bleeding rabbit out of the hat.

He put his arm round her and hugged her as she sat beside him.

'Well done, darling!' How ruthless she was, he thought. She had used the ultimate weapon and of course she had won. How could a gentle soul like Helena hope to compete with Isobel? 'This calls for champagne again.' He half-rose to his feet.

'Not for me, James. No alcohol, not from now on. Not even champagne, I'm afraid. It's water for me.'

'Water it shall be then,' Morton said firmly. 'Doubles.'

Chapter Eighteen

Paddy McGrath, the Irish Commissioner who was in charge of the EEC Budget, was adamant. 'We could never swing it, James. Even if my Budget director would wear it, which he wouldn't, the Court of Auditors would be sure to pick it up. You're talking about a payment which is equivalent to more than £500,000. There's no way you can hide that kind of money.'

'The Germans won't let Kunig testify before the European Court without sureties. Of course they're asking this ridiculously high figure because they don't *want* Kunig to testify. It's quite clear to me that throughout this whole business, the Germans, or at least their Ministry of the Interior, have been hand in glove with Deutsch-Chemie. The Public Prosecutor in Cologne is just acting as a mouthpiece.' A note of appeal came into Morton's voice: 'The Commission has its responsibilities in this affair. Shouldn't we put up bail, no matter how large the amount is?'

'The man made the first advances, didn't he?' McGrath was still far from sympathetic.

'Yes, but I followed them up. He trusted the Commission not to reveal his identity and we let him down.'

McGrath was beginning to see the point. As a politician, particularly as an Irish politician, he was used to treachery of every kind. The double-cross was a load they all had to bear at one time or another, and he knew how painful a burden it could be. He didn't like to see the European Commission be a party to it.

177

'You're sure Kunig doesn't have the money?'

'Absolutely sure.' Morton was emphatic. 'Isobel has been to Kunig's home. It's clear that Kunig is not a rich man. He could never raise half a million pounds on his own account.'

McGrath thought for a moment. There was a trace of humour in his voice when he said: 'If Kunig has to stay in gaol, why doesn't he stay in gaol, in Luxembourg – at least for the duration of the trial? Isn't there some EEC directive which says a man has a right to be imprisoned anywhere he pleases as long as it's in the European Community?'

Morton smiled for the first time that morning. 'You mean, if dentists can practise their profession anywhere in the Community, why can't convicts? If Kunig can't get bail, then at least the Commission should press for him to be able to testify from prison, even if that means it's a Luxembourg prison. And then, of course. . . .' His voice trailed off as the full vista of possibilities presented itself to him.

Paddy McGrath put an expansive arm round Morton's shoulder. 'You British may be slow on the uptake, but if you keep going, you get there in the end! We need some action now, don't we? May be I should be having a word with some friends of mine.'

Morton didn't quite know what McGrath meant when he referred to 'friends', and he wasn't sure it was sensible to find out.

Ten days later the case of the Commission versus Deutsch-Chemie opened at the European Court of Justice in Luxembourg. The interest in this unusual judicial event, already strong, was further heightened by the announcement that Hans Kunig, the man named by the European Commission as being its principal informant, had been transferred to the main, indeed the only, gaol in the small city of Luxembourg and that the Government of the Grand Duchy had given undertakings to its large and powerful neighbour, Germany, that it would hold Kunig in safe custody for the duration of the case. The Court of Justice was therefore treated to the unusual sight of a prisoner arriving each day under armed guard and of *gendarmes* remaining in the courtroom throughout the proceedings.

As with so many other legal battles of this nature, the protagonists conducted their affairs through proxies. The Commission's team of lawyers, headed by Laurent Guimard, built up an exceedingly unflattering picture of Deutsch-Chemie's actitivities over a period of years, relying not only on the documents which Kunig had supplied but also on well-timed and judicious interventions by Kunig himself. Morton, the man behind it all, kept well away from Luxembourg, receiving daily reports – both written and oral – on the progress of the case. By the same token, Ludwig Ritter, the President of Deutsch-Chemie, was seen conspicuously boarding an aircraft at Frankfurt on the first day of the trial for what was announced as an extended vacation in the Caribbean. But Ritter too was kept closely informed of developments by loyal lieutenants at Deutsch-Chemie's Cologne headquarters.

Hans Kunig, the Commission's star witness, lived up to his billing. As the case proceeded it was clear that his evidence was having a considerable effect. Guimard called Morton in Brussels on the tenth day of the trial – a Friday.

'Our man's doing well,' he said. 'He's by far the most impressive witness so far, not only for what he says but for the manner in which he says it. He's made no bones about his dealings with the Commission, and with you in particular. And the fact that the court knows that he is damning himself out of his own mouth as far as the Germans are concerned makes him all the more convincing.'

Morton had barely finished this conversation when the telephone rang again. It was Paddy McGrath.

'The boys are on their way.'

Isobel was standing beside him as he replaced the receiver. 'Are you ready?' he asked.

'Of course. I've been ready for days.' The light of battle was in Isobel's eyes.

'Then you had better get going first thing in the morning.'

'Don't worry. I told you to count on me and I meant it. I haven't had so much fun in years.'

Morton looked at her. He wasn't sure about Isobel's idea

of fun but he was confident that, whatever else might have happened along the long and winding road of their marriage, on this particular occasion Isobel would not let him – or herself – down.

The new prison which had been built in Luxembourg in the late seventies was, Kunig thought, probably a good deal more comfortable than the dark dungeon that had served the purpose for the ten previous centuries. But even if the physical surroundings had been harsher, more medieval in character, Kunig was confident that Saturday afternoon that his morale would have been in excellent shape. He had had good news from home. Helga had apparently recovered from her breakdown, had left hospital and was now staying with her sister, together with the children. They had all sent messages of love and support and these had cheered Kunig immensely.

There had been another message too. Now that Kunig had finished giving his evidence, he could expect that afternoon – so his lawyer had indicated – a visit from James Morton, the Commissioner for Industry.

'It wouldn't have been wise for you two to have met while you were still on the stand, but since that part of the proceedings is over I see no further difficulty.'

When the lawyer had gone, Kunig settled down in his cell to wait for his next visitor.

Morton was surprised to see how well the man looked. He hadn't seen Hans Kunig in person since that day in Holland when Kunig had given him the caseful of documents which had formed the basis of the Commission's case against Deutsch-Chemie. Kunig, outwardly at least, had not changed much since then. His face was perhaps somewhat paler, a trifle more tired, but that was not altogether surprising. He had already spent several weeks in prison in Germany before being transferred to Luxembourg. Morton doubted whether the conditions in the gaols of the Federal Republic were quite as comfortable as those that obtained in the Grand Duchy.

'Hello.' Morton held out his hand as soon as he came into the prison's visiting room and saw Kunig sitting the other side

180

of the wide table. (The prison authorities had dispensed with the traditional glass barrier but there were still certain formalities to be observed.)

Kunig leaned across the table to conclude the handshake, then settled back again in his chair with an expectant look.

'Well? Did I do all right?'

'You did splendidly. We couldn't have asked for more. Now it's up to the Advocate-General and ultimately the judges themselves. But if the Commission has a case, you made it for us.'

It was obviously the news that Kunig wanted to hear. There was a pause and then he asked: 'What about me, then? You gave me your word as a man of honour. I'm not saying that you personally let me down – although in a certain sense you did because you failed to protect my identity – but the Commission certainly is responsible. I'm in prison now and if I go back to Germany I'm likely to stay in prison for a very long time. Does that concern you, does that concern the Commission? It ought to.' A note of rising anger was beginning to enter Kunig's voice.

Morton looked around. The guard at the far end of the room was reading a newspaper and in any case seemed totally uninterested in their conversation. Morton doubted whether the man was listening, or could understand what they were saying. Even so, he lowered his voice and leaned across the table.

'We're not going to let you down. I can promise you that.' He spoke quickly, urgently, conveying to Kunig in short precise sentences all that he needed to know.

When Morton had finished, Kunig nodded.

'I understand. I hope they're going to move fast. I have to attend the court one last time on Monday but I've been informed that the German authorities are insisting that I be returned into German custody by Tuesday at the latest.'

'Don't worry,' Morton reassured him. 'Things are well in hand.'

Before he left there was one question which Morton had to put to Kunig.

'I remember you told me that day in Scheveningen that you

181

once had met Ritter in person because of some article you'd written. Can you tell me the background? It could be important.'

Kunig looked at him in surprise. 'In what way?'

Morton quickly summarized the situation which Helena had described to him a few days earlier. 'Something odd is happening to the Rhine downstream of the Deutsch-Chemie plant,' he concluded.

Kunig whistled. 'That explains it!'

'Explains what?'

'Why Ritter wanted to see me. One of the things I pointed out in my article was that the production of 2,4,5,T, which is one of the basic ingredients of the herbicide Agent Orange, involved the distinct risk that a runaway reaction might give rise to the production of lethal dioxins. What puzzled me was why Ritter should have been interested since Deutsch-Chemie, like every other chemical company in the world, has been totally banned from producing Agent Orange.'

As Kunig spoke, Morton remembered the piece he had seen in the *Herald Tribune* the day he flew back from Portugal, and the Rhine barges at Rotterdam laden with chemicals from Germany. 'What's your own explanation,' he asked, 'for Ritter's concern?'

Kunig thought carefully before replying.

'So much of chemistry,' he replied finally, 'is a matter of structure. Take a chlorinated hydrocarbon ring, for example. If you put the chlorine atom in at, say, position seven rather than six, you can change the whole nature of the molecule. In terms of production processes, you only have to jiggle the reaction around a bit and you can find that, working with the same basic feed-stocks, you've got another substance altogether. A plant which was organized to produce, say, an ordinary weedkiller could quite possibly be switched to producing 2,4,5,T and only the engineer in charge would know.'

'With the attendant dioxin risk?'

'Exactly.'

Kunig appeared reluctant to say any more and Morton did not press him. In any case, he had heard enough to know that something very wrong was going on and that, just possibly,

182

there was a disaster in the making which could make Bhopal seem like a minor blip on the screen.

Morton said goodbye to Kunig and returned to Brussels in a sombre mood.

The following Monday, the eleventh day of the case of the Commission of the European Communities versus Deutsch-Chemie, the black maria, which had been in the habit of fetching Kunig from the gaol each morning and depositing him on the steps of the court high up on the *plateau de Kirchberg*, failed to arrive. The President of the Court, Professor Cornelius van Rijn – the man who a few months earlier had presided over the new Commission's Inauguration – waited for half an hour and then adjourned the hearing for the day. The be-robed justices filed from the room to their chambers where they waited patiently (for justice is nothing if not patient) for news of any further developments. By lunchtime the embarrassing truth had emerged. Hans Kunig, having delivered himself of the bulk of his evidence, was apparently no longer in Luxembourg – or at least not in the prison where he was meant to be. Precisely how he had escaped was not clear. For want of any more plausible culprit a Turkish cleaning woman who had been the last to see Kunig in his cell and who had now failed to turn up for work was being blamed. But nothing was certain. What was clear was that a row of monumental proportions was brewing between Luxembourg and Germany. The German Government, with justice, accused its tiny neighbour of falling down on the obligations which it had solemnly undertaken. The Government of the Grand Duchy, after considering the matter in a hastily-convened session, had not much to say by way of reply to the charge except to suggest, somewhat disarmingly, that they probably weren't as good at running prisons as the Germans were but, anyway, a full inquiry was in process.

Late that night Morton received a telephone call from Paddy McGrath. 'I've had word that he's arrived safely in Spain.'

'Thank God for that.' As he spoke Morton was conscious of an overwhelming sense of relief. Of course, it was unfortunate that Kunig had disappeared before the end of the trial. The Justices of the European Court were probably as prickly and capricious as judges anywhere else in the world and they would certainly resent the disappearance of a key witness who had in some sense been in their custody. But Kunig had had his say. He did not believe that the man's absence at this stage would have a crucial effect on the verdict one way or the other.

'How did they do it, Paddy?'

There was a deep, throaty laugh at the other end of the line. 'You know, I'm not really sure myself. The boys are pretty experienced at this kind of thing and of course they've got their contacts just about everywhere. I think maybe some people looked the other way. Luxembourg may be a tiny little country, not much bigger than County Cork if you come to think of it, but these people don't like being leaned on by their neighbours, and particularly not by Big Brüder!'

Morton left it at that. He doubted whether he, or anyone else, would ever know the full story. What mattered was that the plan had worked.

'Did you pick up the children all right, then?' McGrath asked.

'They arrived here this afternoon,' Morton reassured him. 'They're sleeping now.'

'And Isobel?'

'She's asleep too.'

Morton remembered the moment when the car had pulled into the drive and he had caught sight of his wife's face on her return from Cologne. There had been tears in her eyes as she brought the children, shy and bewildered, into the house. She had spent the day fussing over them like a mother hen, totally absorbed in her new role, while Helga Kunig stayed in the sitting room, dazed and bewildered.

'Isobel will leave with them tomorrow,' he told McGrath. 'The paperwork is all done. She's going to fly staight to Madrid – Spain has no extradition treaty with Germany – and their father is going to meet them there.'

Morton had one thing more to say. 'We didn't see absolutely eye to eye on this at the beginning, Paddy, but I want you to know that I'm grateful for your help. I couldn't have done it without you. I wouldn't have known where to turn.'

'Aw,' McGrath brushed his remarks aside. 'It was the least I could do. You're a bit like a charging bull at times, James, but on the whole you're charging in the right direction.'

Gerry McLoughlin called for them early the next day. Morton went to the airport with Isobel, Helga and the children. Isobel was still keyed up, tense, teetering on the edge of happiness. She squeezed Morton's arm as she walked with him to the check-in counter. 'I don't think I have done anything as important as this in my life.'

Morton wanted to say: 'You're dead right, my dear,' but he refrained. The new Isobel, the tender thoughtful Isobel who had been born that day she told him she was pregnant, was still a recent phenomenon, a delicate plant that might very well wilt before the blast of an unkind wind.

Murray Lomax was waiting by the desk where passengers were checking in for the Air Iberia flight. 'I've been on to my press friends in Bonn, Commissioner.' He spoke in a low voice, steering Morton to one side while the others went through the formalities. 'Apparently the Germans are hopping mad.'

'Do you think they know the grisly truth about Kunig's escape?'

Lomax laughed. 'No, Commissioner. Brussels bureaucrats are credited with many things, particularly facelessness, sloth and cupidity. But they are not generally imagined to be capable of decisive action *à la* James Bond. Most people seem to reckon that Kunig simply bribed his way out.'

Morton heaved a sigh of relief. Whatever his moral obligations to Kunig, there was no doubt that what he and Paddy McGrath had done fell fairly and squarely outside the law.

Hoping that there was no one around to put two and three together, Morton went with them to the plane (Commissioners rated certain privileges at airports) and saw them safely on board.

'Come back soon, darling.' He kissed her with real affection. For a moment Isobel dragged her attention away from her small charges. She smiled at him. 'I will, Jimmy.'

185

Morton watched the plane pull out towards the runway. It seemed to him that, whether they liked it or not, the James and Isobel Morton show was condemned to succeed. It would take more nerve and energy than he had to cancel the billing now — and in any case he was not sure he wanted to.

Lomax rode with Morton back into town. 'I hear the court's going to adjourn,' he said. 'And give its judgement later. After the summer recess, in fact.'

'Is that so?' Morton was genuinely surprised. He had supposed that, like an Old Bailey trial, the jury would deliver its verdict at the end of the proceedings. Journalists, he reflected, were often better informed than principals. 'What's the reason for the delay?'

'The European Court makes a habit of deferred judgements. It gives the Justices time to collect their thoughts, I suppose, as well as having the translations done into all nine languages!'

'When the court does give a verdict, which way do you think it is going to go?' Morton asked. 'You've been following the case as closely as anyone has. I'd value your opinion; I'm too close to the whole business to see it clearly. What odds would you give?'

Lomax gazed at the grey and grey-brown buildings as they slid past, watched the burghers of Brussels taking their dogs for their morning constitutionals. What a lot of dogs there were! No wonder the *trottoirs* were so foul.

'Sixty to forty,' he replied at last. 'Against you, of course. Kunig was good but he wasn't good enough. Deep down, no one likes a sneak and in the end that's really what Kunig was.'

'Oh, shit.'

Lomax felt sorry for the man. 'Odds can change, Commissioner.'

It was cold comfort but better than nothing, Morton supposed.

Chapter Nineteen

It was like the Phoney War in the summer of 1939. Belligerence had been signalled on either side but outright hostilities had yet to commence. Within the Commission itself, it was clear that there were two camps. There were those who believed that Morton had done, and was doing, the right thing. They included Helena Noguentes, Larsen the Dane, Paddy McGrath, Ippolito Camino and, somewhat to Morton's surprise, that walking monument to antiquity, old Dimitrios Kafiri. Ranged up on the other side were the President of the Commission, Dr Horst Kramer, who now regarded Morton with a venomous dislike which he made no attempt to conceal, the Frenchman Pierre Duchesne, who clearly felt Morton had gone too far, and the haughty young Spaniard Ariosto Rivera Azul de Balaquentes, who still remembered with gratitude the effort Kramer had made at the beginning of the Commission's mandate to accommodate his wish for a more substantial portfolio. And then there were the floaters like the Commissioners from the Benelux countries who had yet to make up their minds which way to jump. As far as this last group was concerned, the only thing that was at all clear was that the judgement of the court would be decisive. If the court found for the Commission or, more precisely, for Morton, they would be the first to applaud his tenacity in pressing the affair to a successful conclusion and, by implication, his willingness to challenge many of the accepted conventions of bureaucratic behaviour. If, on the other hand, Deutsch-Chemie escaped scot-free or, at worst, with a derisory fine, then they would have no hesitation in concluding that Kramer had been right after all. In such circumstances, Morton knew, his own position within the Commission would be very shaky indeed.

At the beginning of August the Advocate-General of the European Court gave it as his opinion that the Commission had failed to make out its case against Deutsch-Chemie. For Morton – and others who had worked with him, like Laurent Guimard – the news came as a solid blow. The opinion of the Advocate-General was not, of course, conclusive. Later in the summer, the judges would in their wisdom either confirm it or reject it. But Morton could not pretend to himself, or to Isobel, that the omens were specially propitious. He knew that nine times out of ten the verdict of the court followed the opinion of the Advocate-General.

'Why is that?' Isobel realized to her surprise that she cared almost as deeply as he did about the outcome of the case. Throughout all those years when Morton had been at Westminster, even when he had held that junior ministerial job, she had never been wholeheartedly involved. She had at the start put up a fairly good show but later, when Morton seemed to be going nowhere rather fast, she knew she had been happy to remain in steadfast ignorance of both the major and minor preoccupations of her husband's political life. Christ, she remembered the occasion when Morton had been making a statement about something (Northern Ireland, wasn't it?) and instead of being up there in the Gallery like a loyal wife, she'd been in bed with Tim Kegan in that ghastly little flat in Dolphin Square. Whatever had happened to Kegan by the way? She hadn't heard from him in ages. No doubt Lily or Edna or Phyllis (or whatever Mrs Kegan was called) had him firmly nailed to the floor once again.

She brought her thoughts back to the present with a jolt as she heard Morton answer her question.

'It's their way of spreading the load, I expect.' Morton sounded cynical. 'When one old boy does a lot of work, the others aren't likely to overturn him without good reason. If there is honour among thieves, there is solidarity among judges!'

'Why *did* Pantaloni find against you?' Isobel couldn't suppress her smile as she recalled the name of the Italian jurist who was Advocate-General on the court.

They were sitting on the terrace of their villa on the outskirts of Brussels, enjoying a morning of rare sunshine. Morton pulled the pot of Oxford marmalade towards him. Such routine gestures helped to disguise the cosmic gloom that had enveloped him.

'It sounded to me like a lot of legal mumbo-jumbo. As far as I could make out, Pantaloni's main complaint was that the Commission had based its evidence on purloined documents. Apparently, they don't do that kind of thing in Italy! The essence of his argument was that since the theft of the documents was illegal, a case based on illegal evidence could not be allowed to succeed, no matter what the intrinsic merits might be. There's some Latin tag for it, I believe. *Materiae causa* or something like that.'

'Sounds like rubbish to me.'

A few minutes later Morton's gloom deepened when Laurent Guimard rang.

'I've just heard from the Commission's office in Spain that Kunig is going to sue the Commission for damages.'

'What on earth for?'

'He's claiming that the Commission failed properly to protect his identity. By allowing his name to be known to Deutsch-Chemie or to the German authorities, or both, he says that the Commission exposed him to severe loss, both material and psychological.'

'Good grief!' Morton could hardly believe this latest turn of events. It was true that Simpson had told Kramer about Kunig. And it was probably true that Kramer himself had tipped off the Germans even though the President of the Commission had contemptuously refused to discuss such a suggestion. But goddammit, they had tried to make amends. Kunig was a free man now thanks to Morton and McGrath. And the Kunig family – Helga and the children – who might have been kept back in Germany for years, had been whisked away to safety thanks to Isobel and some efficient organization.

'Kunig's right, of course,' he heard Guimard say. 'The Commission let him down badly. He is entitled to seek redress.'

189

Morton put down the telephone in a state of shock.

'What's the matter?' Isobel asked when he came back to the terrace.

'Kunig's suing the Commission for failing to protect his identity. In practice, that means me. Any cross-examining lawyer will have a field day. Can't you hear him? "So you left the *Herald Tribune* in your office, Mr Morton, with the time and place of the rendezvous in Holland circled in black ink? And the combination number of the safe was based on your wife's date of birth, was it? Did it not occur to you that Mr Simpson might think of that?" ' He sat down heavily opposite her.

'You know, Isobel, I think I had better resign before they throw me out. This could ruin us, you know. And I mean ruin us. Financially and in every other way.'

Isobel threw her napkin at him. 'James Edward Morton, let's get one thing straight. You have personally displayed more courage and more determination than anyone else I can think of within the Commission or outside it. Don't throw it all away now. Fight back, for heaven's sake. Surely you can think of a way.'

Morton picked up the napkin and handed it back to her. He felt strangely cheered by Isobel's outburst.

The following morning when Morton arrived at his office he found a book on his desk.

'The library sent it up,' his secretary explained. 'Apparently it was out on loan when you asked for it, and the person who borrowed it has only just sent it back.'

'What did I ask for, Vivian, and when?'

'Books on the chemical industry. Months ago. The library sent you a print-out.'

'I remember now.' Morton looked more closely at the book which he held in his hand. The title was *An Illustrated History of I. G. Farben*.

For the next few minutes Morton was absorbed in a study of the book. He had of course heard the outline of the story before, both from Lomax and Kunig. Indeed, he was surprised at how closely the tale Kunig had told that day in Holland resembled the one he was now reading. It was almost as though Kunig himself had established or at least confirmed his facts by consulting the treatise he now had before him.

Thinking back to that long afternoon on the dunes at Scheveningen, he found he could remember with almost total clarity the sad tale Kunig told, the passion with which the man had spoken. He realized with hindsight that the critical moment had been when Kunig had told how his parents had died in the concentration camp at Auschwitz, and how Ritter had been there as an aide to one of the I.G. Farben bosses. It was Kunig's desire for revenge, for justice, as much as anything else that had made him believe in what the man was saying.

He turned from the text to the photographs. Two or three of them seemed familiar. Examining them more closely, Morton saw that they were precisely the same as the ones Kunig had shown him. That by itself was not surprising. The pictures came no doubt from some of the company's archives (wherever they were now); if the author of the *Illustrated History of I.G. Farben* had access to them, there was no reason why Kunig should not have made use of them as well.

The author of the *Illustrated History* had put names to the faces and these, Morton noted, corresponded to those that Kunig had recited: Schmitz, Kuehne, Krauch, Ter Meer, Herman Abs – they were all there.

And that, thought Morton, is the youthful Ritter, standing modestly in the rear. He turned to the text beneath the photograph, expecting to find either a mention of Ritter's name or at least the author's intelligent surmise as to the identity of Krauch's aide.

'In the background,' he read, 'standing behind Krauch, is another I.G. Farben executive called Oberndorfer who died at the end of the war. See also the photographs on the following pages.'

Morton turned the page. There was another picture of Oberndorfer, this time a head and shoulders portrait. There was no doubt that it was the same man as in the group photo of the I.G. managing board; but – equally clearly – there was no doubt at all that Oberndorfer was not Ludwig Ritter! Morton had met Ritter face to face and however much a man's features might change over the years, he knew that the picture in front of him could not have been of Ritter.

Puzzled, he turned to the index. There was no reference to Ludwig Ritter, or indeed to any other Ritter. There were, on the other hand, several references to Oberndorfer, who had clearly been one of the rising I.G. Farben stars before his untimely death.

Morton shut the book at last and stared dazedly out of the window. What a fool he had been, he thought! What an unbelievable blundering idiot!

He picked up the telephone. 'Can you get me Murray Lomax please, Vivian? Yes, it's rather urgent.'

Chapter Twenty

While Morton grew increasingly entangled in the ramifications of the Deutsch-Chemie affair, Isobel – unusually perhaps for someone in the early stages of pregnancy – found herself enjoying an almost euphoric sense of energy and well-being. No sooner had she organized her personal life (the grand opening of her new shop *Isobel de Bruxelles* had been a great success with Chiko and her team stealing the show) than she determined that she would also take on official assignments appropriate to her status as the wife of the British Commissioner.

The British community in Belgium welcomed this development. They were delighted that Isobel, whom they were quite prepared to consider as a sort of 'honorary Brit', was ready to take on engagements which her husband might otherwise have declined.

'How about going to Arnhem?' he had asked her one day. 'I've been asked to open an extension to the War Museum there, but I can't leave Brussels that day. Could you go instead? Of course, you're an American and it's bound to be something of a British occasion.'

Isobel had bristled. 'Our boys died there too, didn't they? I saw the film. I'll represent the Allies.'

In the event, Isobel had done just that. She stood on the platform in the new wing of the museum, surrounded by veterans and dignitaries, and delivered a homily as full of zest as it was of historical inaccuracies. The audience loved it. The only awkward moment came when she decided to compare the battle of Arnhem with the Spartan defence of Thermopylae. When she sensed from the muted reaction of her audience that she was eulogizing the wrong side, she paused in mid-flow, took a long deliberate drink from the glass of water which had been set beside her, and started talking instead about *The Guns of Navarone*.

'What the hell?' Isobel told Morton when she returned to Brussels. 'They were all heroes, weren't they, no matter what side they were on.'

Morton had patted her on the head in a paternal way. 'Have a drink, darling. I'm sure you did very well.'

He had began to pour her a stiff whisky, but Isobel had stopped him.

'I'm still on water, I'm afraid. Ghastly, but good for me. . . .'

Late that night they took the wagon-lit from Brussels to Auray, on the far western coast of Brittany. From there, a taxi brought them to Quiberon where they stayed only long enough to hire a boat to take them to Hoëdic.

'There's no hotel so we are staying in the home of one of the islanders,' Morton had told Isobel. 'One of the local fishermen, I believe. We should have some good lobster while we're there.'

'I hope he doesn't have a telephone. We can do with a break from all that, Jimmy, even if it's only for a week.'

'Don't worry,' he reassured her. 'Apparently there's hardly a telephone on the island.'

The crossing took about three-quarters of an hour. The sea was calm, the weather warm. Though, in terms of latitude, they were not far south of Brussels, they seemed to be a world apart as far as the climate was concerned. There was something almost tropical in the breeze which pushed up into their faces and in the abundant vegetation which greeted them as they put in at last to the tiny harbour on Hoëdic.

'I love it,' Isobel said as the gulls swooped to their nests on the towering cliff-face, screeching and shrieking against the wind. 'I love you.'

Morton took her arm and steadied her as she stepped down the plank on to the quayside.

*

As they ate their dinner that night, the fisherman in whose house they were staying came to join them at their table. He was about sixty-five years old, a Breton born and bred, with leathery skin and pale blue eyes that spoke of a Celtic past.

'Once they planned to build a port here, but in 1930 when I was still a lad, a big ship was wrecked off the island; many people were drowned. I can remember it now. The fishing industry died after that. People said the lobsters had fed on the flesh of the drowned men.'

They listened, fascinated, as the man told stories of pirates and shipwrecks, of days long past and of men and women, giants in their own way, who had carved out a harsh living from the rocks. 'You see us with the sun shining today; most of the year it's a very different story. It's not cold, so much as rough and wet. The future doesn't look so bright either. Most of the young people have already left for the mainland.'

Later that evening they walked along the cliff-tops. In the distance they could see the lights of the French mainland – of Quiberon, Trinité-sur-Mer and other towns along the coast. They might as well have been astronauts looking down from space. Morton took her arm.

'Don't get me wrong,' Morton explained. 'I'm not a fanatic. I just think there has to be room in the world for places like this – and for people like that old boy who talked to us at dinner. If the Commission loses the case I shall be sorry not just because I think we deserve to win, but because I think we *need* to win. The Deutsch-Chemies of this world have had their own way for too long.'

Out of the night, a swirl of kittiwakes beat their way back to the narrow ledges of the cliff beneath them.

Chapter Twenty-One

L omax caught the one o'clock Sabena flight from Brussels to Washington DC.

He landed at Dulles International Airport late in the afternoon and took a taxi into the city. As they turned off the Dulles access road on to the Beltway, then hit the George Washington Memorial Drive along the Potomac, a flood of memories came back to him. Washington was a city where he had served his journalistic apprenticeship; cut his teeth, as it were. He had been there for Watergate – from the first break-in at the Democratic Headquarters, through the hearings on Capitol Hill, the drama of the missing tapes and the long-drawn-out agony leading to Nixon's disgrace and resignation. Those had been heady days. Journalists had discovered a power which they had not known they possessed. If you could break a President, you could do anything.

They passed the CIA headquarters at Langley (how much did *they* know about what was going on, Lomax wondered?) and headed across Key Bridge on to M Street. He still had friends in town he could have stayed with but he didn't want to advertise his presence. Someone would be bound to throw a party for him and questions would be asked about why he was here – so he made for the Washington Marriott on 22nd and M. At almost two hundred dollars a night anonymity didn't come cheap, but short of pitching a tent on the banks of the river, he couldn't see the alternative. Lomax checked into the hotel, swam fifty lengths in the pool, ate a meal in the restaurant, made some telephone calls and went to sleep.

Dr Thomas Barnard was waiting for him in his office at nine the following morning. As Vice-President for Science of the World Wildlife Fund's North American Organization, Barnard was a busy man who still managed to find time for his own original research. 'Hell,' he told Lomax, 'if I can't get my hands dirty, I'm not going to be able to do my job You can't run an organization if you don't know what you're talking about at the scientific level.'

Barnard was in his early forties and at the top of his profession. He had received just about every conservation award North America had to offer, knew the forests of Central and South America as well as most people knew their local supermarket; more important, he had an ability to communicate and to enthuse. When, on the previous evening, Lomax had reached him by telephone at his home, Barnard's immediate reaction had been one of intelligent interest. 'It could be. It could just be. Come in tomorrow and we'll talk about it. I'll make the time available.'

In the event, they did more than talk. 'Let's get out and take a look,' Barnard said. 'No good sitting here in an office on Connecticut Avenue when the evidence could be staring us in the face.'

So they took Barnard's car – a battered Land-Rover which had seen action in half the countries of Central America – and drove into Rock Creek Park, the two-thousand-acre wooded stream-valley which bisects the nation's capital.

'When I was a child,' Barnard told him after they had parked the car and were walking up through the ravine, 'we used to build tree-houses and creek-bed dams in this valley. I can remember that in the spring and summer the woods were filled with birds. Of course you still see the year-round residents such as bluejays, cardinals, titmice, nuthatches, chickadees and woodpeckers, but what I'm missing now in recent years are some of the breeding species which used to be commonplace, particularly the species which migrate to the neotropics.'

'Neotropics?'

'The Caribbean and Southern Mexico, through Central

197

America down to Central South America. There are six hundred and fifty bird species in the United States and half of those spend half to two-thirds of their lives in that part of the hemisphere. And one hundred and seven species – and that includes many of our familiar songbirds – are associated with and dependent upon tropical forest. The Audubon Society has been conducting annual censuses of breeding birds on a sixty-five acre tract here at Rock Creek Park and they've found sharp drops in the numbers of some breeding neotropical migrants. It's a new silent spring. Once tropical habitats for these species are gone, the species will also be gone regardless of how much breeding habitat we have up here.'

At last Lomax put the question he had been waiting to ask. 'I can understand that you're losing forests in Central America because of population pressure, commercial logging, slash-and-burn cultivation and so on. But are there any other causes of deforestation or defoliation which could be resulting in species-loss?'

Barnard looked at him sharply. 'Why do you want to know?'

Lomax wasn't sure how much to tell him. So much of the evidence was still speculative. It was not clear that there were causal interconnections. But in the end he decided that if he wanted Barnard's help, he would have to trust the man, tell him what he suspected – or rather, what Morton suspected.

Half an hour later they were seated together in Barnard's office in the World Wildlife Fund's headquarters on Connecticut Avenue, high above Dupont Circle. Barnard had spread a series of charts on his desk and was explaining their meaning. 'What we have here,' he said, 'is an attempt to relate each migrant species as it appears in the Nearctic Zone to its breeding ground in the neotropics. As you can imagine, it's a massive undertaking. We've had naturalists and scientists working throughout the hemisphere; in fact this survey has been one of WWF's major projects. Up till recently the US Government was participating, through the Fish and Wildlife Service of the Department of the Interior, but last month they suddenly withdrew their funding.'

'Any reason given?'

'No, it rather surprised us. We swallowed hard, put it down to general budgetary restraints, and managed to make up the difference ourselves.' He looked at Lomax. 'Now I've heard what you've told me, I wonder if someone out there in the Government was beginning to get worried about what the research was showing and so decided they had better try to torpedo the project. Yes,' he continued, with concern in his voice, 'that could be it! Look at the distribution patterns here, for example.' He pointed his finger at the charts. 'We see a general decline here in the migrant birds coming from the neotropical forest regions and that, as I have said, can be explained by the continued process of deforestation in the area. But if you take the species which are particularly related to the regions of El Salvador in what we call the montane and premontane areas, we find that there has been a virtual wipe-out far in excess of what one might expect. Destruction of bird life on this order – as we can deduce it from studying the arrival of migrants up north – is an altogether exceptional occurrence and it *could*' – and here Barnard chose his words carefully – 'be explained by the deliberate and widespread use of defoliants.'

'What precisely would the effect be?'

'Two-fold,' Barnard replied. 'In the first place, you would have the loss of vegetation, an accelerated rate of deforestation and the elimination of food sources necessary for the particular species. But you could also have a direct toxic impact on avian life resulting from the use of the defoliant. My guess is that what we are seeing here is a combination of the two.'

Barnard put the charts away and stood up. 'As you can imagine, Mr Lomax, WWF is a non-political organization. Our concern is the protection of wildlife. But I want you to know one thing. If I or anyone else here can help you to pin down this Agent Orange story, we shall be only too delighted. What you've got here is circumstantial evidence and you're going to need more than that.' He held out his hand. 'You can count on us for anything we can do.'

Lomax shook the man's hand warmly. 'This is one morning I shall never forget.'

Murray Lomax was not on the whole given to emotional

199

speeches, but he meant every word he said. As he walked back to his hotel he thought how strange it was that history should repeat itself in this way. First, Vietnam; now El Salvador. But then he thought, maybe it wasn't so strange after all. In the nature of things, guerrillas tended to take to the hills, the forested mountainous regions, where they were hard to find. Defoliation – whether in Asia or in Central America – was clearly an effective weapon if you wanted to crush guerrilla movements. The United States had tried it in Vietnam; wasn't suprising that they should try it again in El Salvador, only this time the cloak of secrecy would be complete. Unless. . . .

The following morning, Lomax left Washington for Delaware. Quite why so many of America's great industrial operations were headquartered in that state, Lomax didn't know. It was, he supposed, more to do with a favourable tax regime than any inherent environmental advantages. Ponting Chemicals was one of the three largest concerns to be based there. Lomax had visited the company in the past, at the time he was researching his book on the pharmaceutical industry, so he was already familiar with the massive installations on the banks of the Delaware river. He was familiar too with the smooth-talking hypocrisy of Ed Murphy, head of Ponting's public relations department.

'We didn't much like what you did the first time round, Murray,' Murphy had told him. 'We think you got the story wrong. People *need* pharmaceuticals; they *want* them. You made it out like we force these things down their throats. But if the second edition of your book is going to be an improvement on the first, then of course we'll help. There is more joy in heaven over one sinner that repents than over the other ninety-nine, eh?' Murphy had chuckled insincerely over the phone, promising himself that this time any information the British journalist picked up would be spoon-fed and premasticated.

'Even journalists can admit the error of their ways.' Lomax meant to sound mollifying and he succeeded.

The two men had a long lunch in the executive dining room

while Murphy tried to put Lomax straight on the basic facts of life in the pharmaceutical industry in general, and in Ponting Chemicals in particular. At the end of the meal Lomax asked, as casually as he could: 'Do you remember a man called Hans Kunig? He gave evidence for the European Commission in the Deutsch-Chemie case you may have read about recently. I believe he worked for Ponting once.'

Murphy hesitated a fraction of a second before replying: 'No, I can't say I remember the name. Hell, we have several thousand employees in our headquarters building alone, not to speak of the people in Ponting plants around the world. Kunig? Sounds German.'

'His parents were German.'

Murphy laughed. 'That's no surprise. Have you ever met a pure-bred American?'

Lomax let the matter drop. He had an instinctive feeling that Murphy was lying but he had no wish to excite suspicion by challenging him.

Later that day he went to the local library. The annual reports of Ponting Chemicals were on file and he began to read through them. Like many American companies, Ponting treated its annual reports as an opportunity to promote good public and staff relationships as well as indicating profits (never losses) for the year.

After about an hour, Lomax found what he was looking for. There was an article by Ed Murphy, Vice-President for Public Relations – entitled 'Gold Award Winners of the Year'. There was also a photograph of five sombre-suited executives receiving a medal from Oscar Harman Jnr, Chairman of the Board of Ponting Chemicals.

One of the award winners, Lomax noted, was called Hank King. Studying the photograph with care, Lomax tried to recall the description Morton had given of his meeting with Kunig. They had covered so much ground the day they had lunch at the Villa Lorraine that it was hard to be sure whether Kunig's physical appearance had featured prominently in Morton's account. He seemed to remember that the Commissioner had mentioned dark hair and spectacles. Well, that fitted as far as it went.

201

There was a short biographical description of each award winner. Hank King, Lomax read, had been with Ponting for thirteen years. 'Born in Cedar Falls, a small town in Iowa, Hank graduated from the State University of Iowa, before taking his doctorate in Chemistry at Johns Hopkins.'

Lomax was so absorbed with his research that he failed to realize the library was closing for the evening.

'If you want to come back tomorrow, I'll keep them on one side for you.' The librarian was a friendly man. He had been filing Ponting's annual reports for years. It was good to see that someone had a use for them.

'No, I've finished. Thanks very much.'

Lomax walked out of the air-conditioned cool of the build-ing into the muggy evening air.

Twelve hours after leaving the library Lomax found himself in Cedar Falls, Iowa, a township with a population of 1031 inhabitants (so a sign on the outskirts indicated with probably spurious precision) about thirty miles from Iowa City itself. It was a place of hogs and corn, of Amish families riding their buggies along the highway as though time had stood still for the past two hundred years; of white clapboard churches shimmering in the heat of the summer sun. Small though it was, the village was not unused to tourists; in any case Lomax, as a professional newsman, knew how to melt into the back-ground when this was required. He talked to the locals in friendly terms, sticking as close to the truth as possible. He was a British journalist, working on a story about people that fled Europe at the time of World War Two to settle in America. Had their hopes been fulfilled? How many of them had stayed, how many had gone back?

Late that afternoon, when the sun – huge and red – was already dropping to the flat horizon of the plain, Morton found – tucked away at the corner of the churchyard on the outskirts of the town – one particular tombstone whose inscription interested him intensely. As was customary, it gave the names of the couple who were buried there as well as the date and place of births and deaths. Underneath the inscrip-tion was the line: 'At peace after life's troubles'.

Chapter Twenty-Two

Piet Lummers, a tall bearded Dutchman who had just passed his fiftieth birthday, had worked for the last fifteen years at the Water Monitoring Centre in the small Dutch village of Hagedorp situated on the banks of the Rhine just across the frontier with Germany. His was not a very difficult job. Nowadays, monitoring was a highly automated business. At Hagedorp, computers kept track of twenty water-quality parameters on a regular basis, ranging from temperature and turbidity to the presence of toxics such as arsenic, mercury and cadmium. They also sampled for 'drins', the popular name for a collection of pesticides, such as aldrin, dieldrin and endrin.

Lummers was a conscientious man and he took his job seriously. He was aware that much of Holland's drinking water depended, directly or indirectly, on the supply of surface water which came down the Rhine and that there was, therefore, a paramount need to verify the quality of the source. Of course, you could do a lot with modern treatment methods. You could take out some of the suspended solids, for example; you could distil and purify. But there were some things – he and his colleagues tended to call them the 'ultra-nasties' – which no treatment could touch. The only thing to do in such circumstances was to make sure that you closed the valves on the intakes and waited until the pollutants, whatever they were, had been carried on downriver and safely out into the North Sea where the fish could worry about them.

Because the centre at Hagedorp was the first place on the Dutch side of the border where water coming down the Rhine from Germany was monitored, the authorities had taken special care to ensure that the system worked. Computer readings which exceeded certain specified levels for the key pollutants, and in particular the 'ultra-nasties', automatically triggered an alarm system. This system not only alerted the men, like Piet Lummers, who worked at the centre; it also led to a shut-down of the water-intakes downstream, thus giving the authorities time to investigate and take whatever evasive or corrective action was necessary. The system of course operated at weekends when the centre was unmanned. On more than one occasion over the last several years, Lummers had come into work on Monday morning to discover that a pollution 'episode' had taken place during his absence and that the intakes had been closed until the danger had passed. There were times, of course, when he was uneasy about leaving quite so much to machines. Just as a pilot likes to believe that he is, if not indispensable, then at least useful for the flying of an aeroplane, so Lummers occasionally expressed the view to his colleagues in the centre that it was perhaps unwise to leave the responsibility for protecting Dutch drinking water during the long weekends to some robot, however capable and well intentioned that robot might be. As Lummers saw it, the element of interpretation remained important no matter how crafty the computer was. There were blips on the screen, lines on the graph which might mean nothing to the automatic scanner but which, to the trained eye, might nevertheless indicate that the river was not running as sweetly as it should. His colleagues, who had no wish to find themselves spending their weekends at work, on the whole tended to pooh-pooh Lummers' fears. If the system had worked up till now, they suggested, there was no reason why it shouldn't continue to work in the future.

On the third Monday in August, Lummers cycled to work, just as he had for the last decade and a half. He propped his bicycle against the brick wall of the water monitoring centre, undid his bicycle clips and stowed them in the pocket of his jacket, donned a white overall in the centre's vestibule and walked into the control room to check on the weekend's readings. As far as he knew, no alarms had occurred during the

204

course of the weekend. It had been business as usual, a situation which he expected to find reflected in the print-out which, as a matter of routine, he inspected first thing each Monday morning.

It came, therefore, as no surprise to him to discover that at least as far as the normal parameters were concerned the graphs and print-outs revealed nothing unusual. Like the great river outside the door, the lines flowed strong and even. Tracking events hour by hour, he couldn't help thinking what a far cry it was from the days when he had first come to work at Hagedorp. That was a time when the state of the art was nowhere near as developed as it was now, when sometimes you had – quite literally – to dip a bucket in the water at the end of a rope, and pull it up and see what you had. But the technology had evolved and the pattern of life, as well as the pattern of work, had evolved with it.

Piet Lummers went through the first batch of print-outs and turned to the next. He had begun on the records of the previous Saturday when he recognized the tell-tale signs of a pollution 'episode' which – though not serious enough to trigger the alarm signals – was quite unmistakable for anyone trained to interpret the data. He pulled the sheets towards him so he could study the lines more closely.

'Hello, hello, hello,' he said. 'What have we here?' He could see at once that something very strange had occurred around 10 p.m. the previous Saturday. The sensors had detected a high level of 'drins' as well as two or three of the 'ultra-nasties'. Lummers scribbled a note on his pad. It was not the drins and the ultra-nasties which worried him in this instance; they had, after all, been below the 'emergency' levels. What worried him was the fact that the sensors had also recorded the presence in large quantities of an unknown pollutant which they were unable to identify through the programmed analytical methods. The data sheets read simply 'sampled and stored for subsequent analysis'.

Lummers scribbled again on his pad, swearing furiously under his breath. It was precisely the situation which they all hoped to avoid. An unknown pollutant coming downstream over a weekend when there was no one minding the shop. Of course the sensors had done what they were trained to do; there had been no failure in the system; the problem was, the system itself had been inadequate. He looked one last time at the data sheet. The pollution 'episode' involving the unidentified substance had lasted, as far as he could see, for twenty-five minutes. In other words, it had taken twenty-five minutes for the stretch of contaminated water to pass the monitoring point. He looked at his watch. It was now 8.35 on Monday morning. The river Rhine was flowing at, say, ten kilometres an hour. That meant that by now the problem, whatever it was, would have long since arrived at the North Sea. For the last thirty-six hours or more towns like Arnhem, Rotterdam and Amsterdam had been taking in polluted water from the reservoirs which served them.

He felt the sweat breaking out on his forehead as he punched the buttons on the console in front of him which would sound the alarm down the length of the river Rhine. There were three grades of danger, ranging from WARNING to SERIOUS ALERT to MAXIMUM PERIL. He hesitated for a second – no one liked to be accused of crying wolf – but then, trusting his instinct, he selected the highest classification. Within seconds the valves and stop cocks began to turn on the water-intakes and outlets, on the reservoir conduits and water-treatment plants. The system, involving a capital investment of billions of guilders, was designed to function perfectly in emergencies such as this and it showed itself to be equal to the task. Lummers pulled out his handkerchief and mopped his forehead. How much damage had already been done, if any? And if some dangerous chemical had got into the water supply of half of Holland, was there still time to do something about it?

He picked up the telephone to call his wife. When she came on the line, he said, fighting to keep the note of alarm out of his voice: 'Don't, I repeat, *don't* drink the water. Don't let the kids drink it, either!' He slammed down the receiver and ran to the laboratory which they had built, five years earlier, next to the control room. The technician still hadn't arrived, so Lummers went through the test-results himself. In theory, the laboratory provided a sophisticated back-up to the more conventional monitoring undertaken by the centre. For example, it was pro-

206

grammed to analyse pollutants which fell outside the normal scope of the centre, subjecting water samples to more complicated investigation than was possible in the course of the centre's routine operations. Of course, these more sophisticated techniques took time; they sometimes involved complex chemical programmes, and, even where the tests had been performed, the results were not instantly available. Lummers knew that there was only a small probability that any extra samples of Rhine water taken at the time of the pollution 'episode' had been fully analysed, but he decided that it was worth taking a look anyway.

Again, it was a question of bringing the data up on to the screen. After two or three abortive attempts, he finally had what he wanted.

'Sample 220,' he read. 'This is a vertical sample of the water-column in the river Rhine at Hagedorp Water Monitoring Centre at 2210 hours on August 19th. Previous sample was taken at 2010 hours, and subsequent sample at 2310 hours. Sample 220 is still being analysed. Results expected 0845 hours.'

Piet Lummers looked at his watch a second time. It was, he noticed, precisely 0845 hours. Almost immediately, the screen in front of him began to pulsate and a bright red star appeared in the top left-hand corner. THIS SAMPLE CONTAINS DIOXIN TO ACUTE TOXICITY LEVELS. ALL EMERGENCY PROCEDURES SHOULD BE ACTIVATED.

Lummers found that he was trembling uncontrollably as he realized the sheer scale of the disaster which could lie ahead. If there was one nightmare which a water engineer feared more than any other, it was that some dangerous pollutant would find its way into the system. And when that pollutant was dioxin, a substance ten thousand times more dangerous than cyanide, all other fears seemed inconsequential. To his certain knowledge such an accident had never happened before. Why it had happened now, he had absolutely no idea and he didn't propose to start finding out. As far as Piet Lummers was concerned, the only sensible reaction was to push the panic button and then push it again.

He stood up as the technician came into the lab. She was a

pretty girl, six months pregnant, with a cheerful open view of life (which was one of the reasons she was expecting).

'Do you know the village priest, Cathy?' Lummers asked.

She looked at him with surprise. 'Father Smeets? Of course, I do. He's going to baptize the baby when it comes.'

'Go and find him then,' Lummers urged her. 'Tell him to ring the church bells like they did in the war.'

When she stood there, bewildered, he suddenly lost his temper. 'Get moving, Cathy,' he shouted. 'People's lives may depend on it!'

The girl didn't wait to be told a second time. She turned on her heel and ran out of the laboratory as fast as she could, leaving the door open behind her.

Max van Tromp, the young and athletic Dutch Minister for the Environment was incredulous. 'Are you telling me that you can't predict what's going to happen?'

The senior civil servant, summoned to an urgent meeting in the Minister's office in The Hague, shook his head despondently. 'There's never been a case of oral ingestion before. At Seveso, it was a case of external exposure to dioxin and that was true of Bhopal, too.'

'I thought it was methyl-isocyanate at Bhopal,' the Minister interrupted sharply. He was a stickler for detail.

'I stand corrected.' The civil servant, who had seen ministers come and go in his time, including young athletic ministers as well as old crumpled ones, wasn't going to be browbeaten. 'The point I'm making is that, in spite of everything that novelists have written on the subject in their wilder flights of fancy, there's never been a case of a major health disaster resulting from contamination of the water supplies. There was that Spanish disaster a few years back but the cause then was adulterated cooking oil, not polluted water.'

The telephone rang on the Minister's desk. 'Your conference call, Minister,' a voice said when Max van Tromp picked up the receiver.

For the next ten minutes the Dutch Minister for the Environment was engaged in tense discussion with four of the world's leading experts on dioxin. From a purely technical point of view the multi-sided conversation, which included the Director of the Centre for Disease Control in Atlanta, Georgia as well as scientists in England, Switzerland and Japan, was a triumph. Audibility was good and the participants managed not to talk all at the same time. But, from a substantive point of view, the hook-up achieved little or nothing. The Minister, at the end, was near despair. 'What you're saying, gentlemen, is that you just don't know. Dioxin, if swallowed, may attack the vital organs beginning with the liver and spleen; may give rise to tumours and deformities, including genetic deformities in pregnant women; but on the other hand it may not; we've no way of telling until it happens. There are no antidotes available. In a nutshell, we've either got a major catastrophe on our hands or we haven't. We just have to wait and see.'

When the Minister replaced the telephone he was white and shaken. The senior civil servant couldn't suppress a feeling of sympathy. He knew a broken career when he saw one.

'I'm sorry, Minister.'

'Don't be sorry for me, Jan. Be sorry for all those people out there, who will have to live in fear and uncertainty for months.' He picked up a pen. 'We'd better get started on a draft of a resignation statement. If a Minister for the Environment can't safeguard the nation's water supplies, he's not much good, is he?'

Max van Tromp scribbled for a few minutes and then handed what he had written to the civil servant. 'Get that typed up for me, could you, Jan – and then I'll sign it.'

The Minister rose to his feet and walked stiffly from the room.

Chapter Twenty-Three

On their fourth morning on the island, Morton went down to the beach to watch the few remaining fishing vessels come back in to the tiny harbour. He was surprised to see the familiar figure of Murray Lomax aboard one of the boats.

'Good heavens! What are you doing here? Not looking for me, I hope?' For perhaps the first time in his dealings with the journalist, Morton sounded more than a little cross.

Lomax stood his ground. 'I've not tracked you half-way across Europe, Commissioner, to be given the cold shoulder now. Forgive me for interrupting your vacation, but when I tell you the reason, I think you'll understand.'

As the men of the island unloaded the morning's catch on to the quayside, Lomax explained: 'During the course of last weekend there was a major spill of dioxin in the Rhine. The water supplies in Arnhem and Rotterdam and several other Dutch towns may have been contaminated. People are looking, as you can imagine, for the source of the pollution. The Dutch believe it came down the river from Germany. The Germans say they have made inquiries and can find no evidence of any accident. The German authorities are suggesting that the Dutch monitoring system has produced an erroneous reading – apparently the incident was tracked by only one station. In the meantime the scientists and the public health specialists are having the mother and father of a row because they can't decide what the consequences of oral ingestion of dioxin are likely to be; this is the first time it has ever happened. The politicians, of course, are caught in the middle.

The Dutch Environment Minister has already resigned.'

'I'll come back to Brussels at once, of course,' Morton turned away from the harbour and began to stride up the path towards the house where he and Isobel were staying.

As he followed, Lomax realized that he was doing for Morton what he would have done for very few other men. At the beginning, perhaps, his motives had been largely journalistic, but by now so much else was involved. He felt a loyalty to Morton, an admiration for the way the man never gave up. What's more, though journalists were not on the whole paid to entertain ideas of that kind, he believed that Morton had got it right.

'I'll bet a thousand to one,' he said, catching up, 'that the reason no one is owning up to having spilled dioxin in the Rhine is not just the question of legal liability; it's also because an admission of guilt would reveal the manufacturing processes involved.' They paused as they reached the top of the cliff. Down below, the seabirds were hovering around the fishing vessels, waiting for their turn at the offal. Across the water, forty minutes away in a fast craft, a continent beckoned.

'Can we pin it on Deutsch-Chemie?' Morton asked. This could be the breakthrough he was looking for. 'I mean, really pin it on them.'

Lomax smiled. 'Journalists like their stories to be exclusive, but this time I thought I had better spread the word. Right now' – he looked at his watch – 'I'd say that there are some fifty newspaper men and women of different nationalities working on the leads which I've given them. It was enough to tip off the wire services. After that, the system takes over. My guess is that at least thirty newsmen and half a dozen television crews will at this precise moment be nosing around Deutsch-Chemie's headquarters in Cologne. If an accident happened that is now being hushed up, they'll find it. After that, you can be sure, all hell will break loose.' He paused and then, still smiling, asked: 'Could you give me a lift back, Commissioner?'

Morton didn't immediately take his meaning, so Lomax explained.

'I've arranged for a coastguard helicopter to land here twenty minutes from now. It will bring you to a French military base just outside Quiberon. There's a Mystère standing by to take you on to Brussels.'

Morton was back in his office by five o'clock that afternoon. A small crowd was gathered round the television set in the corner of the room. Laurent Guimard was already there waiting for him, as well as other officials involved in the Deutsch-Chemie business. The sense of excitement was palpable.

'We shall have the *Journal Télévisé* in a minute on the French channel,' said Guimard, making room for Morton on the sofa beside him. 'But I expect the Dutch and German stations will be carrying the story as well.'

In the end it was the Dutch channel which they watched. Somehow the principal TV station in the Netherlands had managed to get a team of reporters inside the plant and, through carefully selected interviews with Deutsch-Chemie personnel (some of whom had themselves been directly involved), had been able to reconstruct the nature and scope of the accident. It appeared that a chemical reaction had gone wrong, the substances had overheated, venting had taken place, but, unlike Bhopal, none of the gases had escaped into the atmosphere; on the contrary, the cooling systems had worked and the gas had been liquefied. The accident happened when one of the containment vessels ruptured, causing a spill of contaminated water into the Rhine. There had been some exposure of workers within the plant (though the management had done its best to hush this up, together with any information about the accident itself); the prognosis was that any persons exposed would be ill, though how severely no one seemed to know.

'What we *can* say with certainty,' said the Dutch commentator, 'is that this is an accident which should never have happened. People are suggesting here tonight that Deutsch-Chemie was engaged in the manufacture of illegal chemicals and in particular the notorious Agent Orange. If this story is confirmed, then it adds a new dimension of horror to what is already a sufficiently macabre incident.'

As the commentator continued speaking from his vantage-

212

point in front of the gates of the Deutsch-Chemie factory, Guimard said to Morton: 'This may clinch it for us, Commissioner.'

Morton leaned back in the sofa and shut his eyes to block out the images from the screen. 'Do we really want to win like this?' he asked.

He walked quickly from the room, consumed by a sense of anger and outrage.

When he returned home that night he found Isobel glued to the television.

'They're interviewing people in Arnhem, trying to find out how many might have been exposed,' she told him.

Morton sat down next to her to hear a bearded Dutchman who apparently worked at some monitoring station just on the Dutch side of the border explain how his suspicions had first been raised.

'There is always a danger that something like this could happen at a weekend. This time we were unlucky. Anyone who drank the water here in Arnhem last weekend took a risk he or she could not possibly have known about.'

'Heavens, I was in Arnhem myself last Saturday,' Isobel exclaimed. 'Just before we went to Brittany. It seems so long ago now I'd almost forgotten.'

Morton was concerned. 'I hope you didn't drink the water.'

'Don't worry, I always stick to Perrier.' But then she remembered and went pale.

'Jimmy, I had a glass of water when I was making that speech. It wasn't Perrier. It was ordinary water. Tap water. I thought at the time it tasted funny.'

'Oh God,' Morton groaned. What had the experts said? If there were going to be consequences from swallowing dioxin, they would be most likely to affect pregnant women most of all. Thalidomide times ten, that was the way one of the scientific experts had described it.

He walked over to her and put his hand on her shoulder.

'I'm not going to get rid of it, James.' Isobel had never sounded more determined, more inflexible. 'This is our child, the only one we've managed to produce in six years of marriage, and it's going to be born the way nature intended.'

213

Ten days later Morton and Isobel drove down to Luxembourg to hear the verdict of the European Court of Justice in the case of the Commission of the European Communities versus Deutsch-Chemie. Isobel, though depressed and anxious because of the uncertainties of her own situation (there seemed to be as many opinions as there were medical experts), had insisted on coming with him.

'If you're going down to defeat, James, I want to be there too. And I'll make a statement to the press afterwards saying that you were right even if the Court finds against you.'

They took their seats in the courtroom while the judges filed in, resplendent in their robes and regalia of office. Apart from the Italian Advocate-General, Ernesto Pantaloni, who looked agitated, the members of the court had impassive, almost bored expressions. It was almost as though there was some inverse relationship operating: the more interesting and important the verdict they had to deliver, the less excitement or animation was to be displayed. When the learned Professor Cornelius van Rijn, President of the European Court, began reading no less than ten or twelve preambular pages, even Morton found his attention beginning to wander. 'Get on with it,' he muttered inwardly. The tension in the courtroom was beginning to mount. The press up in the gallery were waiting with their pencils poised; it seemed unreasonable that a matter which could have been dealt with so summarily should be delayed by a load of legalistic rigmarole. He caught sight of Murray Lomax on the tribune above him and nodded a greeting.

In the end, as the audience began to fidget, the President of the Court came to the operative paragraphs. 'We therefore find,' he intoned, 'that the Commission's case is well-founded and that Deutsch-Chemie are guilty of the charges set out in the indictment. It is the decision of this court that Deutsch-Chemie should pay within thirty days the sum of five billion Deutsch Marks by way of fines and reparations, while giving guarantees of future good conduct.'

The Dutchman looked up from his notes. 'The court would, in conclusion, like to congratulate the European Commission

214

and in particular. . . .'

'You've won!' Isobel, sitting next to Morton, hissed in an excited whisper.

'Shhh!' Morton laid a warning hand on her arm.

Cornelius van Rijn seemed not to have noticed the interruption '. . . congratulate in particular the Commissioner for Industry, Mr James Morton. It is possible that, without his courage and dedication and sense of conviction, this case would not have been brought. Europe would have been poorer for it.' Van Rijn picked up his papers and stood up to indicate that the session was at an end. He looked in Morton's direction as he did so with more than a hint of a smile.

Jackpot! thought Morton. It's the bloody jackpot! He'd taken them all on and he had won and what's more, they had thrown sweet-smelling bouquets at him as well.

Later that morning, before driving back to Brussels, he walked across the road to the great building which the Luxembourg Government had put up specially to house the European Parliament. Though the Parliament still spent most of the time in Strasbourg, Luxembourg had managed to keep one or two plenary sessions a year for itself and it nursed the hope that over time this number would increase.

Almost as soon as the verdict of the European Court was announced – in fact he was still in the courtroom receiving the congratulations of colleagues and officials – Morton had received a message that a delegation of Members of the European Parliament wished to consult with him urgently – and in any case before he returned to Brussels.

While Isobel waited for him in the Holiday Inn, Morton learnt – from the horse's mouth as it were – that the MEPs were planning to propose for immediate adoption a resolution censuring the President of the Commission for his conduct of the Commission's affairs – based in particular, so far as Morton could understand, on the Parliament's indignant understanding of Kramer's role in the Deutsch-Chemie case. Since the MEPs came from a broad spectrum of nationality and political opinion, it was clear to Morton that the move could not be lightly discounted even though, from a strictly constitutional point of view, the Parliament had no power to

215

censure individual Commission members.

'Why are you telling me this?' There was no one else around in the lobby of the hemicycle but still he spoke in a low voice. This was as near to conspiracy as he ever wished to get.

'We wanted you to be informed in good time.' Morton recognized the speaker as a young German radical, a woman who had once led the Green Party from obscurity at least part-way down the road towards power.

'Well, thank you.' Morton had sounded abrupt and he had meant to. He rejoined Isobel feeling both puzzled and exhilarated. Were there yet more battles to come?

They hardly spoke during the course of the long drive back across the Ardennes to Brussels. Both were enveloped in their own thoughts. Somewhere near Namur, Isobel asked: 'Why did the court change its mind?'

'It didn't change its mind. It simply decided not to follow the opinion of the Advocate-General.'

Isobel would have none of it. 'You know what I mean,' she insisted. 'If it hadn't been for the accident on the Rhine, for the threat of dioxin poisoning caused by Deutsch-Chemie affecting thousands and perhaps tens of thousands of people, Pantaloni's opinion might have prevailed. It's ironic, isn't it, that one of the reasons, perhaps the main reason, you won your case is because I might be carrying a deformed child.'

He looked at her. She didn't seem angry or hysterical. Her mood, as far as he could gauge it, was subdued and reflective.

He leaned forward in his seat, anxious to avoid any further conversation. The morning's euphoria had evaporated. His triumph, if indeed it was a triumph at all, was bitter-sweet.

'Let's have the news, Gerry.'

Gerry McLoughlin wasn't listening. He was thinking about the white-fronted stone cottage perched high up on the cliffs of Connemara which he knew would be his one day. As he drove, he could almost hear the great Atlantic waves breaking on the rocks below. Another couple of years and he could be on his way with a fat EEC pension behind him.

'The news, Gerry.'

'Of course, sir.' McLoughlin brought his mind back to the present and turned the car radio to the BBC, knowing that

216

Morton liked to hear the PM programme.

The newsreader led with the story of the European Court's verdict in Luxembourg. Morton was pleased to hear that political leaders in Britain of all parties (including his own) had paid tribute to the Commission's role, as well as endorsing the warm comments made by the President of the European Court about the Commissioner for Industry. In the circumstances, of course, with Isobel sitting glumly beside him, it was all cold comfort.

The traffic thickened on the motorway as they approached Brussels. Isobel had her eyes shut and seemed to have gone to sleep. Morton realized that she was in fact listening to the car-radio when she clutched his arm:

'Listen to this, James.'

Morton heard the newsreader say: 'The European chemical industry has, of course, been under fire in recent weeks particularly on account of the recent spill of dioxin into the Rhine. The good news today is that a survey recently completed in the affected areas of Holland indicates that there has been no increase in the occurrence of abnormal births while tests carried out on a large sample of pregnant women – who it is thought might have been exposed to the pollutant – show absolutely no sign of any foetal irregularities. Scientists are saying tonight that dioxin may in fact fall into that very small class of toxic compounds which may be ingested orally with comparative safety at very low concentrations, while other forms of exposure – such as through the skin or lungs – may result in permanent impairment or even death.'

Isobel grasped his hand. 'It's going to be okay, Jimmy. I know it. I'll go and take the test myself but I know now it's all right.'

Two days later Isobel, who until then had firmly resisted the idea, had an amniocentesis which appeared to reveal completely normal foetal development. When the doctor asked her whether she wanted to know the sex of the child as well, Isobel had replied in her typical full-blooded way: 'Hell no, as long as it's a baby!'

217

Chapter Twenty-Four

In the end Dr Horst Kramer, ninth President of the European Commission, went quietly. He announced his resignation at the meeting of the Commission which followed the over-whelming vote of censure in the European Parliament. As he made a brief farewell speech, Morton reflected that nothing became Kramer's conduct of office so much as the manner of his leaving it. He would never feel friendly to the man, but at least he could recognize that Kramer had mustered a certain bulky dignity for the occasion.

'I shall not comment on the so-called Deutsch-Chemie affair,' Kramer told them, 'except to say that I believe, and will continue to believe, that I acted properly. Nor shall I comment on the European Parliament's resolution, except to say that those who turn against me now may, if you let them get away with it, turn against any one of you later. It is clear that the resolution is *ultra vires*, whatever political importance it may hold. I offer you my best wishes for the future.'

With that, Kramer was gone, leaving the remaining eleven Commissioners staring fixedly at the polished oak table in front of them as though observing a minute's silence for a departed friend. Out of the corner of his eye Morton noticed that Leopold Brugmann had slipped quietly from the room after the President. How like the man, Morton thought. Whatever Brugmann's own opinion of Kramer might be, he would ensure that the dignity of the office was properly respected. Ex-Presidents of the Commission were an honour-able band. They included the good and the great, past and present. If you devalued one, you devalued them all. But Brugmann would also, Morton knew, loyally serve whom-so-ever the Commission now elected in Kramer's place.

His thoughts were interrupted as he heard Dimitrios Kafiri break the silence. 'I believe I am the *doyen d'age* here. Under these circumstances, I propose – as is usual – to take the chair.' When he saw that there was no dissent to the proposition, Kafiri continued. 'We are obviously today in an unpre-cedented situation where there are no rules or guidelines. My own view is that we must without any further ado proceed with the election of a new President. What is more, to avoid all speculation and outside pressures of whatever kind, I propose that we do this here and now. I believe, moreover, that it is important, even vital, that the man or woman' – and here Kafiri made a deferential nod in the direction of Helena Noguentes just as Kramer had at that first meeting in the castle a few months before – 'should command the support of the largest possible number of his colleagues. I suggest, therefore, that the requirement for election should not be a simple majority of the votes cast, but that on the contrary the next President of the Commission should receive the votes of at least three-quarters of his colleagues, abstentions to count as a vote. The ballot will be held in secret; there will be no coloured voting papers, as I'm afraid has been the case on other occasions' – he permitted himself a wry smile as he recalled the last occasion that the Greek Parliament was called upon to elect a President. 'The first ballot,' Kafiri continued, 'will take place immediately after I have finished speaking, and subse-quent ballots will ensue at intervals of half an hour.' He looked around, an old man at last coming into his own. There had been some elderly caretakers, thought Morton, like Adenauer or Deng who had gone on to hold supreme power in their own right. He doubted whether this would be true of Kafiri, but it amused him anyway to see that the old boy was getting a good run for his money.

Kafiri looked around. 'Are there any questions?'

Pierre Duchesne, sharp as a whip as always, put the obvious question. 'Who are the candidates in this election, Mr Chair-man? If there are no candidates, how can there be an election?

Should we not have time to consult our governments?'

'I don't see what the governments have to do with it,' Kafiri rebuked him sharply. 'There will of course have to be another German member of the Commission to replace Dr Kramer and governments, at least the German Government, will no doubt be involved in this. But I see no other reason to disturb the ministries and chancelleries of Europe. This Commission is, after all, not at the beginning of its mandate.'

They were all of them, Pierre Duchesne included, clearly impressed by the firmness with which Kafiri spoke. Bully for you, Morton thought. It amused him to see the smirk wiped off that clever young Frenchman's face.

Kafiri was still speaking. 'Let me reassure you about one thing,' he said with a smile. 'I do not propose to offer myself for election. I am too old for that. But perhaps I could invite some other nominations.'

Helena Noguentes was thinking about the great golden eagle circling high above them in the mountains of the High Sierra. Perhaps she should have held on to Morton while she had him. Perhaps she should have stood her ground and slugged it out with Isobel, toe to toe. Perhaps she should have got herself pregnant too! Poor old James, how would he have handled that? She looked at him across the table. So the man had run back to his wife. Could she truly blame him for that? As far as the rest of it was concerned she was quite clear in her own mind that nobody else could do the job. 'I propose James Morton.'

Morton shook his head in disbelief, not so much at the notion of his becoming President of the European Commission, (he felt strangely capable in that respect) but at Helena's generosity in proposing him.

As he smiled his thanks across the room, Kafiri asked: 'Is that proposal seconded?'

'It is indeed.' Paddy McGrath, now a sure ally, was keen to be in there ahead of the field. But at least three other Commissioners had their hands in the air. There was a small burst of applause. Commission meetings could often be long, turgid affairs. At least this one would go down in the annals as something special.

220

'I see it is,' observed Kafiri, and he continued: 'If it is not improper, I should like my own name to be recorded as one of those who seconded Mr Morton's candidature.' He paused and looked around the assembled Commissioners again, this time with markedly less enthusiasm. 'Are there any other nominations?'

As the silence in the room lengthened it became increasingly obvious that there would be no other nominations. Kafiri rapped on the table with the Presidential gavel. 'There being no other nominations, we shall proceed to a ballot. In the event that Mr Morton fails to attain the necessary three-quarters majority on the first ballot, I shall invite new nominations and we shall continue with the vote.' He turned to the Commission's Secretary-General who, by now, had resumed his seat. 'Mr Brugmann, are we ready to proceed?'

James Morton was expecting to hear Brugmann say 'Aye-aye, sir' or words to that effect when Pierre Duchesne held up his hand to ask for the floor.

'Mr Chairman, may I have your permission to make a suggestion?'

'Go ahead, Mr Duchesne.'

The Frenchman knew that, whatever happened now, he would live to fight another day. He could see, as clearly as he could see anything, that the tide was flowing strongly in Morton's direction. He had no wish to weaken his own position in the future by a false move now.

'I'm not precisely clear under what rules we are operating — perhaps we should ensure that for future situations of this kind we are better prepared. But, as far as the present is concerned, could I suggest that it might be possible to dispense with the formal ballot? Could we not elect Mr Morton by acclamation?'

It was not entirely obvious to those present whether Duchesne's proposal was to be taken as a procedural motion, preparing the way for a subsequent decision, or as a substantive motion standing in its own right. Lacking clarity, the Members of the Commission either raised their hands or applauded or attempted to do both. Kafiri waited until the hubbub had died down. Then he said simply: 'I declare Mr

Morton elected and have great pleasure therefore in asking him to take the chair at this meeting.'

If James Edward Morton, formerly Member of Parliament (Conservative) for Newbury and one-time junior minister in Her Majesty's Government, felt any reluctance in stepping forward to pick up the wand of office which Horst Kramer had so recently laid down, he showed no sign of it.

'Thank you, colleagues.' He took his seat in the President's high-backed chair. 'Shall we get on with our business?'

Chapter Twenty-Five

The following Wednesday, after the first full meeting of the Commission under his Presidency, he invited Isobel to a celebration lunch at Comme Chez Soi.

Some people believed that it was the finest restaurant in Brussels even though the location – tucked in behind the statue of the Mannekin Pis ('that little boy peeing' as Isobel had proclaimed in her anti-Brussels stage) – was hardly the most salubrious in the city. As they worked their way steadily through the *Menu Dégustation*, the conversation turned inevitably to the events of recent months and weeks.

'But what happened to Kunig?' Isobel asked. 'I thought he was going to sue the Commission for breach of confidence.'

Morton smiled. 'Do you remember that line in *Murder in the Cathedral*? About doing the right thing for the wrong reason?'

Isobel shook her head. As the prettiest co-ed of her year she hadn't had much time for T.S. Eliot.

'Get on with it, James,' she said sharply. She hoped being President of the Commission wasn't going to go to his head. She was quite keen on the new James Morton – certainly a sharper, more confident man than the one she had known in those Westminster years, better in bed too (where did he get that from, huh?) – but still a proper balance had to be maintained in any relationship, particularly one in which she was involved.

'I'm sorry, darling,' Morton tried to mollify her. 'What I mean was that Kunig was an industrial spy right from the start.

He was planted by Ponting within Deutsch-Chemie with specific instructions to build up a dossier of information on that company's crimes and malpractices and to make that dossier available to the Commission. Which is precisely what he did. And I swallowed it hook, line and sinker. It was, as I said, a question of doing the right thing for the wrong reason. There's no doubt that Deutsch-Chemie was guilty and the European Court of Justice quite properly found against them. But equally there's no doubt in my mind now that Kunig's motives all along were of the basest kind. He was an industrial mole in the pay of the Americans and he succeeded brilliantly. After the court case, after the dioxin business, Deutsch-Chemie is virtually finished as a company, which is precisely what Ponting wanted. Either they'll buy it up in its weakened state, and thereby gain a major foothold within Europe's chemical industry – or else it will go to the wall altogether in which case it will cease to manufacture and sell products competitively. Which is also good news from the Ponting point of view.'

He poured himself some more wine. A bottle of very decent Pouilly Fumé between the two of them went a long way, particularly since Isobel was still on the wagon. The smile on his face broadened. He enjoyed this Hercule Poirot bit, waiting for the guests to assemble in the drawing room as it were and then telling them what really happened.

Isobel prodded a forkful of poached turbot into her silky, petulant mouth. She had rather lost her appetite since being pregnant, but Comme Chez Soi was, as she put it, something else again. She chewed reflectively on the delicate flesh, savouring the aroma of the herbs.

'When did you first suspect Kunig?'

'Not soon enough, I'm afraid. When I first met him I vaguely realized that he was younger than he should have been if his story was true, but I rather put it from my mind. It was only when I discovered that he had lied by pretending that Ritter had been at the I.G. Farben plant at Auschwitz that I began to catch on. Ritter was never at Auschwitz. And Kunig's parents never died in a concentration camp in Auschwitz. They were buried, under the name of King, in a small mid-western town in the United States outside Des Moines, Iowa. I can prove that too.'

For the next few minutes Morton went on to explain what Lomax had learned in the course of his visit to the United States, as he put it, in search of 'the real Hans Kunig'.

'How did Lomax know that the Kings who were buried in Iowa were Hans Kunig's parents?' Isobel asked.

'The birthplaces and birthdates matched. Both Kings were born in Germany in the twenties. And besides King is König in German.'

'Elementary, my dear Morton,' Isobel smiled.

'It all fitted. What Kunig had to do, above all,' her husband concluded, 'was to convince me of his sincerity, of his moral conviction. And there's no doubt he succeeded.'

'So Kramer was right? He didn't want to block the merger, nor did be believe that the Commission should act solely, or even mainly, on the basis of Kunig's evidence.'

'Hey, wait a minute.' Morton was genuinely upset that she chose to see things that way. 'Deutsch-Chemie was found guilty and they were guilty. Don't forget that.'

She was not convinced. 'That may be so. But the long and short of it is that Ponting comes out on top. Don't get me wrong, James, I'm an American. I grew up there among the smokestacks of New Jersey as you know very well. But if you're talking ethics, I doubt if there's much difference between Ponting and Deutsch-Chemie. Was planting Kunig ethical?'

Morton sighed. He hadn't wanted to tell her. It wasn't official yet. 'Keep this to yourself,' he said, 'otherwise I'll be done for insider-dealing. Deutsch-Chemie's not going to go under. Nor is Ponting going to buy it. This morning the Commission approved the merger with United Chemicals. Actually, it's not so much a merger. More a takeover. United Chemicals is picking up the shares dirt cheap and the Commission's all in favour. The lawyers have backed off. Even the most ardent advocates of an effective competition policy can see that it's better to have a European chemical giant operating in Europe than an American chemical giant operating in Europe. Helicopters are one thing. They're on the fringe of

Europe's industrial policy and at the end of the day no one really cares. But the chemical industry is something else. If Ponting took over Deutsch-Chemie, it would only be a matter of time before the others – Hoechst and Bayer, United Chemicals and Rhone-Poulenc – went their way too. Of course Sir Gordon Cartwright is absolutely delighted with the way things have turned out.'

'A huge donation already on its way to Party funds, no doubt?' Isobel still sounded sceptical.

'Come, my dear,' a patronizing tone crept into Morton's voice (after all, he was President of the Commission; he could afford to be patronizing). 'You can hardly imagine it was all planned this way.'

'Can't I?' Isobel sounded tired and a little bored. She wanted to go back to the house in Rhode St Genèse – she thought of it as home now – and make some curtains for the nursery.

'Forgive me, Jimmy,' she said. 'I never was much good at all the ramifications. But if you think it's going well then I'm sure it is. Thanks for lunch. It was a sweet thought.'

She gave him a quick peck on the cheek and swept out, leaving him to pay the bill.

Chapter Twenty-Six

Lomax had been postponing the evil moment as long as he could. He knew what he knew and Morton's election as President of the European Commission only made matters worse. If he had a scoop on his hands before, then it was plain that he had a much larger scoop now. Not perhaps a mega-scoop. Not yet. But it was moving that way.

Ted Smith, the news editor who had no time for the niceties of personal as opposed to professional relationships, pressed him relentlessly. 'Christ, Murray,' he shouted at him one day over the telephone when he heard about Morton's elevation. 'The story will go cold if we don't use it. Who the hell's going to remember who Kunig is two weeks from now?'

Lomax could see Ted Smith's point. In the end, he had rung Morton's office for an appointment. It was unfortunate – for Morton of course – that the erstwhile Commissioner for Industry had taken him so much into his confidence. Doubly unfortunate – again for Morton – that he had asked Lomax to do the devilling for him in the United States.

Lomax recognized that he himself had participated with considerable enthusiasm but that did not mean, when all was said and done, that you threw the cardinal rules of journalism out of the window. A newsman was a newsman was a news-man. Morton had never sworn him to secrecy and indeed had no right to do so.

Morton came back from his lunch with Isobel to find the journalist waiting for him. He sensed immediately that something was wrong.

'Come in, Murray.'

Lomax came straight to the point. 'We're going to run the story, Mr President. The whole thing. The presses are set up and ready to roll, as they say.'

Morton felt the hot flush spread across his face. He didn't know what to say or think. This kind of thing didn't happen in Berkshire.

'I don't work for the Commission,' Lomax continued quietly. 'I work for a newspaper. We have to sell copies or we go out of business. This story will sell a lot of copies. "Commission duped by industrial spy." "Newly-elected President of the Commission James Morton admits he acted in ignorance.' I can see the headlines now.'

All the muscles in Morton's face seemed to have frozen solid but somehow he managed to force a smile.

'Murray Lomax, I congratulate you. You're a damn fine journalist. You've got a job to do, so go and do it. If your story makes me look a fool, well, it won't be the first time and I don't suppose it will be the last time either.'

He stood up. He could have kicked that dirty rotten fat-arsed Scotsman from Brussels to John O'Groats.

Murray Lomax returned to his office in a despondent frame of mind.

'Well,' he thought, 'Ted Smith can bloody well decide what to do.' That's why Smith was news editor and he, Lomax, wasn't. He went to the telephone and asked to be put through to London.

'You lost your bet, Ted,' he said. 'Morton didn't try to stop me; didn't say the Commission would withdraw all journalistic privileges from all *Times* correspondents; he didn't even say "publish and be damned". He just said "congratulations", though I could tell it cost him.'

There was a long silence the other end of the line.

'Ted, are you there?' Lomax thought the call might have been interrupted.

'Of course, I'm here. Shut up for a moment; I'm thinking. I may have to go to the editor with this one.'

'Don't overdo it, old man.' Lomax waited impatiently as the minutes ran on.

Finally Ted Smith came back on the line. The man sounded unusually subdued.

'I just had a word with the editor and we've decided to spike it. The editor's rather a pal of Morton's, it seems. Apparently they were in the Bullingdon together whatever the hell that may be.' Smith sighed. 'I hate to kill a good story Murray, but. . . .'

'Actually I'm glad you spiked it, Ted. Morton has just begun here. There aren't many people like him, not in this town anyway. You just gave him a break, but he deserved it.'

'Just one. No more.' The old Ted Smith had returned, tougher and harder than ever. 'From now on, you give him hell.'

Late that afternoon James Morton received two telephone calls in his office.

The first was from Lomax. The journalist, sensing the barely-disguised hostility in Morton's voice, came straight to the point.

'We're not going to use the story. If you'd tried to stop us, we would have run it. But you didn't.'

Morton heaved a sigh of relief. 'Thanks, Murray. I know you were doing your job, but I'm glad you didn't press it. It could have made things difficult.'

'For you?'

'No, for you. I want you to be my Chef de Cabinet. You might have had an awkward time, with the new President of the Commission under attack!'

'Are you serious?'

'Of course I am. I need someone I can trust. Your first job, by the way, will be to get on the plane to Madrid to tell Kunig that if he doesn't withdraw all charges against the Commission, we'll have him indicted for industrial espionage before the courts of half a dozen countries. So do you accept?'

Lomax didn't hesitate. 'I'm not sure that I can do the job, but I'll give it a damned good try.'

The second call was from the British Prime Minister.

'Ah, James, back from lunch already? I'm lucky to find you in. I know how much you people in Brussels enjoy your meals! I thought I'd ring you because we haven't been in touch for some time. I just wanted to let you know how much I admire the way you've been getting on over there. That's what we want. Someone who will fight his corner. I always knew you were the right man for the job and now you're actually President of the Commission, a *British* President, James. That's what counts. . . .'

As the Prime Minister pressed determinedly ahead without waiting for him to respond, Morton couldn't help thinking that she had never sounded friendlier towards him nor spoken in such honeyed tones. Why did she sound so pleased when he could hardly be said to have toed the Party line? As his mind wandered back to that Sunday lunch at Chequers, a stupefying thought occured to him: could the whole business after all have been some deep-laid plot to replace a German President of the Commission by a Briton, a devilishly ingenious scheme hatched up by some deeply cunning man like Sir Oliver Passmore and blessed by the Prime Minister herself? Could they have known, in appointing him to Brussels, in allowing him to take the industrial portfolio, in *insisting* – perhaps – on the industrial portfolio, that sooner or later he would clash with Kramer?

Could Peter Simpson actually have been ordered to precipitate such a clash by spilling the beans as he did? And could they, whoever 'they' were, have foreseen the subsequent course of events: the collapse of Deutsch-Chemie, the takeover by United Chemicals? Had they known all along that Kunig had been planted by the Americans, with instructions to dig out the dirt on Deutsch-Chemie and to make sure that the Commission – led by the heroic and gullible Commissioner for Industry – moved headlong into a prosecution while they stood smugly by, waiting to pick up the pieces? He felt a flush of anger spread across his face as he recalled the bombing of his apartment. Surely that could not have been part of the game-plan?

He shook his head, trying to clear away the horrendous enveloping images of double and triple dealing. No, it was all too incredible!

'. . . a *British* president of the Commission,' the Prime Minister was saying. 'We wouldn't have had a British President for the next forty years if we had stood our turn in the queue, not with all the other countries waiting in the wings. Bravo James! And give my love to Isobel. I'm so pleased about the baby!'

No! Morton repeated to himself, it couldn't be true! Not even *she* could be so devious or so astute.

'Thank you, Prime Minister,' he began at last to reply, only to realize that the redoubtable lady had already moved on to other business.